THE CASE

OF

COLOURFUL

CLOTHES

AND

KILTS

RRGall

My thanks to Chris & Carol for their help.

Cover: detail from a painting of Dumfries by Irene Gall
www.artist-irene-gall.co.uk

THE DUMFRIES DETECTIVE TRILOGY
PART 1
THE CASE OF THE PIG IN THE EVENING SUIT

PART 2
THE CASE OF COLOURFUL CLOTHES AND KILTS

PART 3
THE CASE OF THE HERMIT'S GUEST BEDROOM

More information at RRGall.com

MYS
Pbk

Thursday 13th July 2006

Jimmy Mann – we called him Manfred – died of a heart attack yesterday, out on a walk in the country: found on a bridleway by a woman on horseback. He could only have been sixty-two or thereabouts. It came as a great shock to us all. He was a nice man, tall and thin, who seemed genuinely interested in what you had to say and even waited until you had finished saying it.

Shortly after taking early retirement from the railway, Manfred's wife passed away. It was twenty four days to be exact. Despite this, there appeared to be no hint of bitterness towards the cruelty of life and no sign of feeling sorry for his situation.

Instead, perhaps to cope with the loss, he kept busy, venturing out with a couple of black bags in an attempt to stem the blight of Dumfries – litter. It took only a few seconds to fill each one and with very little walking required: but it was a step in the right direction.

Once, on a raw, February morning, I spotted him wading in the Nith, just below the caul, dragging bike frames, rusty supermarket trolleys, and battered bollards to the bank, ready for lifting away. And I wasn't the only one watching either as the thrill of the unusual had brought others to a gawping standstill. They marvelled at his courage as he took on the cold and the currents with little more than a pair of green chest waders and a pair of yellow rubber gloves. It must have stirred a guilty nerve for word of his deeds sped through town faster than a boy-racer and people began volunteering in their droves to join in.

Manfred obtained bright orange t-shirts from somewhere and he and his merry troupe marched out to tackle the mess. They began to personalise their shirts with mottos like: *say no to refuse – the little bitta litter hitters – clean rubbish – out with*

5

the lout – and such like. They may have had their own, wee competition.

At first I was worried that all this bonhomie would give the miscreants an excuse to discard even more anti-social debris – keeping the good folk of Dumfries happily busy – and so the effort would be counter-productive, but, as the weeks progressed, I became increasingly duty bound to join up – and did. It was enjoyable and somehow the grottiest, unpleasantest tasks offered up the cheeriest rewards.

The cleansing wave became so popular that Manfred had to coordinate his litter patrols by placing ads in the local paper, The Standard, giving the location and date of the next clear-up.

It was then that bureaucracy showed its ugly face. Health and Safety sidled in on the act and he was forced to fill out masses of forms dealing with matters such as risk assessment, protective clothing, and liability. Before long it was deemed necessary for everyone taking part to be insured and have proper stout gloves. Then, when the direct use of hands was outlawed for being too dangerous, we were forced to use awkward grabbers, and, to add salt to the wound, or, as we say round here, to add Gretna to the Scottish First Division, we had to pay for them out of our own pockets.

Eventually, it became too much of a bother and Manfred gave up. He went back to his simple life. Needless to say, without his driving force, our good-hearted intentions waned quickly and the rubbish is back with us once more.

Manfred's simple life included attending to his vegetable garden and, at the very least, a twice weekly drink at the Globe Inn, with his mate of long-standing, Charlie Menzies. It is said they met at Lauriknowe Primary School playground when Manfred was in P2 and Charlie was just starting out on the education ladder, and then remained firm friends ever since.

This might not be too surprising in a wee town like Dumfries, except that their paths took quite different directions.

Whereas Manfred lived with his wife in a council house and worked manually, Charlie remained single, broadcasting sport on the radio, whilst becoming a property tycoon, not just in Dumfries and Galloway but throughout the whole of Scotland. No-one is really sure how much he is worth but it must be a few million by now.

Although Manfred's slender shape stayed fairly constant, Charlie's shorter, squat physique did not: it expanded horizontally, his stomach extending out as far as his enormous cigars. And while Manfred dressed mostly in black, Charlie kept with his mission of wearing every colour known to man – and usually all at the same time.

A forlorn Charlie Menzies is standing in front of me at this very moment. He is at my back door. It is eight in the morning. He has never visited me before so it came as a surprise to open up and see him there. I invited him in. He looked like a lost puppy.

For the sake of balance, Charlie's shoulders are always arched well back from the vertical: making him walk like the big drum player in a marching band, and his extensive belly breached the threshold of my home a few seconds ahead of the rest of him. I offered a cup of tea: he accepted with a half-hearted nod.

His attire was much more subdued today – normally he makes a bird of paradise look drab – so, at this sad time, he had taken to wearing red slip-on shoes, dark green trousers, a navy-blue blazer, a cream shirt, no tie, rounded off with a pink handkerchief and chunky cigar, both poking out from the breast pocket of his jacket. His usual florid complexion was quite mottled and his age sagged his face. Summer had yet to pull the starting trigger and our nights have been cold of late, yet beads of perspiration bobbled on his brow.

He pulled the kitchen chair a couple of feet away from the

table, allowing plenty of room to manoeuvre in, before lowering himself down with all the trepidation of someone easing onto an ancient rope bridge across a high chasm. The chair gave out a few gasps but as soon as he was satisfied with its fortitude, he allowed his considerable weight to collapse down.

I laid a mug of strong tea in front of him, switched off the radio, and sat down at the table opposite, asking what I could do. It was a sad-eyed, hesitant Charlie who answered, his jaw quivering, 'You heard about Manfred.'

It wasn't a question, so he went on, 'He's left everything to me in his will.' He took a sip of the tea to ease the lump back down his throat. 'Not that there's much.' He added, quickly, 'Not that it matters, of course.' He sighed. 'I've sorted the funeral out for Monday. You'll be coming?'

I gave a nod.

'But there's still the house to be cleared out. The council want it done as soon as possible to get the next tenant in. I'll be honest with you Jin, even if I had the time, and I don't, I doubt if I could handle it by myself. I'm finding all this very difficult, I don't mind saying.' He took a longer gulp of tea. 'You're still in the business of helping folk out, aren't you?'

When he saw me nod again, he continued, 'I'm asking if you could help *me* out – see to the house, you know, look out anything of value, bundle up any documents, and get one of those house-clearing firms in to do the rest. Do you think you could do that?'

I hesitated. I'd certainly had the practice: both my uncles died leaving me with the job of tidying up after them. I sold their large houses, put the money in the bank, and now live comfortably off the interest. And before that it was my parents' house: the house I'm in now. But the memory of going through their things is still vivid: even after ten years. Perhaps it wouldn't be such a big deal this time – not being family – but I doubted it would be easy.

'I don't know, Charlie. It's not something I would care to do.'

'I understand.' He shuffled in his seat and fingered the cigar in his top pocket – perhaps needing to fire it up. 'He had no kids, not even a distant relation, I'm all he has... all he had, I mean.' He gave me dejected look and I knew I was going to say yes.

He went on, 'I'm honoured, of course, to be doing it. He was a good man. Always paid his way when it was his turn. Never allowed me to always foot the bill, as some do.' Charlie straightened a little and his tone became business-like, 'I have to be away for a day or two, you see, tying up some loose ends. I'm going in for my operation in about two weeks' time, so I don't know how long I'll be out of commission after that.'

'Oh, I didn't know. Nothing serious?'

He wafted an unconcerned hand through the air. 'No, it should be fine. Lionel has assured me the risks are quite low. The ticker needs a bit of a service, that's all. Lucky it's not the stomach: they'd need a drilling rig to get down into there.'

I gave a brief laugh – his weak smile deserved that, at least. 'Lionel?' I asked.

'My nephew.' His tone was lighter. 'All the family's brains have been filtered into him.'

We both knew it was fine to joke now.

'He's a surgeon up at the hospital,' he went on. 'I'm in good hands there.'

'Always best to keep it in the family, eh?'

'Too true. All the family I have now, in fact. So I'm lucky; it makes quite a difference, I can tell you. He used to work up in Edinburgh until recently; and he's one of the best in the country. So will you help me out with the house?' Another sip of tea. 'I imagine the only thing of real value is his car. It's still parked where he left it for his walk. Maybe I could give you a

9

lift out there right now and you could drive it back to his house – if you're not too busy. I have the keys with me.'

'In fact,' he added, almost as an afterthought, 'if you sold it, you could keep half of the money – for all the trouble.' He raised his hands to stop me from answering, saying quickly, 'I know, I know, you wouldn't do it for the money. You're a bit like me in that respect – you have enough to be secure – but the offer is still there. What do you say?'

Five minutes later I was in Charlie's Porsche heading out into the countryside, sneaking an amazed look, out the corner of my eye, at the way the steering wheel gouged into his stomach and the way he had to breathe in to turn corners. It was just as well we weren't on one of those corkscrew, hairpin-bend roads they have on the continent or else he would have ended up hyperventilating.

It wasn't really out to the countryside: it was only to the edge of town. We passed the hospital and then the Crichton Golf Club where I play. I glanced at the car park on passing and spotted Doc Halliday's car. This is my day for a game. In fact I should have been here, unloading my clubs at this very moment, but that wouldn't have been fair to Charlie. I had kept quiet about it.

He drove on and, after the Crichton Campus, turned left into a narrow lane with a dead-end sign at its entrance. Two hundred yards further on, a lonely blue car sat in a passing place. He pulled up behind, yanked hard on the hand brake, and sat rigidly still, eyes forward. I ask him where the body had been found and he pointed, without looking, to a bridleway off to our right – as the worn, wooden sign, sticking out of a hedge, indicated. When I climbed out I saw a large wreath on the ground no more than twenty yards along the track. I didn't need to ask who had arranged for it to be put there.

It was awkward getting the cars turned and I stalled this unfamiliar one in reverse a number of times – but then I've never been much of a driver. Eventually, though, we made it out and I followed him over to Manfred's house on Terregles Street, parking on the newly created red-bricked space in the front garden, by the front door, Charlie leaving his vehicle out in the street.

It was a typical row of council houses: silver roughcast, two up and two down. Although, judging by some of the other front doors, a few of them had been bought over.

He handed over the house key, saying, 'I'm not going in, Jin. I'll wait 'til after the funeral. D'you want a run back over?'

I refused his offer, deciding on some much needed exercise, and pocketed the key. Charlie was about to leave when he leaned out of the car window. 'Could you do me one more favour, if you don't mind? Come with me tomorrow – I need to tell Manfred's mother that he's passed away.'

Asa Murdoch and I arrived at our local, The Bruce, at the back of eight: Asa likes to have an early beer so he's not starting a session on an empty stomach. And we were discussing some important matters: the differences between chutney, pickle, and relish, and whether the majestic Queen of the South would end up above Gretna, our newly installed, cocky rivals, when the new football season gets under way. We were toying with a new bet.

But, before we could get into our stride, an interruption arrived in the form of a very beery and bleary-eyed Jackie Gittes staggering his way in our direction. The black leather jacket over his brown t-shirt looked new, as did his jeans. Jackie's centre parted, ear-covering, greying hair sat firmly on his head like a saddle, and the years had rounded his shoulders a touch; yet there was mirth embedded in the deep lines radiating from the corners of his large, watery and slightly bulbous eyes. For decoration, he wore a necklace made from a white bead threaded onto a leather strap.

11

'Jinky...Asa...' he slurred, giving each of us a nod in turn. He was a touch below average height. He had to look up at Asa but was level with me.

'Don't often see you here,' Asa stated.

Jackie's eyes wandered from my face to Asa's and back again. He'd had a few. It was as if he was on the deck of a ship in rough seas and we were watching from the shore. A couple of times I had to land a propping palm on his chest to stop him falling onto me. Each time his loosely held pint of beer splashed onto his light brown shoes – narrowly missing mine – but he didn't appear to notice.

'Just come to see... how the other... half live," he said, his words uttered in glissando-like bursts.

'What have you been up to then? Must be a wee while since I saw you,' I said.

'Bit of this... and a bit of that,' he said. Then added, using mostly 'sh' sounds, "It's a special... occasion.' And, with an exaggerated nod, continued, 'That's right... that's what it is. That's why... I'm here. A special occasion... it is.'

The nodding continued for a while longer as he tried to drag the reason for the occasion up from the bottom of the ale-filled well of his soggy mind.

'And what might that be, Jackie?' I enquired, cawing the handle of the well.

He tapped the side of his nose and gave a wink. 'Now that... would be telling... wouldn't it?'

I remembered Jackie was one of those people who liked to wink a lot – even when sober – inviting you to the doorstep of a secret but no further.

We went to the same school; he was three years younger. Nevertheless, I could recall him, which was unusual, as it tended to be the older ones who made an impact. But Jackie *did* have some kind of appeal. Even then he was a wee bit dodgy, roguish, always getting himself into scrapes, and out again.

12

The girls liked him – he was good looking in those days, I suppose – and there was the hint of danger, which must have been very enticing for them. The belle of our school was undoubtedly Jill Jones. She was a year younger than me and, therefore, two older than Jackie but that didn't stop her falling for his charms, and they started going out together: much to the dismay of the rest of the boys at the school. They were of similar height, both slim, both with longish, wavy hair. At times, from the back, and with only a quick glance, it could be difficult to tell them apart. Of course, they were called Jackie 'n Jill – even if there was only one of them present.

Every lunchtime they could be seen propping up a wall, Jackie's hands all over her as though he was turtle-waxing a car. I'm told there was a thrill in watching them go at it – not that I ever did. Back then I thought that, after a while, Jill would stare beyond Jackie's good looks and see his lack of future: but I was wrong. Despite the many bust-ups they eventually married. The last I heard they had separated after nineteen or so years of wedlock.

'I've got a... job for you... Jinky,' Jackie was saying.

I was about to tell him that I didn't do marital problems, when he went on, his words continuing to stumble out, as though responding to slow prompts from inside his brain – like a very forgetful actor on stage, 'I want you... to find the owner... of a red Corsa... L reg. He's quite an... old man... like the car. In his sixties... maybe.'

He gave Asa a long look. 'Nothing risky... about it... mind.' Asa works for the police, as a civilian, on the computers.

I wondered if I should mention to Jackie that he must be approaching, or have reached forty by now and that sixty is only a short slide down the other side. I chose to go with, 'I would need to know why, Jackie.'

He gave me an assessing look for a moment, his head moving back an inch or two, before producing another wide

13

grin. 'That's no problem... Jinky. I bashed... into him... the other day... in my car... dented his front wing... coming out of... Terregles Street... turning right... never saw him... bad corner... that one. He was minding... his own business... Jinky... and... bash... right into... the side of him.' To simulate the accident Jackie clapped his free hand against his glass, causing a wave of beer to flow up over his wrist.

He went on, unperturbed, 'Nowt much damage... to mine... the bumper took the force. But I'm worried... at the time... I can tell you... and he's getting out... of his car... and me not having... any insurance... you see... didn't know... what would happen.'

I gave a tut and Jackie nodded several times in agreement before adding, '*But* I can assure you... *and* Asa... that I have since... taken care... of fixing myself... up with some good... coverage. And do you know... the surprising thing?' He leaned towards me with a tilt of the head, like a parrot spotting a fancy nut.

I shook mine and laid a restraining hand against his chest yet again.

'It was... that when he got out... you know... to have a look... at the damage... on his machine... and I got out... with a bit of a sweat on... he just shrugged... said not to mind... it was an old car... and it could have happened... to anyone... no hard feelings... nothing to worry about... and do you know... what he did next?'

Asa and I shrugged in unison.

'He held out... his hand... for me to shake.' Jackie took a wobbly step back to create space for a demonstration of handshaking, at the same time saying, 'Then he was off... and away... before I could utter... a word.'

Jackie's hand remained out in front of him. Instead of grasping it, I asked, 'So why do you want to find him, then? Seems like a lucky break for you.'

14

His hand turned to point a wavering index finger at me. 'Ah... that's just it... I want to... pay him... that's what I want... A nice man... don't you think... he was a nice man? I want to give him... a wee bit of money... maybe fifty quid... something like that. It's the spirit.' Jackie's hand dipped into his jeans' pocket and swirled around.

'You must be doing well, then, Jackie, if you're handing out money for no reason,' Asa remarked.

Jackie gave a smile and muttered, 'Doing fine... Asa. Doing fine. And it looks... as though... you're doing... fine also.' He tugged his hand out and started patting Asa's extensive tummy as though clapping a dog. It was not a good idea and I could see Asa's large, bulky frame prickle. Quickly, I pulled Jackie's hand away.

'What about a drink... you two?' he went on, oblivious to the offence, reaching into his pocket once again, producing a fat roll of notes.

I declined, showing him my nearly full glass. 'So that's all you know about him – he drives an L reg. Corsa?' I asked.

'And it's red... don't forget. Here... take the £50... out of that... and a couple of extra... for yourself.' He slapped the roll of money against my chest.

I grasped the notes to stop them falling to the ground, but also to shield them from view. The Bruce is a good pub and Dumfries folk are normally fine but you can never be too careful: flashing stacks of money about is never recommended, anywhere.

I peeled a £50 note away and handed over the rest, guiding them back into his pocket with a hand on his wrist, saying, 'You can pay me after the job, Jackie. Okay? I don't usually take any money up front.'

Jackie went on, 'As well as that...' I don't think he heard me groan, for he continued without a break, 'I would like you... to find out... about a Don Gardiner. See what... you can dig up...

15

He's new to the area.'

'Good one, Jackie,' I muttered. His blank look almost made me point out the digging and Gardiner pun but deciding against it, I said, 'Again, I would need a reason, Jackie.'

'Do I... have to?'

'If I find out any information I would need to be sure it's not going to be misused.'

'Aw... come on. You know me.'

'Exactly,' Asa and I replied together.

'All right... all right.' There was a pause as he took his first long pull from his now half-empty pint. The sleeve of his jacket dealt with the small amount of froth on his lips; the rest of the head lay over his shoes. 'I thought... you might say that. And I can tell you... in front of Asa... as well... it's no problem... nothing illegal. He wants to... join our poker group. Yeah... that's right. He'll be the first... outsider... we've had... so I need to... make sure... he is... okay... will pay debts... you know... a solid character... just need... some background info... on the guy... that's all.'

'Poker group?'

'Strictly for those... in the know... sorry... can't invite you... Jinky... others wouldn't... like it.' He tapped the side of his nose again. 'Can you... do it? Let's say... £50... for both jobs.'

'Why don't you do it yourself, Jackie? It's not likely to be all that difficult: a few questions here and there.'

He thought for a moment. 'And I know... how to wallpaper... and paint a room... doesn't mean... I want to spend... my time... doing it... right? Especially... when I can... afford it. Do you know... at this very moment... my brother's decorating... my room. Better here... than there... wouldn't you say?'

When Jackie left suddenly to visit the toilet, Asa said, 'You going to take it?'

I gave a shrug to signify 'why not' and said, 'You won't mind getting me details of the car, will you? There'll be a drink in it. Do you think he'll be all right?'

Asa didn't answer, but a grin spread across his face as he asked, 'Do you remember the time Jackie was at that dance at school?'

'Which one?'

'You must remember. Him and Jill were going at it big guns in the corner: the endless kissing, the frayed lips stuff. You remember the kind of thing?'

I was about to shake my head when he answered for me, 'No, of course you don't: you never did it, for some reason.' He gave a weary sigh before going on, 'And, somehow, in the meleé, Jackie managed to dislodge one of Jill's capped teeth, and it stuck in his throat, choking him. He had to be rushed to hospital. His first visitor was Jill, asking if her cap had been found, adding that, if he'd swallowed it…'

'… could he keep a lookout and return it to her as soon as possible as the dentist would be able to cement it back into place,' I finished off.

I downed the rest of my gafoni. 'Look, Asa, I'm going to see to Jackie, talk him into going home, and give him a hand back. It shouldn't take too long.'

Asa gave me a knowing stare but said nothing. He knew my concerns. Earlier in the year I'd had a couple of bad experiences after leaving the pub in an unfit state. But, on top of that, with Jackie throwing his cash about, I wanted to make sure no harm came to him.

Asa muttered, 'If you start helping anyone who's had a few too many, Jinky, you'll be at it all night, every night.'

'You're right. But, then, none of them have just offered me a job. So I need to keep him safe or else there'll be no payday for me. Do you want a beer before I go?'

He shrugged. 'Does a fruit punch, does a side kick, a book mark, a…?'

'Okay, okay, Asa, I get it: it was a daft question.'
17

Andy Wishart, the barman, served me. As he laid the pint delicately on the counter – Andy takes great pride in every drink he pours – he said, 'Oh, by the way, there's a message for you from Onion Sanny. He wants you to go and see him soon. He's got work for you.'

Onion Sanny is a bit of an eccentric, a recluse. I did a job for him once before, so he must have been pleased enough with the result to ask me back. Although, what a man who is rarely seen and whose private life is a mystery would want with me again was a wee bit puzzling – but then I do like mysteries.

'Just out of curiosity, Andy, how does Sanny get in touch?' I couldn't imagine him phoning, and certainly not by coming into the bar.

'Same as last time. There was a bit of paper pinned to the cellar door when I arrived this morning. Nice handwriting.'

Friday 14th July

The front door key for Manfred's house weighed heavily in my trouser pocket as I walked down Buccleuch Street, on my way to Charlie Menzies' house. I passed the red sandstone building of the Sheriff Court and gave it a long look as always. Its intricate carvings are fascinating: the way the stone has been expertly sculpted to resemble coils of rope. It must be nice to produce something so beautiful and enduring.

It didn't feel right to be scruffy when telling a mother her son had died so, as a mark of respect, I was in trousers instead of the usual jeans, as well as a smart white shirt and polished black shoes. It was hot under these clothes: and the warmth wasn't solely down to the alcohol distilling in my system from last night, it was the fact that Dumfries had woken to a fat sun in cloudless, blue-grey sky. The summer show was about to make an appearance at last.

And what a performance it was going to be. The forecast was for steadily improving temperatures – records to be broken – with, at the very least, a staggering 30°C expected over our area on Wednesday. That might just be a bit too much for us: in Scotland we wait expectantly all year for the heat to arrive, and then when it finally does, we remember that we don't really like it all that warm. It's like craving an ice cream only to be reminded, on the first taste, that the mouth is filled with sensitive teeth.

There had been no hint of this sudden change in the weather last night as I'd dropped off an increasingly squiffy Jackie back at his home. At times it was like guiding a butterfly through a gale but he did manage, with a lot of prodding, to give me some snippets of information on this Don Gardiner guy and I was back in the pub in good time to watch Asa's face turn as smiley and bright as today's sun.

Charlie's home is on Station Road – through the town and

across the river – in one of the many new, impressive bungalows built there. Why he needs such a big place when he lives alone is beyond me. However, as he designed it personally, it must have been exactly what he wanted.

In a similar way, my dad, his two bothers and my mother's sister all bought large houses with their spouses, and in the same street as well; however, I was the only child produced. I daresay it must have been a great disappointment to them not to have created more. Fortunately, they had enough friends calling in and staying over to make sure the space in their homes wasn't totally wasted.

This was my first visit to his house and Charlie's doorbell gave a hearty, welcoming chime. After a few moments he rolled into view, malformed through the frosted glass door. He gave a grim, 'I suppose we have to do this' shrug before beckoning me in. It was cooler inside, and I followed him along a corridor, ending up in the heart of the house, passing a small room with a grand piano on the way.

Charlie had gone for a sober appearance today also: a dark green shirt, a pair of brown and purple checked braces holding up light blue, slightly flared trousers, with a pair of red shoes peering out from underneath. He was finishing off a cup of tea in his large, ultra modern kitchen, where the highly polished steel hob and surrounds gleamed my reflection, as oodles of fancy gadgets, sitting on every surface, waited for work; while a chunky, wooden, circular table, surrounded by six robust chairs, stood patiently in the centre of the room, ready for its next meal.

He offered me some tea but, as I was hot enough already, I declined for once, with a shake of the head. After a final gulp from his mug, casting the dregs into his stainless steel sink, he asked, in a heavy voice, 'Do I need a jacket?'

I spotted a yellow blazer on a peg on the back of a door. 'No, you'll be fine. It's really starting to fire up out there.'

Those were my first words of the morning: it was probably the same for Charlie. When you live alone it can be quite late in the day before any are required, and you're never quite sure how they will come out. I noticed we both gave short coughs afterwards.

Charlie clapped his hands firmly and a distant beep sounded from another room. I followed him as he continued to clap, the beep growing stronger. He found his keys in the sitting room, under a cushion.

On the way out we passed the room with the piano again. This time I couldn't help lingering for a longer look. 'You play?' I enquired, knowing the answer was almost certainly in the negative as the piano was covered, head to toe, in framed photographs: even the keyboard lid held several pictures, standing in a line like dominoes. It would be too much of a footer to take each one off every time to play. An expensive table, indeed.

'It was my Mum's,' Charlie replied, moving slowly into the room. 'I wish I'd stuck at it, though. It's a great skill. My father bought it for her in an auction. Couldn't resist it, he said.'

There was a small brass plaque just above the keyhole on the lid. It said: *'To my darling Celia, from your loving husband Colin xxx.*

The piano was the only piece of furniture and the room was just big enough to hold it: designed with it in mind no doubt. There were other photos on the walls as well, showing a beaming Charlie shaking hands with various dignitaries.

All this is quite a contrast to my own home as no-one in my family owned a camera: so there are no photos of me growing up and I have no pictures in the house at all. It saves on dusting, I suppose.

Charlie picked up one of the photographs from the piano and cradled it in both hands. 'Sad business,' he said. 'This is my brother and his wife. They died in a car crash on the A76. It'll

21

be coming up for fifteen years ago now. D'you remember?' I gave him a tiny nod back: I had only a vague memory. 'It's a terrible road that one – so many deaths. He was three years younger than me,' he added.

The people in the picture weren't wearing colourful clothes.

'So Lionel the surgeon is their son?'

He nodded back. 'He had graduated medical school by the time of the accident.' He pointed to the next frame. 'That's him on his graduation day with us...' His voice faded away.

'He'll be coming to the funeral on Monday?' It was something to say to break the building silence.

Charlie shook his head. 'No, he's very busy with his work. I suggested he doesn't. It's not like he knew Manfred, or anything like that. There's plenty of other people needing his help up at the hospital.'

I examined the photograph of Lionel with his gown and diploma, and then the next one in the line. It was an old black and white picture of a couple on their wedding day: the man, smart in his soldier's uniform, standing arm in arm with his new bride. She held a nice bouquet in her free hand and wore a small dark hat at a jaunty angle.

'My parents' wedding day,' Charlie said, noting my gaze. 'They look so young. She was a bonny, bonny woman.' He gave a shake of the head and he would have talked me through the rest of the photos, and I would have gladly listened but this wasn't the time.

We left his house.

'Are we really going to see Manfred's mother?' I asked, opening the car door.

'I'm afraid so. She stays in a home, on the road to Moffat.' Charlie groaned as he levered himself into the driver's seat, using the steering wheel as a handle. 'Not really compus mentis. The staff there have tried to tell her but they don't reckon they've got through. They thought I might make a difference. Sometimes, it seems, although it's not very often now, she'll remember things from the past. She might recognise me – but I'm not all that hopeful. It's been a long time. Only fair to give it a shot, though.' He wiped at his eyes with the back of a hand, started the engine with a roar, and we were off.

Charlie took in a deep breath as he guided the car round a roundabout, before saying, 'Poor soul. It's very sad. She was so lively, busy, always good to me when I was growing up. I was round there playing almost as often as Manfred was round at mine. She used to bake twice a week. You know, I can still smell the cooking even after all this time – rock buns, soda scones, treacle scones. Great cook, she was. We could never leave them long enough to cool down, him and me, always right in there. I don't think Manfred's dad ever got to see any of them.' He gave a ghost of a smile in remembrance.

'You may be in luck,' said a very stout, bustling woman, carrying a cup of tea in one hand and a tower of biscuits in the other. Her undersized, blue, nylon uniform gaped alarmingly down the front, throttling the necks of the buttons as they tried desperately to keep the garment shut. In the gaps I could see her underwear: I didn't want to.

As she showed us through, the rustle of her uniform created enough static to power a small village. Cleverly, she had pinned her hair firmly into a bun, stopping any of the electricity escaping through the ends. 'She seems quite bright today, Mrs Mann, compared to yesterday: but then that's not saying much.'

She led us into a large room with armchairs spaced round the walls. A few of her clients sat, slumped, fingering their cardigans, staring into space, ignoring the loud television, fixed on the news channel. The nurse raised her voice over the TV, 'Some days it takes a lot of coaxing to get her out of bed. This morning was quite good, really. Over there – by the window.'

She motioned with her head towards another large room filled with white-haired people sitting patiently in another batch of comfortable armchairs.

At the far end, in a bay window, a woman sat in a rocking chair, moving steadily back and forward, staring out at the trees beyond. She had cushions piled up on either side, propping her in place. Her hair had been recently permed, and the white cardigan and tartan trousers both looked new.

We moved towards her, zig-zagging between the chairs – no one paid us any heed – and Charlie pulled over a wooden seat and eased into it, sitting down facing her. I stood to one side.

'Mrs Mann? It's Charlie. Do you remember me? Charlie Menzies.'

She continued to look away. Out into the distance.

He shuffled forward, riskily to the edge of his chair, his legs splayed to accommodate his stomach, leaning over, trying to block out her view, staring into her face. He waited, before saying it again, this time touching her delicately on the arm. It took a while before she turned from the window to gaze blankly at him.

'I used to come round, Mrs Mann, to play with Jimmy. Do you remember? It's me, Charlie Menzies?' He was speaking deliberately, and louder than was probably necessary: there was no indication she was deaf.

'Wee Charlie?' She spoke in a weak, throaty voice and her hand lifted off her lap towards him. He grasped it and nodded frantically.

Her expressionless eyes stared at him. 'I know a wee Charlie.'

'It's me, Mrs Mann, it's me.' He took a hard swallow. 'But I have some bad news for you.' He paused, unsure if she was listening, but continued anyway, 'It's Jimmy – your Jimmy – he's passed away.'

The words appeared to bounce off her. She stared at him, her
24

face unmoving.

'Do you know what I am saying, Mrs Mann?' he asked despairingly.

There was a pause and then she turned her head towards me. I stepped forward and laid a hand on her thin shoulder. 'I was a friend of Jimmy's as well. I'm very sorry for your loss.'

'You should tell his real mother,' she said, staring straight up at me. And with that her eyes moved away, her head turned back to the window, her hand regained her lap, and the rocking started up once more.

Charlie dropped me off at my home. On the way back, after a few miles in silence, I'd asked him what he thought she had meant. He dismissed her comment straight off, his eyes never leaving the road, saying that she wasn't in her right mind anymore. Then he gave a tired shake of the head and the matter was closed. The trip had taken a lot out of him.

It was nearly four o'clock in the afternoon when I drove over the Buccleuch Bridge, wishing my sunglasses weren't in a drawer in the kitchen. I wasn't going to do anything with Manfred's house for the moment – it didn't feel right until the funeral was over – but I wanted to get a rough idea of the size of the task before contacting the clearing company.

Manfred's car sat in its space in front of his house. There wasn't enough room for two vehicles, so I parked in the street, and with a great deal of trepidation, turned the key and stepped into his home. The weather had turned the place stuffy but I didn't feel I had the authority to open any windows.

A quick inspection showed it to be very neat: the only thing out of place was a half drunk cup of tea, standing on the kitchen table. There were faint marks on its rim where his lips had taken their last sip. I placed it in the sink and filled it up with water. It wasn't comfortable here, but I forced myself on

25

through the rooms.

It didn't look too big a job: there was no real clutter anywhere and a filing cabinet upstairs in the back bedroom held neatly labelled folders with all his important documents. That was enough snooping; I needed to leave.

There was a library book sitting under the phone in the hallway. I picked it up. It was overdue, so I took it with me and was standing at the front door, assessing Manfred's car, when the next-door neighbour came over to the fence for a blether.

He was a man in his fifties with little hair left and a puckered brow. Judging by his dusty t-shirt and trousers he worked on a building site. The trousers had once been part of a pin-stripe suit. He wore no shoes, and his socks had holes in them. Shaving had not taken place on this day and his fingernails held generous amounts of dirt. I didn't know him and I doubted if he knew me, so, as is the way, he needed to get enough information to satisfy his curiosity.

'You a relation of Manfred's, only I didnae think he had any?' They like to be direct around here. He gave me his most penetrating stare – meaning he wasn't going to be fobbed off with anything but the truth, which he reckoned he was entitled to due to the fact that he lived next door.

'You knew him well?' I asked in return. I would give him what he wanted, eventually, but sometimes I like to play them along.

'Aye, been here six years now. He was a good neighbour to have. They say he's lived here thirty-five years.' That statement was a question.

'I'm not sure,' I replied. I knew the answer but asked, 'Been working today?'

'Aye, we're on bonus right now.'

I didn't ask him to elaborate, giving, instead, the necessary details: who I was and what I was doing here. He nodded continually as I spoke as though confirming everything I said made sense.

'So you'll be selling the car, then?'

'That's right. You don't want to buy it, do you?' I joked.

His ears pricked up at this, sensing a bargain. 'How much?'

I backtracked a little. 'Oh, I'm not sure right now. I'll have to take it round a few garages to see what's on offer.' I would only be taking it to my friend Tread Dunlop.

'It seems a pity,' I went on. 'He spent a lot of money getting this car-bay put in, and then never got the full use of it.' I tapped my foot against the red bricks a few times.

'How do you mean?'

'It looks almost brand new. These things don't come cheap: I had a quote for my front garden not so long ago, but it was too much to stump up.'

'Naw, it's not new. It's been here as long as I have. In any case, the council would have paid for some of it. Remember they had that fancy idea of getting rid of the clutter on the streets? They wanted everyone to have their own driveway.' He pursed his lips and mimed drinking tea from a fancy cup, pinkie extended – the other hand holding the saucer.

'He never used it, that's all,' he went on, after replacing the cup. 'Kept it nice and tidy though. Manfred had one of them power-hoses. But he never had the car on it. This is the first time I've seen it here – and that's a fact. He never reversed, did Manfred.'

I thought he was having me on, but he continued when he saw my disbelieving expression, 'It's absolutely true. I dinnae really ken what happened to start it – but he never reversed. Wouldn't talk about it, mind.

He always parked out on the street and drove off the way he was facing. If he went to Tesco he parked at the far edge, well away from the store, where it was quiet, so that he could pull-through and be sitting ready to leave. I've seen him do it. Never went near at Christmas, you know – too busy.

27

If he ever needed to turn back – he wouldn't. He'd go on until he came upon a roundabout or circled round the block. He never went into a cul-de-sac, that's for sure. Never. Parked at the bottom and walked up. That's the God's honest truth. Do you want to ask the wife?'

I told him it wasn't necessary, said goodbye, and hurried off. If that was true then why had Manfred ended up in a dead-end road before going on his last stroll?

Quickly, I drove away from the house with my mind churning over this piece of unexpected information. The car was hot: the sky had turned into a deeper blue and the sun beat down with a spiky energy, suitably invigorated after a nice long holiday away from Scotland. My clothes were heavy and uncomfortable. I could have done without being in the car today but I had another visit to make and that was on the other side of town.

The open window whooshed noisy warm air across my right ear as I drove over to see Onion Sanny – Andy the barman had said he wanted to see me and I didn't like to disappoint. To be granted an audience with him at any time was as rare as a friendly wasp, so to have a second meeting with the man within the year made me feel honoured.

It took less than ten minutes to negotiate the traffic and park at the rundown driveway of the old hotel, off the Lockerbie Road. It was a relief to get out and walk in the shade, up the overgrown path, to his abode.

Sanny's weather-beaten caravan sits in a corner of the grounds of a ruined hotel. No-one is sure when he moved in or where he stayed before: it seems this has been his home since records began. I knocked on the grey-white door and jumped back off the wooden step, wondering if he would be in. He would do his poaching at night so there had to be a reasonable chance.

Sanny was quick to open up, his head peeking round the

edge of the door giving me no chance to see inside. 'Ah, it's yersel.' His sharp blue and grey eyes locked onto me again. He got straight to the point. 'A've got a job fer ye.'

In one swift movement he was out onto the top step, closing the door behind. He was remarkably agile for his age – whatever that might be.

Sanny's summer collection was the same as his winter one: an off-white nightshirt tucked into heavy, faded black trousers, held up by a set of brown braces, fastened to the top of his trousers by buttons. His feet were bare, well maintained, and hairless; unlike his head, where his long white, unkempt locks fell almost to his shoulders. His skin held deep wrinkles: circling his face like contour lines on a hilly map. It might get quite hot in the caravan for the few odd days in summer, but he didn't seem unduly flustered at this moment.

'Ye ken the hotel up there's to be demolished and they're building new hooses?' he started. The finger he pointed towards the hill was trembling.

I nodded.

'Well, that means A hiv to go.'

I was taken aback; my voice was slightly shaky. 'You're going to leave here?'

'Aye. That's whit A said, didn A?'

It wasn't right. The end of an era – like the end of the dinosaurs. 'Sorry to hear that. I really am. It must be quite a wrench for you, after all this time.' I shoved in a sneaky, 'How long has it been now?'

He dismissed my concern with a flick of the hand. 'A've been meaning tae move in ony case. Thought aboot it on November 23rd, nineteen seeventy-echt an never quite got roon to it. It's aboot time. A'm getting stale here. A've seen enough. They've fixed me up with another place – the construction company hiv.'

As my last question was likely to remain unanswered, I went

with another one, 'And what can I do for you?'

'A'll need me stuff shifted. A want ye tae help me. Ye dae that, don't ye?'

First it was Manfred's house and now this. These are not the kind of jobs I normally undertake, but, again, I couldn't possibly turn this one down. It was a once in a lifetime chance: an opportunity to peek into the mysteries of Sanny's life, to delve into the full workings of his caravan, to understand something of the man. I would, at long last, be in a position to find out if all the rumours about him are true.

'I don't really do removals but I'll give it a go,' I said, trying to hold my excitement at bay. 'You know you can get people in to do that kind of thing? Professionals.' I felt obliged to point it out.

He shook his head violently, shut one eye, and stared ferociously with the other one, as though peering into a microscope and not liking what he saw. 'Dinnae want strangers messin aboot with ma stuff. Why wid A want that, eh?'

Fortunately, he went on, saving me from coming up with an answer, 'A want ye tae hire a van to tak ma things over tae the new place. A cannae drive, ye ken.'

'You'll have to pay – with money – for the van.' When I'd helped Sanny before he had paid me with two bottles of liqueur. It was wonderful stuff and I wouldn't be complaining about receiving more of the same – but it was unlikely that the van hire people would be as accommodating.

'A ken aboot payin. Am no daft.' He fixed onto me again, gauging if I thought he was. A few seconds later he added, in a slightly softer, inquiring tone, 'Wid ye be able tae dae that?'

'Certainly. No problem. What day did you have in mind and how big a van would you need?' I took a step back to size up his very small, battered caravan.

'Better get the biggest ye can.'

'Do you want me to bring round some empty boxes?'

'Naw. A'll see tae all that.'

We made arrangements. The hotel was scheduled to be demolished on Thursday, six days from now, Manfred's funeral was on the Monday before that, and I hoped to have his house cleared and finished by Tuesday or, possibly, Wednesday morning at the latest, depending on the removal firm. We decided to go for Wednesday midday. I was to pay for the van and Sanny would reimburse me – with actual money, he said.

I left, thrilled; even the knowledge of working in record high temperatures on that day couldn't take away the excitement. It would be well worth it. We hadn't discussed a fee for my troubles, in fact, I might even do it for free: it's not as if Sanny can have all that much money. Come to think of it, the construction company may very well pay for the hire of the van if they were asked nicely. I must remember to mention it to Sanny the next time I see him.

Helping the living to move is a much better task. It was another job to keep me busy. Soon I would be able to find out if Sanny does, indeed, keep his meat, fruit and vegetables under large pyramids to keep them fresh, and if he still eats a raw onion every day to keep him healthy. There might even be the chance to discover what's in his liqueur and how he makes it.

Other rumours circulate as well: Tread says Sanny has a trained crow to gather worms, and when he's ready to go fishing, it dumps them in a tin cup. Tread also says that Sanny can hypnotise a rabbit at forty feet and make it hop towards him, right into an empty pot. But then you can never tell with Tread – sometimes I think he just makes stuff up.

The fact that Sanny wanted my help buoyed me. He didn't want a removal firm. He didn't consider me a stranger. I couldn't wait for Wednesday.

As I turned the corner into my street my phone buzzed. It was a call from Asa. It had to be important: he wouldn't have phoned otherwise. I'd had experience of that. I parked the car and stepped from its confines.

'Meet me down at the caul in twenty minutes?' It was more of a command than a request.

'Can't it wait?' I knew the answer, but continued, 'I'm just back from Sanny's, I'm roasted and I need a bit of cooling off first. It's as warm out here as The Bruce's beer.'

'Hey, watch it, Andy pours a decent pint of ale, I'll have you know.'

'Can't I at least get a drink?'

'It can't wait, Jinky.'

'I'm in front of my house at this very moment,' I pleaded.

'No. Get yourself down to the caul.'

Deciding to ditch the concentrated heat of the car, I trudged off towards the river, the phone still at my ear: I needed to find out some things about Manfred's death.

Did anyone else think there was something suspicious about it? Would there need to be an investigation? The funeral might have to be delayed. Maybe I should have voiced my concerns straightaway by going to the police with the fact that Manfred never reversed.

'Asa, what's happened with Manfred?'

'How do you mean?'

'Is anyone looking into his death?'

'What are you talking about?'

'No-one thinks it's suspicious?'

'Why would anyone think that? He had a history of heart trouble and died of a heart attack. It's all in the doctor's report.'

'Oh, I didn't know he had a condition – Charlie never said.' I felt a bit silly. Nevertheless, there was still the question of why he would drive up a dead-end road in the first place. Was it simply that he had a premonition that he was never going to return to his car? There's certainly a nice view of the town from out there. Perhaps it was the last thing he wanted to see.

32

I cleared my thoughts and asked, 'Aren't you going to give me a clue as to what this is about, Asa? It better be worth the effort.'

'I'll explain when I see you.'

'So it's a call to the caul then.'

'Funny. Hurry up, Jinky.'

I picked up the pace, increasing the sweaty hug of my shirt, passing through the centre of town, down The Vennel, arriving at The Whitesands – the stretch of riverfront from Devorgilla Bridge to St Michael's Bridge – in good time.

The Nith aims to flood here three or four times in the course of a year so that might be why the riverfront hosts bus stances, a car park, and very little else. Years ago the caul diverted water to the mill but now its function is to end the tidal section of the river.

The atmosphere was sticky and the air around me had gathered up the heavy, pungent perfume of the abundant pink, wild orchids growing on the riverbank. I tried shoogling some clothing free, to allow air to circulate but it was futile in the still and shadeless atmosphere. It was getting close to the point where the shorts would have to be howked out and the cobwebs blown from the sandals. I gave a sigh and looked around.

Despite my agitated state I could sense that this late Friday afternoon held a lazier feel for others. The heat had dragged out time like dripping molasses and had soothed the usual flurry, allowing people an escape from the normal rush. Even the way they were saying hello had changed from the familiar short, sharp 'aye' into a much longer, lengthier slide, making it possible to convey the rather ominous, 'if this is the start of the heat, I'm no looking forward to it getting any hotter' message: the thought uppermost in the minds of Dumfries folk.

There was still no Asa. It was unusual: he's normally very punctual. In fact, he veers on the side of early, but, for once, the meeting place was not in The Bruce so that might have something to do with it.

The Whitesands was busy and a few of the men were already ahead of the game – prancing around in t-shirts and shorts, craftily prepared for the summer onslaught. A late-in-the-day coach from Maryport had pulled in, its door springing open to pour white-haired, permed, cardigan-clad pensioners out onto our streets. As is their way, they will, in time, move three-abreast in a slow, snaking, pavement-clogging meander through town, relentlessly drawn to a café, ending up with a cup of tea and a tray-bake.

Still no sign of Asa. He would need to be contacted. I gave a sigh and glanced down as I fumbled for my phone. The vision at my feet blasted shock waves through me.

Sometimes, on a dark night, I've mistaken a sudden blowing leaf for a rat, and it always sparks a bolt of primeval fright, an involuntary jump, a race of the pulse. It felt the same this time. I was almost standing on it – at one point I might have been. Why hadn't I noticed it on arriving? I bent down for a closer examination.

My birthday was earlier this month – the 2nd – and the passing years are starting to take their toll and my forty-three-year-old eyes are misbehaving at close quarters now: they require the aid of reading glasses, bought from the pound shop. So, squeezing them out of my other trouser pocket, I crabbed down onto my hands and knees for a closer look at the pavement.

Sure enough there was a small photo stuck there and the person looking up at me was very, very familiar. It was the face that often fixes in front of my eyes. It was Chiara. There could be no doubt about it: she is very difficult to mistake. I might be a high handicapper in the looks department but Chiara plays off scratch; and here she was, in a photo, stuck to the ground, at this very spot!

It was a wee bit smaller than the passport type, and roundish

– about the size of a two pence coin. Its edges were rough, jagged: as though it had been torn from a larger picture. The image was slightly faded: it might have been here for some time. I tried to peel it away but it was made from delicate paper and ripped.

What did this mean? I was still down on my hands and knees when my phone gave a brief buzz. A passing woman shot me a funny stare and I sprung to my feet to take the text. It was from Asa: he couldn't make it after all, something to do with work. He'd meet me back at my home in about an hour.

I stood, rooted, wondering what to do next and how to explain the photo. I suppose it could have fallen out of Chiara's purse during her visit to Dumfries back in April – but it wasn't likely – although the photo did look worn enough to have been there a while. If not that, then what? As far as I knew she had never returned to my home town.

We had said our goodbyes in April and we had parted one night in the Dock Park. It was for the best. We live hundreds of miles apart – so what chance was there? How could it possibly continue? At the time I was only thankful for having experienced a stimulating, yet fleeting, encounter with a beautiful woman. I suppose I thought I was entitled to nothing more. I had walked away from her imagining she would fade from my brain, as I would disappear from her thoughts.

But it didn't work out that way – for on that dark, terrible night her face appeared in front of my eyes and would not leave. And then through the long days in the rigid hospital bed, barely able to move, the desire to hear her, to sense her presence, increased by the hour until I could hold back no longer. I persuaded Asa to find her phone number. And I called.

She was surprised to hear from me; I felt immediate relieve in her voice. But I was hesitant, not sure how to continue. It was vital to show her how I felt, to demonstrate her importance to me. I had to tell her how much she meant to me, explain that

I didn't want it to end. So I told her something I'd been yearning to say: for the first time I gave her my mobile phone number.

It was a brand new number as well: too many people had gathered up my old one. Other than my four close friends, she would be the only person now to possess it. Surely that had to be enough to convey my feelings.

After that call in April, we stayed in touch. I played down my considerable injuries: I didn't want her to feel obliged to visit. But I'm not very good with phones. I don't like them: you can't see into the other person's eyes and, in the next few weeks, our conversations became shorter and shorter, and less and less frequent, until they dried up completely.

Chiara did suggest I take the train to see her but I have never managed to venture down: something always crops up. Really, if I ever made that trip, I think it would end up in a disappointment, or, at the very least, I would be.

Certainly, there would be no end of places to stay: she has a number of properties throughout England. She buys into developments before the houses are built and sells them on, a year or two later, fully furnished, invariably at a substantial profit. She moves around and stays in each one from time to time, keeping an eye on them.

I don't even know if she's seeing other men. I would expect so. I imagine she goes about her affairs as normal: a woman like that must have boundless opportunities. As for me, I've had no urge to see anyone else – couldn't care less in fact.

Heavy-hearted, I turned away from the river, in the direction of my house, head bowed, waiting for the green man.

And there she was again!

There was another photo on the pavement at my feet. I crouched down. It was the same pose – a copy of the last one. How could this be? What was going on?

The signal beeped. I crossed the road in a daze. I should

phone her now and find out what this was about. When I turned into The Vennel there was another picture waiting for me. I hadn't spotted it on the way down – but, then, I hadn't been looking. I quickened my pace. Whenever there was a choice of direction, there would be a photo, a yard on, to show me the way through town.

I noticed the one on the bottom step of The Cairndale Hotel, climbed the stairs into the foyer, and stood, peering around.

'Mr Johnstone?' A woman's voice sounded from my left. I glanced over and saw the receptionist. I gave a small nod and she beckoned me across. 'Room 43,' she whispered, and turned back to her monitor. A phone rang. She picked it up and started talking. I stared on. She saw me and gave a shooing motion with her free hand.

I reached room 43 and knocked.

'It's open.' It was a soft voice. It was Chiara's voice.

I stepped inside. Suddenly, I was trembling. She was lying flat out on the bed at the far end of a large room, head propped up on a high pillow, her body covered in a blanket, tucked right up to her chin. At least, I think it was her. I moved in slowly, quietly, for a closer look.

She wore a mask. On it was a picture – the same picture I'd been following from the river. An arm slid out from under the blanket and slipped it off her face. 'What do you think?' she said, a broad smile on her lips.

'I think it's the best mask I've ever seen.' Suddenly, now, in her glorious presence, I wanted to rush at her, hold her, and kiss her.

She must have sensed it: her voice was firm. 'Don't do anything. Stay where you are. You look a bit hot and flustered. Close the door; then take a shower. Everything comes to him who waits.'

I stood my ground: uncertain.

'Go and shower,' she said firmly.

37

I did as I was told.

Ninety seconds later, after the quickest shower ever, I emerged from the bathroom, still flustered, but fresher.

'Drop the towel and let me see you,' she ordered.

I untied it from my waist and let it fall. I wasn't sure where to put my hands. I went for the nonchalant, behind the back look, at the same time turning my right foot out like a model.

'You look pleased to see me, Jin. Come nearer, but go slowly now, tiger. Not too close – not until I explain the rules.'

It was almost unbearable. I opened my mouth to tell her how much I had missed her, how everything changed when I was with her, but she shook her head strongly. 'No touching. Not yet.'

I approached the bed. She wasn't under a blanket: it was a piece of thick paper, like a large poster. Printed on it was a picture of a heavily clothed, spread-eagled body – I assumed it was Chiara's as it matched exactly her position in bed. In the photograph she was wearing a scarf, a chunky sweater, gloves, black trousers and flat shoes. There were numbers printed inside dotted rectangles.

'Did you have an advent calendar last Christmas, Jin?' she asked.

I shook my head. 'Never had one.'

'Never – not even as a child?'

'Never.'

She tutted. 'That's a shame. Well, we can make up for that right now. Normally there's a chocolate behind each door – this one also has a treat.' She paused, gauging me, before going on, 'It's quite simple. I call out a number and you have to tear round the rectangle to open the window. You can only move on when I call out another number. Do you understand? Is that clear? You have one decision to make and that is all: whether to lick or suck. I'll start with number ten, please.'

I scanned the poster and found the number on the left hand
38

glove and started to tear along the perforations. My hands trembled but I managed to open the door. Underneath, Chiara's hand was naked. I decided to lick between her fingers, one at a time. Then I took her thumb into my mouth and sucked. She pulled away sharply and scolded, 'Lick or suck, I said. One or the other. Nothing else.'

I apologised and she gave me a stern look, followed by a smile. 'Number nine, please.'

It was the scarf. I tore away. Her neck underneath was bare and held the wonderful fragrance of her flesh.

'Do you have anything on at all?' I asked.

'Sh, don't say a word. You'll have to find out.' She closed her eyes.

I chose to lick again: the full length of the opening, from ear to ear, lingering under her chin.

'Number eight, please.' Her voice was becoming softer, quieter – almost purring.

It was her sweater this time: at her heart. My hands were shaking now as I prised the big door open. It was an easy call – I sucked. After the effort she'd made to be here, it was the least I could do.

Saturday 15th July

I take my only remaining relative, my aunt, to the supermarket now. We go once a week, on a Monday afternoon. It's a fairly recent development.

She stays only five doors along but I've never been particularly close to her. Quite often, of course, over the last ten years, we'd bump into each other in the street, and have a natter, but nothing more than that: she didn't visit me and I didn't go round. Nevertheless, a few weeks ago, I started going for a quick chat on her doorstep, just to make sure everything was fine: it was clear she hadn't been about as much as normal. Now we spend time at Tesco every week getting in her shopping. She's always been a very independent woman, so it must have been a big step for her to admit to the need for help.

With Manfred's funeral coming up, and the house clearing afterwards, I had suggested we venture out earlier than the Monday this time – she had plumped for today, three o'clock. She was waiting with her shoes already on when I arrived – half an hour late – her toes tapping on the kitchen linoleum like a frantic woodpecker. She didn't say anything: although it was obvious she was a wee bit put out. I had considered asking for a postponement – with the unexpected visit of Chiara and all – but I could see she wouldn't have taken too kindly to the idea. Sometimes I think she actually enjoys our weekly jaunts despite all her talk of supermarkets taking over the world.

I don't get very much and always finish my shopping first, usually sitting quite happily in the car, biding my time, listening to radio 4, watching for her appearance: but not today, not under this burning sun. Despite having the windows open and the door ajar, the soaring temperature made the car almost unbearable and it was not a pleasant wait.

It was then that I spotted Jackie Gittes wandering through the car park about twenty yards ahead, on the far side of the next line of cars: his head sweeping left and right like a metal detector. He was searching for something, probably forgotten where he'd parked – I've done the same. On a similar note I have a rule never to leave the sitting room with the TV remote in my hand. I was about to get out, shout across, and pass the time of day – when I hesitated for two reasons.

For the first time it occurred to me that Jackie might not actually recall much of our meeting in the pub two nights ago, nor the tasks he had given me. And if he did remember, he might want to reconsider his benevolence and demand the £50 back. Of course, it wasn't my money and I didn't have a say in the matter, but it sounded like the Corsa driver was worthy of some sort of compensation for the accident; so I held back.

But, on top of that, there was something else: Jackie was wearing a jacket. A long leather one. It was as unnecessary as a hairdryer in a hurricane. There had to be a reason. I sat tight and watched on.

He completed his inspection of the cars, turned away from me, and moved into the next row. Suddenly the jacketed Jackie dipped from sight. A moment later, he had bobbed back into view and was walking quicker this time with something hidden under his arm. I saw over-clothed Jackie scurry away in the direction of the exit as I slid out and slalomed carefully up the aisles of jutting wing-mirrors. But by the time I reached his row he was nowhere to be seen.

The vehicle in front of me was a blue, four-door Renault. I gave it a quick once over. There could be a harmless explanation for Jackie's behaviour: it was his own car and he was simply taking something out of the boot. I hadn't seen it open – but, then, he might not have needed to raise the lid all that high. It was far-fetched: this car was barely a year old, not what I would expect Jackie to drive despite all his cash, and, most damningly, there were no marks of any kind on it to suggest a bump with a red Corsa. Sadly, my knowledge of
41

Jackie's life steered me towards a less than wholesome conclusion: he was stealing. It was a shade low – even by Jackie's standards.

The Renault had one of those annoying 'Baby On Board' signs stuck to its back window and an Ecosse sticker on the bodywork directly above the exhaust. I examined the boot lock. Jackie didn't have time to pick it. It must have been left unlocked.

There was one way to find out for sure. I extended my hand, giving a quick scan of the car park at the same time. Someone could be watching, as I had been. It might be better to bend down in the same way to lessen the chances of being seen.

I gave another long look around. I shouldn't be doing this. How would I explain it away if I was caught? I glanced round again and this time spied my aunt at the supermarket door. I pulled my hand back quickly and gladly hurried over to help with her shopping trolley.

An hour or so later I had pulled open the doors of The Bruce. It was early evening. I'd missed last night's pub session yet no-one had rounded up a posse to come looking for me, no-one had stuck up missing posters in my street. It was very strange: normally a Friday night absence is only excused by a doctor's certificate. They all had to be in on it.

My text to Asa earlier in the day had brought them out in force. Tread Dunlop, Hoogah MacPherson, Chisel Woods and Asa sat expectantly, hunched like conspirators, round the table by the door, with burst-dam grins on their faces and drinks in their sweaty palms.

I stood in front of them – their eyes travelled the length of my body to the top of my head. A gafoni – gin and fresh orange, no ice – sat patiently for its customer. I downed half of it in one go before easing down onto the stool, facing them. Their eyes followed my movements and four unflagging,
42

beaming faces watched me set the glass back down, taking in its clear thud with the table.

Tread was wearing a white shirt, no tie, and had, doubtless, rushed away early from work at the saleroom. He dabbed his bald head and fair, freckled, damp face with a cotton hanky. Unsurprisingly, Hoogah was waistcoatless for the first time this year and had clambered into a t-shirt with the words *Rock n Roll* blazed across the chest in pointy red letters – just in case anyone failed to spot his beloved ponytail. He's a teacher.

'Okay, okay,' I said, 'you have to stop all this grinning: it's not natural, not for you lot. How did you do it then, Asa?'

This was the new, changed us – everything out in the open – well, almost everything. In the past I would have waited to capture Asa alone before quizzing him. But we had decided, as a group, not so very long ago, that the time for secrets was over. After all, we'd known each other from first year at secondary school, or earlier. In fact, it was as if we had formed naturally, drawn together without thought; our friendship had formed without effort.

Asa gave a shrug. 'You've been looking fairly scunnered of late. Like a person who has lost all their life-savings and has a front gate which doesn't close properly and bangs in the middle of the night when the wind blows.'

He'd put some thought into that one.

'Haud yer wheesht, Asa,' I replied quickly, 'A gate can always be nailed shut, or bricked over, but to lose your savings... That's not something to joke about.' I gave an involuntary shudder.

Asa continued, in the same breath, as though I hadn't said a word, 'So I decided to give her a call and explain the situation. That was before your wee job with Jackie Gittes came along to fill your time, of course.'

And Asa was probably right: I had been a bit down but I wouldn't have cared to admit it to anyone.

43

'Jackie Gittes?' There was some surprise in Hoogah's voice. 'Is he still around then?'

I nodded. 'And there wasn't just *a* round in him either – he'd had quite a few before he collared us the other night.'

Hoogah went on, 'Last I heard Jackie was going to open up a refuge for lost homing pigeons. I don't know what happened to that idea though.' He shook his head and Tread made a similar gesture.

I veered the conversation away. 'I've got some more jobs on the go as well: one with Charlie Menzies and, wait 'til you hear this, one with Onion Sanny.' I gave them a quick description of yesterday's meeting with the recluse.

Hoogah was aghast and rose in his seat. 'You mean Sanny's actually moving out? From his caravan? After all these years?'

'No doubt about it,' I replied.

'Why didn't you tell us about this before now? It could have made the front page of the paper,' Chisel, the newspaper man, scolded.

'Bound to be headline news,' Tread added.

I shrugged. 'There's been no time and I haven't seen any of you. And, anyway, it was well into Friday before I found out. It would have been too late for the edition.'

Tread came in, suggestively, 'So what *else* have you been doing then, Jinky?'

'Oh, you know, I've been busy – tearing around here, and tearing around there.'

Chisel muttered, his head lowered, unable to let it go, 'I can't imagine Sanny being anywhere else. Doesn't seem right somehow.'

We all gave a sad nod in agreement and Tread proposed a toast to 'changing times.' It appeared we were taking the news far worse than Sanny. We clinked glasses and gulped down a mouthful – the beer drinkers finishing off with an 'ah' sound and the customary quick wipe of the mouth with the back of the
44

hand.

I cut away at the following hush, 'The photos of Chiara were a nice touch, Asa. The way they looked old: as though they'd been there for a while. That's what threw me.'

'What photos?'

'Come on. The ones on the pavement. The paper trail.'

Asa shook his head harshly, wobbling his cheeks. 'I don't know anything about that, Jinky. I phoned her and explained what you were like: that your chin was dragging the ground and a farmer could plant tatties in the furrow left behind. She said she'd take care of the rest. So what happened?'

'And don't spare any of the details,' Tread threw in. Hoogah and Chisel nodded eagerly.

As I related the story, I could see them gradually leaning forward. I finished up with, '…and I reached the door and knocked and a woman's voice said it was open. It was Chiara's voice.'

'Go on,' prompted Chisel.

'That's it,' I said.

'You didn't go in?' Tread burst out.

'Oh, I went in all right,' I replied. 'But that's your lot.'

They sat in stunned silence until Tread asked, 'What was she wearing?'

'No, no, that's as far as the story goes,' I said decisively, leaning back, folding my arms. 'But from now on I'll always think of her as my poster girl.'

Their faces bunched in disappointment and they lifted their glasses slowly, simultaneously, and swallowed.

'How did you know I'd find the first photo, Asa?'

'As I just said, Jinky, I didn't know anything about it. It must have been her own work.' He went on, 'She said I had to watch you, keep you at that spot for a while, and then make sure you set off in the right direction. She told me the route you had to take from the caul and I was to look out for any wrong turns. If

45

you didn't go the right way, I had to text you and put you on the right track: I knew where you were heading. As it turned out you did exactly as you were supposed to.'

'So you were spying on me the whole time?'

'Yup.'

'I didn't see you.'

'Didn't think you would.' There was a swelling in his chest. 'I watched you from where you'd never, ever see me.'

'You had binoculars?'

'Not on your life, something much better. Anyone like a guess?'

There were a few efforts involving hot-air balloons and invisibility cloaks but, eventually, we gave up.

'You'll kick yourselves. The Camera Obscura,' he uttered with pride. 'I was in with a family from Sweden. And what a laugh we had watching you.'

Right enough, it was a good place to observe The Whitesands as the Camera Obscura sits on a hill in a converted windmill – now part of the museum – and has a great view along the river, as well as other parts of town.

'And you can zoom right in with it: better than the one they have in Edinburgh,' Asa was saying. 'I pointed out all the landmarks to the family while we waited. They were very interested. And then you came along, all hot and bothered, so we closed in. It took a few minutes before you dipped from view.'

I suddenly thought of Jackie in the car park. 'Down on my hands and knees, looking at the photo on the pavement,' I explained.

'We saw you do it again later on when you were about to cross the road. I thought the woman next to you was about to get her leash out and lead you across.'

'I'm glad you had a laugh,' I muttered, sarcastically.

'Oh, we did, we did,' Asa said, his big face almost splitting in two. 'We were at maximum magnification and could almost make out your puzzled expression. Even the wee-est one of the Swedish kids had good English – great education system they must have there – it was almost as good as mine, in fact – but the father had to explain to him what I meant by 'a study in bewilderment.' And I learned to count in their language as well. We got as far as *sju* for the number of times you scratched your head.'

'I doubt, though, it wasn't nearly as much fun as *you* had, Jinky.' Tread nudged Hoogah sitting beside him, his words oozing with meaning.

The heads round the table nodded avidly.

Chisel said to Asa, 'You could have watched him from your own home, you know, instead of going to the Camera Obscura.'

'How? It's miles away.'

'I know that but there's a web-cam pointing out from the Burns Centre. It's been there for a year now. You could have watched on your computer from the comfort of your armchair.'

Hoogah cut in, 'That wouldn't do, Chisel. There's always a delay on those things. They refresh every 30 seconds.'

'No, no, they've changed it. It's a live feed now – same as the one up at the hospital. Although why anyone would want to watch the hospital car park all day long is beyond me.'

Tread asked me, 'So when do we get to meet her – this woman of yours? Is she really as stunning as Asa says?'

'You've seen her,' I said to them all.

'I caught a glimpse of some brownish hair,' Tread went on, 'as she was leaving the pub, back in March, but that's all. It's not quite the same thing – and that's a long time ago now. It's only Asa who's actually *met* her and been introduced. You're not ashamed of us, are you?'

Chisel and Hoogah looked keenly at me, backing up Tread's aspersion. 'It's nothing like that. There's been no chance: she
47

only arrived yesterday.'

'So, maybe tomorrow then?' Chisel added, taking another slug of his beer and licking his lips. 'If she's staying that long.'

Tread broke in, probably needing a break from the subject, or, maybe to cover up my silence, 'Right then, better be getting back to the wife, too dangerous to be in here from this early on in the evening.'

'Which model is it this time?' Chisel asked him.

'Mary,' he replied, and we all gave knowing nods.

He went on, 'She's quite a bit fiddlier than the others. Surprisingly so. But it'll be well worth it when I'm finished with her.'

He says it every time, so we know that 'getting back to the wife' really means returning to his shed to continue with his long-time hobby of model building. He started in his teens with an Airfix Spitfire and hasn't stopped. Now he's onto the great cruise liners of the world and keeps them in a shed in the back garden, suspended by fishing wire from the roof.

'By the way, Jinky,' Hoogah said. 'I've got a wee job for you as well – if you've got the time. Could you have a look through these bank statements? You're good at that sort of thing. I started to have a squint at them, but it's quite confusing.'

Everything out in the open, right enough.

'If you did it every month,' I mumbled, taking the wad of papers he'd pulled from his rucksack, 'it wouldn't be so difficult.'

He probably couldn't be bothered and knew a mug who'd do the work for him. It was always the same: Hoogah never worried about his finances, always left it to his wives to see to the money side of things. The second one was divorced not so long ago.

How he could be so frivolous was beyond me. But then he has always been a kind of 'live for the day' type of guy, with

48

no thought or plan for the future. However, there does seem to be the hint of a change appearing: he mentioned recently that he'd bought some frozen food and a few green bananas.

'What do you want me to do with these statements then?' I asked him.

'Just see if it all makes sense. It looks to me as though there have been an awful lot of changes over the months. Maybe you can figure it out and I'll go and take it up with the bank.'

'Do you know where it is – the bank?' I slipped in.

Chisel's phone sang to him from his pocket. He answered it, standing up and moving away from our table as he spoke.

'About Manfred's death,' I said suddenly to Asa, as Chisel continued to talk into his machine. 'He had a heart condition?'

'Been at the doctor's with it,' Asa confirmed. 'What's with all this again, Jinky?'

'It's just that I didn't know, and I don't think Charlie did.'

Hoogah and Tread agreed that they knew nothing about it either.

'He probably wanted to keep it quiet,' Asa went on. 'He was like that – considerate. Wouldn't have wanted people worrying about him.'

I didn't say anything in return. It still bothered me. For one thing, if he was too considerate to tell anyone about his heart condition, then surely he was too considerate to park in a passing place, giving someone the bother of retrieving his car. Nor hadn't I forgotten about Mrs Mann words: *'You should tell his real mother.'*

'He could call it Chez Doo,' Tread shouted, out of the blue, a finger raised.

Hoogah rounded on him, 'What are you talking about now?'

'Jackie's home for lost pigeons – Chez Doo.'

We looked to the heavens.

'It took you long enough to come up with that one,' Asa said.

'Fair's fair, Asa, it *was* in another language,' Hoogah stated.
49

'Aye, you're right there: Pidgin English,' Tread volleyed back.

Chisel returned and towered over us, snapping his phone shut. It caught our attention and broke the groans from round the table. 'Bad news,' he said. 'Jackie Gittes' been found.'

'We were just talking about...' Tread's words were swept away by Chisel's hard expression and the grins on our faces froze.

'How do you mean – found?' I asked.

He exhaled heavily. 'It seems he's been stabbed. In some woods. Only discovered a few minutes ago. Pierced the heart.'

We looked at each other.

'What are you talking about? I saw him earlier today,' I said.

It was a stupid comment, but no-one seemed to notice, listening intently to what Chisel had to say next, 'It looks very bad. Expect the worse, lads.'

'But who would want to attack him?' I said, unable to stop a sudden stirring of responsibility. I should have protected him, shielded him from this. The feeling was stupid, it didn't make any sense: I wasn't his guardian angel.

'The police are at the scene,' Chisel continued. 'I need to go. I've a taxi coming. Anyone wanting to come over with me?'

I don't like anything grisly but this time I felt obliged; and Asa would definitely head up.

'Not for me,' Hoogah replied, with a brief shudder. 'I want nothing to with that kind of thing.' He checked his watch. 'Going to the pictures with Lucy, anyway.'

Tread glugged down the last part of his pint, the bottom must have been rancid, judging by the face he pulled. 'You still seeing her – this new girlfriend?'

Hoogah nodded.

'It's not right what you are doing: going about with your wife's best pal.'

'Ex-wife, Tread,' Hoogah reminded him. 'There's no law
50

against it.'

'I still say it's not right. Nothing good will come of it – you mark my words.'

'Anyone for this taxi?' Chisel asked again, drumming his foot on the floor.

I knocked back my gafoni to show I was, as did Asa with his beer, and we marched from the pub. It was still bright and a few degrees warmer than inside: the day had clung onto its heat like a mother holding her baby.

I slipped Chisel a question. 'Was that your office on the phone?' He works for The Courier, one of our local newspapers, and in a newly promoted position as well: proving that his reporting is as sharp as his features.

He didn't answer that, but while we stood in the shade, under the columns of the entrance, he filled us in on the details gleaned so far.

Jackie's body had been found in a clump of trees in a field close to the by-pass. It had been discovered by a Mr Wallace Lemon who stays near-by. He had raised the alarm from a neighbour's house. There had been a lot of blood. It wasn't looking good for Jackie.

I noticed our 'no secrets' policy didn't quite stretch quite as far as Chisel's contact. Some things were off limits, and, I suppose, parts of my job should be too. I must bear that in mind.

The taxi pulled up in front of us. 'We shouldn't be all that surprised you know,' Asa said, bending into the back seat with difficulty. 'He was always one for finding trouble, wasn't he?'

'I know, but it's still a big step to this,' I replied. 'He didn't deserve it.'

'Who does?' Chisel said, edging into the front.

Naturally enough the taxi driver was interested in finding out the reason behind our journey but Chisel kept tight-lipped. Five minutes later we pulled into a short dead-end street, with three, identical, two-story, detached houses sitting on one side of the road. Chisel started to pay the driver and pointed, 'There's a track beside that end house – it leads into the field at the back of the properties. You'll see from there.'

Asa and I made our way down – the heavy hedge to our right blocking the view of the side of the house and its garden. The wooden gate leading into the field was wide open but we stopped. Chisel caught us up, and, for a moment, he was just as reluctant to move on.

The field was large, ran the full length of the backs of the properties, but all the activity was on the far side, about a hundred yards away, on the top of a small rise.

I heard the noise of the taxi belatedly chugging away, its diesel engine rough with use. Chisel looked at me, then to Asa, sucked in some serious air, gave a short shrug, and moved off. We followed on, walking purposefully towards the commotion, stepping along a line flattened by one of the cars. And there were a few other tyre tracks – all pointing in the same, inevitable direction.

The grass was ankle-deep but seemed free of muck: whoever owned it didn't use it for cattle. At the far end three police cars sat menacingly, lights still flashing, and nearby, a few people stood in a group with a uniformed officer.

I had no doubt Chisel, being a reporter, would be allowed in for a closer look and probably Asa as well, so I might be able to tag along but I wasn't sure if I really wanted to. We climbed the small slope at the end of the field and halted at the top, taking in the scene.

The ground fell away into a small wood made up of a few tall, spindly trees. Delicate strips of blue and white stripy ribbon had been wound round some of the trunks, extending up to metal poles in front of us, cordoning off the area. The tape fluttered in the sticky air.

I glanced down and saw Ed, a senior detective, standing

below, unmoving, hands on hips, pondering the scene. I turned away quickly. The spinning, blinking beams of the police cars splattered flashes of blue light across the green leaves of the trees: like a neon sign cruelly advertising the scene of the crime. There was an unreality about it all: as though it was merely a set-up for a film, and we were waiting for the actors to take their places.

Asa tilted his head, lifted a straight arm, and attempted to brush his forehead across the short sleeve of his shirt. He caught half; the rest of his brow remained shiny. He didn't attempt a similar tactic with the other arm, but stood, staring down at the foot of the trees, his face as tight as my innards.

The uniformed policeman looked over from his group and nodded to Chisel, who gave a returning flick of the head. Now, as I forced myself to look down again, I noticed four policemen, on their hands and knees, partly hidden in the trees, conducting a fingertip search of the area. And then I saw it – in the centre of the copse – a large, nearly-brown stain spilled across old leaves, as though paint had been poured. Jackie's body had been removed.

The air was intense and, like an old cemetery, a pall of foreboding dripped from the canopy of trees. I felt sick and turned away, retracing my steps across the field, wondering why the police had allowed people in so close: they could easily have had posted someone at the gate to stop us.

Glimpses of an alive and winking Jackie passed through my mind: happily drunk in the pub, staggering and chattering along the pavement. Did he have any inkling this was about to happen to him? Was there a warning somewhere of his imminent fate? Was there something behind his words: a hidden code? I tried to focus in on him, capturing chunks of conversation from that night. He was happy – that was all I got.

I stopped and turned. Chisel was no longer in view; Asa was talking to the policeman. I trudged on, slowly, but Asa caught
53

up with me before I could escape the field. 'He's dead – Jackie. He died before the ambulance arrived at the scene. There was nothing they could do.' He pulled a hankie out, spread it across both his palms as we walked, and buried his whole face in it, rubbing away the grotty sweat.

I didn't have anything to say. I wandered on, head down, not knowing where I wanted to go, but understanding I didn't want to be here anymore. Asa added some more news, unaware that, at this moment, I couldn't have cared less about any of the details. I was barely listening.

'The Lemon guy, the man who found the body, lives in that house over there.' He pointed to the middle one in the row of three. The houses were large, solidly built, with, probably, three bedrooms upstairs. Their rear gardens were large also and backed onto the field, each with a gate. Solid hedges grew between each property, shielding the gardens from each other, making them private, allowing only a blinkered view of the field.

'He's got a bad leg, Mr Lemon,' Asa was saying. 'So it took him a wee while to get back across the field to raise the alarm. But they don't reckon it would have made any difference – if the ambulance had arrived sooner.'

Asa waited for me to say something but when I didn't, he added, 'Jackie would have died quickly: I suppose that's something. They found a brown-handled, long-bladed knife beside his body. A common kitchen type.'

I stopped and looked at the houses. Someone at a downstairs window would have a limited view but anyone looking out from upstairs would have a clear sight of the field; although not down into the hollow.

'This Mr Lemon didn't have a phone on him, then?' I felt Asa wanted me to make a comment.

'Couldn't have. He went to his neighbour's house, Mr Redditch – the furthest away one – and got him to call. Mr
54

Lemon was quite shaken up, apparently. Who wouldn't be, coming across that?'

Asa followed my gaze towards the houses. 'There might be a bit of a breakthrough, though. Mr Lemon reckons he saw someone running in the field, a jogger, passing the houses – and then he, or she, disappeared. You never know someone else might have witnessed the same thing.'

We moved on again. Asa added, 'The neighbours on either side of him are retired, so they might have been home: with it being the weekend. We're getting statements from them right now.'

'What's the weekend got to do with it?'

'Retired folk don't go out then: too many people about. They like it when it's quieter – in my experience, that is.'

When we reached the open gate, Asa said, 'It's quite swampy on the far side of the hollow and beyond that the Nith curves round, cutting it off. So really the only way to get down into that wood is through this field. And there are two gates: this one here and another one, along from the houses: where the jogger disappeared.'

'Come on, Asa, I need a drink.'

I glanced round. Chisel had moved into sight and was talking to Ed. It wasn't worth waiting for him – he'd be making up a detailed report for his newspaper. It would take time.

Asa and I walked back along the pavement. 'It's dreadful,' I said. 'I know you deal with this kind of thing every day but when you're right up close…it was almost as though I could smell the blood.'

'Naw, we don't deal with this all that often – you know that. How many murders do we have round here? One or two a year, if you're lucky.'

'Lucky?'

'Not what I meant.' Asa gave a shake of his head. 'He was a silly boy that Jackie. Always was. And do you know the

55

strange thing? I didn't tell you this, but the killer removed Jackie's clothes, trousers and all, threw them to one side, in a pile, leaving him naked. Then he draped a kilt over him like a blanket!'

It took us fifteen minutes of hard graft to return to The Bruce. I needed a shower to separate the grime from my skin but I wanted a drink even more. It was worth while putting up with sticky clothes for a wee bit longer.

We'd been quiet for most of the way: the murder hanging heavily like a yoke across our shoulders. Yet, although harsh to say, if we hadn't met up with Jackie recently, I doubt if his death would have affected us all that much. We would have been saddened, of course, but that's about all. It was different now. The sighting of him a few hours earlier, in the car park, made it much worse. There should be a great distance, a huge divide, between a healthy person and his death but here was a fit, able Jackie suddenly gone. There was no chasm between the two: death was with him, right behind all the time, following him, sheltering in his shadow, shaded from the sun. Maybe Hoogah's 'act for the moment' attitude isn't such a bad idea after all: if all our lives are this flimsy.

I hauled at the big door, allowing Asa to enter. The pub had filled up considerably since we'd left and there were no seats free. Laughter sprung from a group of men nearby. It made me flinch. Further explosions of fun burst through the pub, sparked from the touchpaper of a Saturday night. It didn't seem right.

Asa bought the round while I searched out the quietest corner. The first sip made me feel better and, eventually, some thoughts on the matter began to flow. I had no doubts about wanting to find who had done this terrible act.

I started by giving Asa a description of the earlier events in Tesco's car park. 'Do you think I should go up to the police station and make a statement? It might be important.'
56

He gave a nod.

'It's weird, Asa, the way he was found – naked and all that. And what's with the kilt? They're not cheap, you know. Why would anyone do that – leave it lying? It *has* to mean something.'

Asa shrugged. 'Maybe it doesn't.'

'Explain it then?' I challenged. But before he could answer, I went on, 'Well, what if it's a fetish sort of thing? I've heard a little bit about those kinds of goings on. Is it possible? In Dumfries? A rendezvous with someone who's hooked into that sort of thing?'

Asa gave me a shake of the head. 'What sort of thing is that, Jinky? You haven't got a clue what you are talking about, have you? I doubt if you even know what fetish means.'

I replied, keeping my voice low, 'Maybe not. But there *is* someone who might give me an insight into what Jackie was about – his wife, or ex-wife. Did they divorce?'

'Hold on there. A wee bit of advice for you: leave it to us. That's the way it should be – always. This is strictly for the police, Jinky. And, on top of that, it's likely to be dangerous getting involved.'

'Okay, okay, I know that – but if I hadn't kept poking my nose in last time…'

He gave a sigh. 'Jinky, why would you want to put yourself through that again anyway, eh?'

'That was a one-off, Asa.'

He started to say something but decided against it, taking a slug of his ale instead.

I went on, 'And this is one time I'm not going to be looking up the internet for information.' I gave a shudder. 'Goodness knows what I'd find if I searched for anything along those lines – fetishes.'

'Well, we'll soon know if Jackie was naked when he was attacked or if his clothes were removed afterwards. That's

57

bound to be important. Don't forget, it might just be a robbery, simple as that. He was flashing a lot of cash around, wasn't he? Never a clever thing to do – even in here. It could be a theft gone wrong. They said his watch was still on him but we don't know if any money's missing. There were no wads of cash certainly, only coins in his pocket.'

'That's what's bothering me Asa – if he hadn't brought out all that money to pay me… But it still doesn't explain why he was naked.'

I bought another round.

'And why would Jackie be at such a remote spot anyway?' I started again, as I handed over his fresh pint. 'Surely it means he was there for a meeting with someone. A meeting well away from prying eyes.'

Asa gave a shrug. 'It could be a woman who did it, of course. Jackie wasn't all that big, and with a knife…'

'But why would he meet up there if it was a woman? He had a flat of his own.'

He paused for a moment. 'So they're actually divorced – him and Jill?'

'I don't know for sure,' I replied, and took a long gulp of my drink. 'Right, I'll head up to the station now. Then start looking into it tomorrow.'

His mouth puckered sharply. 'Don't you think you're getting a wee bit ahead of yourself, Jinky?'

I raised my eyebrows to indicate an explanation was needed.

'It'll be handled well enough by us. It's not likely you'll be of any use. You might even get in the way.'

'One thing you seem to forget, Asa, is that I'm able to do things the police aren't. Some people are more likely to talk to me than them – you know that. We're talking about Jackie here. How many of his associates are likely to come forward, eh? We want to get this guy, don't we? So I have to do what I can. It doesn't stop me passing on information to the police, though.'

Asa grabbed my arm as I was about to go. 'Has she gone back down to England then?'

'Who?'

'Your woman, of course. Who else would I be talking about?'

'Chiara? No, she's here for one more night. The boys wanted to meet her tomorrow – were you not listening? I might be able to arrange it: depending on her plans.'

'Jinky, what's wrong with you, man? You've got a woman waiting for you right now.'

'Chiara,' I insisted.

'Right. But why aren't you with her?'

'We spent the morning together – and a bit more.'

'And now?'

I shrugged. 'She was going to spend the afternoon looking at new property developments in the area.'

His sigh was lengthy and I felt my hair move. 'Is she staying at the hotel tonight again?'

'Yes. What are you getting at?'

He gave another sigh. 'I know you're not used to any of this but you need to start thinking about *her* as well. And this hotel – isn't it a bit of an expense? Why doesn't she stay at your place?'

'She'd booked it beforehand. The room's all paid for.'

'Has she, in fact, seen where you live?'

I shook my head.

'You're not embarrassed by it, are you?'

'No,' I replied, indignantly, and thought for a moment. 'Maybe I should be getting back to her first. I'm a bit late.'

Asa gave off one of his 'humph' sounds. 'You mean you haven't even contacted her, to say you were delayed?'

'No.'

'You've a lot to learn.'

I pulled my phone out. It was switched off.

'You've left a woman like that alone – after all the effort she's put in coming up here?' Asa's voice had moved up a register. He gave another of his sad shakes of the head.

I held up my mobile. 'I must have switched it off when I came into the pub earlier – force of habit.' In the past only the boys had my number, so when we were all together there was a distinct pleasure in turning it off and saving the battery. But I'd given Chiara my number months ago: so why had I done it this time? Was it an unconscious signal: like a troubled, recurring dream is a sign of turbulence in one's life?

'Jinky, I hate to say it, but there's no time for the police station right now. It can wait 'til later. You get yourself back up there to that hotel, straightaway, and see her. And my advice…take a bunch of flowers with you.'

I tapped on the door of room 43. Chiara opened it. She was wearing a fluffy white dressing gown and carried the TV remote.

'Watch you don't leave the room with that,' I said. 'You might not find it again easily.

She turned back, sat down heavily on the bed, clicked off the TV, and threw it down beside her, next to an almost empty plate. She'd had a sandwich – one crust was left – white bread.

I gave a weak smile and held out the petrol station's finest flowers: making sure the half price sticker was facing me. 'I got caught up,' I said. 'Sorry.'

She stared at my face, then the flowers, and back to me. 'You had your phone with you…'

'I know, I know. I should have contacted…'

She held a finger to her mouth and I stopped talking immediately. 'Don't say anything. There's nothing for you to say. What *I* was going to say was that I could easily have contacted *you* to find out where *you* were – but I didn't. I went for a massage instead.'

I didn't know what to do. Should I tell her it was switched off? I went with, 'You can get massages on Saturday evenings?'

She nodded. 'Always busy at the weekends.' She stood up, coming over to land a kiss on my cheek. 'I like the flowers.' She added, thoughtfully, 'Now, if only we had a vase...' Then, noting my puzzled expression, said, 'Look, I'm a big girl. I can make my own decisions and I'm used to being on my own, don't forget. I'm not dependent on you. We can go our own way whenever we wish.'

She took the flowers and ambled into the bathroom. I heard the tap running. She returned with a shower cap, filled with water, tied on like a bubble to the base of the unwrapped flowers and balanced it carefully on the windowsill.

'Quite nice. What do you think?' Chiara kept her eyes on the flowers and tilted her head as she spoke.

I thought the new ruling of no secrets should be extended: I told her what had happened to Jackie Gittes. She listened without interruption, and then said, 'What are you going to do about it?'

'You think I should do something? Asa doesn't. He keeps telling it's none of my business.'

'He was a friend, this Jackie?'

'Not really a friend – more an acquaintance. We went to the same school.'

'But you *knew* him. You should try to help.' She paused for a moment; then became excited. 'I know. Why don't *I* help you? We can do it together. I've a meeting with a developer in Dorset on Thursday, but that's all I've got this week. I'm going to be free until then.'

I shrugged it away quickly. 'No. Definitely not. It's too dangerous.' I started pacing the room. 'Not when there's a murderer out there.'

61

'But look what happened to you before – when you were on your own. We can keep an eye out for each other. And I'm not as soft as you might think. I did karate when I was ten – for two years. What have you got? And aren't two brains better…'

'No, I don't like it Chiara. You can't tell what might happen or how things will go.'

She was becoming increasingly animated. 'We don't let each other out of our sight so it'll make it much safer that way. What do you say?'

'What about the cost of staying here longer?' This wasn't nearly as good a reason – but it was better than emphasising how dangerous the investigation might be. Nevertheless, as soon as I uttered the words I heard Asa's voice: *'you're not ashamed of your house, are you?'*

I stared at her. I should ask her if she wants to stay the rest of the week at my place: that's what couples do.

'There are more important things than money,' she replied, moving swiftly to the phone, lifting the receiver. 'I'll see if there's a room available for tomorrow tonight – for a start.'

I'd had a female companion on my last major case and I couldn't have done without her: she had found something I could never have uncovered. I was starting to be won round. 'The police might have the killer locked up already, for all we know,' I said.

There was another thought persuading me: I didn't want to disappoint her, not when she was so eager. And it meant her staying longer in Dumfries. I shrugged. 'Okay, then.'

She beamed back at me. 'How do we start?' She hadn't dialled through yet.

'We interview anyone who might have seen this jogger. I think he's the key to it.' I wandered over to the window, smelled the flowers, and slipped in, casually, 'This person who massaged you – was it a male or a female?'

Sunday 16th July

I woke earlyish, in a double bed, in the heart of The Cairndale, with Chiara sleeping beside me. I left her lying. It had been a habit in the past – and I was doing it again. A sneak round the blazing curtains confirmed another glorious day.

It was strange to be staying in a hotel in my own town, and so close to my house – in fact, I could see one of its chimney pots from the window. This felt like an unnecessary luxury: like aftershave balm. I hadn't slept well either. I wasn't convinced about Chiara helping: she shouldn't be put in danger. And there was another concern: it was the phrase Chiara had used last night, *'we can go our own way whenever we wish.'*

Was our time together coming to an end, with this weekend a mere delay? I couldn't really expect it to continue, but I had no way of knowing: as Asa had pointed out, I'd had little or no experience with women. I knew they were different from men, of course. I knew they held their mugs comfortingly in both hands no matter the air temperature and I knew they looked far better in shorts and sandals – but that was about it. So, if this was to be our last time together, I had to make the most of it. In fact, depending where our investigation led, Chiara might experience enough excitement to give me an edge over any other boyfriends: enough to make her come back here sometime, at least.

I assumed she was seeing other men: I didn't like to ask. There had to be a man in every port, waiting for her to hit town – it would be too lonely otherwise. And in some ways it was comforting to think she wasn't on her own in the dark and emptiness of the night. It was safer this way: I wouldn't wish her to be as isolated as a Gretna centre forward.

I dressed quietly and left her there. The visit to the police station was first on my list as I hadn't managed last night: the craving for a wash had been overwhelming and then I'd been

63

hijacked by a bubble-bathed babe armed with a loofah.

The walk through town confirmed the fiery forecast. Even at this young hour, nearly all Dumfries males were clomping around the streets with naked legs sprouting up from clunky sandals. Their shorts would not be returned to the closet for a considerable period now – not even if a sudden snowstorm blasted through – as the need to give them a decent outing was paramount, making the effort of hunting them out worthwhile.

It was Ed who saw me. I wasn't surprised he was in on a Sunday and it was good to be speaking to the man in charge. He wrote down my account of Jackie's movements at Tesco and the colour and make of the car. I had the first two letters of the number plate as well, so that should be enough to find it – if it's local.

He thanked me for coming in and we shook hands on leaving. Sadly, he'd been quite guarded about any progress made, evading all my questions. The best I got was, 'all avenues were being explored at the moment' which I took to mean that they didn't have any suspects for the murder thus far.

I made a quick visit home for a shave, picking out a thin, short-sleeved shirt along with a pair of light cotton trousers from the back of the wardrobe. The clothes were crumpled but I figured the heat would do the ironing for me. After a visit to the supermarket, I was ready for the drive out to the countryside.

Fifteen minutes later I had parked and started the walk. The sun blazed down but in a friendlier way: as though it was much happier being out here in these hills. And the day had puffed out its chest, compelling me to take in a few deep breaths and contemplate its cloudless magnificence. I stood and stared down the valley for a long time. I wasn't sure what I had done to be so lucky.

Forty minutes on I was in the streets of the town again. A text came through from Asa; I pulled over to read it. He'd found the address of the man Jackie Gittes wanted me to find –

the man with the Corsa he had bashed. He must have been of the same mind as me: Jackie's wishes should be carried out and the £50 handed over. It also meant Asa was at work: probably called in on the murder case. But there might be another reason for this information right now: to keep me occupied and away from other things. It was something he had tried before. It hadn't worked then and it wouldn't work now. Nevertheless, I would need to thank him in the time-honoured way – beer.

The gist of his longish message was that there were only three cars of the right make and age around Dumfries, and only one with an elderly owner. I dropped my car back home, deciding again to walk.

I had to admit it was good to be back doing my proper work of helping. Manfred's house-clearing felt more like a favour; yet, when his car was sold, it would end up paying a vast amount more than any other job I'd ever done before. Actually, there had been only one proper task since leaving the hospital in April: finding a missing wheelie-bin for an elderly lady.

It didn't sound like much at the beginning and any other time I might have been reluctant to take it up but it was better than nothing and a good way of easing myself back in. From her sad face you'd have thought it was her cat, dog, or even husband who had disappeared. Although, she must have been attached to it right enough for she had gone to the trouble of wallpapering it with a flower and leaf pattern – to make it blend into the garden, she said.

At first I imagined it would be nothing more than a prank by some kids and the bin would be round the corner, but, after talking to neighbours, refuse collectors, and the council, it soon became evident that it was a growing problem.

A couple of days later, after a lot of conversations with a lot of people, I was directed to a farm near the village of Collin where I found the wheelie bin in question, along with a number of others, waiting to be put to good use – in a way.

65

The culprits were a group of teenagers. They had been taking and customising the wheelies. A process which included: detaching the lids, cutting out the front panels, giving decoration and adornment, fixing a harness to the handle, before hooking them up to ponies for the fun to begin.

It was chariot racing – round one of the flat fields of the farm – Ben Hur style. They even had a track marked out like the Circus Maximus in Ancient Rome, they told me, and they held their fiercely competitive races every weekend for those in the know.

I explained the situation to the farmer father of one of the boys, making it clear that I didn't think it was right for an elderly lady to have to stump up for another bin – and he agreed. The man said he hadn't paid too much attention to the boys' pastime: other than thinking it was a good way of keeping them off street corners, out of trouble, as well as getting his horses exercised at the same time. He told me he had been unaware of any theft. Whether I believed him or not didn't matter as I managed to persuade everyone involved to chip in for a new bin for the lady.

The job was finished when I ordered a new one online. Unfortunately, I didn't realise at the time that there was a delivery fee and ended up out of pocket as I had said there would be no charge for my services. Nevertheless, the smile on her face when the shiny, new arrival arrived was enough to make me appreciate how much I had missed helping people.

Strolling along Lovers Walk and over the railway bridge, I realised I was really looking forward to meeting with Mr Burbage, the driver of the Corsa: he seemed like a nice man. And when I arrived at his home it was obvious Asa had the right address: a dented car stood at front of his ex-council house.

He remembered the incident, of course, and when I explained the reason for my visit – over a cup of lukewarm tea – he was
66

more than happy to take the cash. Although, he did make it clear that he had no intention of fixing the dent as the car was getting too old to bother – and so was he.

We chatted for a while and said goodbye, the job finished. Jackie was right: Mr Burbage was a genuinely nice man. In fact, he reminded me a lot of one of my long-gone uncles. When I was a boy, Uncle James always managed to find a sweetie for me. I wasn't bothered then that it had no wrapper and probably shared a pocket with his used hankie: but, I suppose, I would now.

I arrived back at the hotel room just over two hours after I'd left. Chiara was in her dressing gown once again. She'd been down for breakfast and was about to go for a swim. I handed over the present. It was in a large cardboard box with a red bow on the top.

'Just a small thank-you,' I said. 'It's not a lot. It's nothing compared to what you must have spent coming all the way up here.'

'You shouldn't have,' she replied, tugging on the ribbon. 'But it's nice. It's the thought...' She motioned me over and gave me a kiss on the cheek as she laid the ribbon delicately on the bed. The gold wrapping paper came away easily and the lid slid open. She peered inside. 'No, really, you shouldn't have.'

I used my shoulders to offer a, 'it was nothing' gesture.

'No, I mean it. You shouldn't have. I've a pair in the car. They're dirty but they're fine.' She pulled out the new, green wellington boots, holding them aloft, staring at them, and then at me.

I shrugged. 'Never mind. They'll always come in handy. I doubt if your feet'll grow much more now.'

'I need them for visiting building sites,' she explained. 'So I always keep a pair handy in the boot.'

She sat down and slipped them onto her bare feet and stood up, quickly undoing her robe, dropping it to the floor. She was
67

wearing a black bikini. It fitted all her curves, and she had the correct number – I'd counted them many times. Then she paraded back and forward with all the style of a model on a catwalk, asking my opinion. She could easily have been one – a model. In fact I must ask her sometime if she ever tried. Though she might not be tall enough: in these boots she was the same height as me.

'If they're not pinching your toes, I think they'll be fine for what I have in mind,' I said.

'And what *do* you have in mind?' she teased, before adding, 'Do you want me to keep them on just now? Do you like that kind of thing?' She looked down at them and banged the toes together.

Half an hour later we were on our way to Glenkiln Reservoir in my car. I parked up the hill, beyond the Henry Moore statue, and pulled on my hill-walking boots. Chiara fitted into her own old wellies: no point getting the new ones dirty, she had remarked.

With my lack of experience with women, I wasn't sure if my thought processes were travelling along the correct lines, but I had started to gauge the strength of my feelings towards her by mentally ticking or crossing boxes – depending on whether there was a match with my view or not. And the fact that she didn't want to waste the new pair of boots definitely put a mark in the positive box. In fact, almost everything she did ticked the right boxes. I only had two in the 'against' column: her love for extremely expensive champagne and her mad hobby with cars. I was hopeful that, given the time, I might be able to talk her out of the latter at least.

I took Chiara's hand to help her over the cattle grid and onto a track leading through the middle of the field. The path was dry and dusty but, with the vast number of sheep and cattle roaming freely, boots were a necessity. We continued to hold hands.

'I've never been up this way before,' she said, delight showing across her face, as she sucked in a deep lungful of air and expelled it in a long, light, satisfying sigh. The sound sent a tingle to my spine.

'And what a view down the valley,' she exclaimed. 'I always take the road along the side of the reservoir. Is that why we're here – for the view? Or is there something else? You're being very mysterious.'

When I didn't say anything, she asked, seriously, 'Apart from finding the jogger, what else should we do? What about the knife? Couldn't we find out where it was bought?'

'From what Asa said, it sounded like an ordinary kitchen knife. We can try, but there must be lots of them sold – even in Dumfries. And it might not be a new one either.'

'What about the kilt then?'

I gave a nod. 'That'll be more promising. It'll be away for analysis right now. It might be something we can look into when the details come back – that's if I can talk Asa into revealing anything. It might not be all that easy though. That's where you might come in handy.'

She understood my meaning and I went on, 'The first thing to do is to talk to people, the witnesses, Jackie's wife, and gather as much information as we can.'

'So how come I've never seen *you* in a kilt? I would like that.' She squeezed my hand. 'You have one, don't you?'

'Of course.'

'Okay then, why don't I take a picture of you in it and get one of those advent calendars made up and then see if it's true what they say about Scotsmen.'

I tried to deflect her playful smile. 'I might need to get a licence for my sporran first?'

She gave a quick laugh. 'Yeah, right. And I suppose it needs to be taken for a walk twice a day as well, and looked after
69

when you're away on holiday. I might be English but I'm not falling for that one.'

'I never go on holiday. But I'm serious about the licence. It was on the radio the other morning. The best sporrans, the most expensive ones, are made with otter, seal, even hedgehog skin and these animals are protected now, so it's illegal to use them – unless you can prove they were killed lawfully. Hence the licence.'

'Hedgehog? That doesn't sound like a good choice. Surely that could cause some serious damage.'

I experienced an inner wince at the thought. 'You can even get badger tassel ones – with the heads of the poor creatures still attached. Who would want that? They sell for hundreds of pounds as well.'

She shook her head absently at the madness of the world, still taking in the scenery. We had reached our destination. I stopped. At first Chiara didn't see it sitting in the small cluster of trees, looking out to the hills beyond. Then she gave a shout and burst into a bouncy run, stopping in front, staring intently into its face.

It was a statue – hidden away. A greened bronze of a slightly bowed, young woman with bulging, cheerless eyes, with hair in bunches. She is dressed in a long, shabby dress with a shawl gripping her shoulders, and stands with her hands out in front like a praying mantis.

'She's sad, don't you think?' Chiara shouted excitedly as she stroked a hand down the statue's hair. 'I feel sorry for her.'

'It's called The Visitation,' I said as I neared. We stood on either side of the woman. I went on, 'The sculptor is a man called Epstein. He must be well known: he has other pieces in the Tate Museum in London. I looked it up this morning. I didn't think you would have seen this one before as it's a bit out of the way. Do you want to hear some more about her? It's quite interesting.'

70

She nodded without turning away from the statue.

'This is the original but there's another one in that museum. This one was going to be melted down to be made into a bust of Winston Churchill but the landowner here happened upon it and offered a decent price – and now she rests at this spot. That's the story anyway. A good place for her, don't you think?'

Chiara noted the bump in the front of the dress. 'She's pregnant.' She ran her hand over the swelling. 'She looks poor and distraught, not knowing how she is going to manage with a child to feed.'

'That's exactly what I thought – until this morning. In fact, she's the Virgin Mary visiting her cousin, Elizabeth, to tell her she's pregnant. You have thought she'd be happy. I'm not up on the Bible: did she know she was about to have God's baby at that time?'

Chiara shook her head. 'We should find out.'

As she continued to study the sculpture, I tiptoed off to one side to retrieve the picnic basket I'd hidden earlier. I'd flapped out the blanket by the foot of a Scot's pine before Chiara realised what was happening. She came over. I handed her a glass. She accepted it without a word. I patted the space beside me and she sat down.

'I know you are used to only the best of Champagne, Chiara, but I couldn't get any this morning: it was too early. And, really, I don't think I could have forced myself to buy some, not at those prices.' I popped the cork, the wine fizzed out. 'This is from New Zealand. The man in the shop assured me it was good. I bought it for my birthday but never got round to drinking it….'

Chiara placed a finger over my lips to stop me talking and gave my face a long, lingering stare. 'It'll be perfect,' she said.

I thought the statue would have an affect on her – and I was right. There was a tear in her eye as I handed her a tomato

71

sandwich.

We dropped my car back at the hotel and took Chiara's this time: its air conditioning giving us some protection from this sun-baking, limp-kite day. We had stayed in our comfortably-shaded, peaceful spot by the statue for a restful portion of time. We had talked and we had breathed in the quiet and Chiara had thanked me in her special way – but only after she'd used a paper hanky to blindfold The Visitation.

Parking in front of Mr Lemon's house – the man who had raised the alarm – I led Chiara down the track by the end house to give her the lie of the land. I pointed to the area on the far side where Jackie's body had been found: the blue and white tape was visible on top of the rise, wilting in the calmly boiling air. She decided it wasn't necessary to walk over.

Instead, we walked into the field, along its edge, behind the houses, trying to gauge how much each hedge impinged on the view, estimating how long it would take someone to jog its length down to the other gate.

'Even if the man seen running away isn't involved,' I said, 'he might still have spotted something important.'

'Wouldn't he have talked to the police then?'

I nodded. 'That's the problem: we don't know what's going on right at this moment – always one step behind. We have to hope Asa will keep us up to date – and that means plenty of beer. We can arrange to meet up with him in the pub later on, if you want. He'll like that.'

She made no reply but turned and glanced again towards the trees of the copse.

I threw in, 'My other pals are keen to meet you as well, you know.'

She remained quiet, taking cautious steps through the grass.

I returned to more pressing matters: her serious expression wished it. 'If this runner hasn't come forward, we have to find him.'

She gave a slight nod.

We reached the gate at the bottom end of the field. There was a path beyond, leading onto Edinburgh Road. I said, 'He would have gone through here but after that it's difficult to tell which way. Any thoughts?'

Her brow had creased; she was strangely quiet.

I continued, giving her time for an answer, 'Mr Lemon often walks round the edge of the field – even though he has a bad leg.' I put an arm round her shoulders and led her back along and out into the street. There was a man in the front garden of the furthest away house. I assumed it was Mr Redditch, the neighbour who had phoned the emergency services.

As we approached he gave off a friendly wave with a gloved hand but continued with his work, watering containers with a large green can held in his right hand. There had been talk of a hosepipe ban coming into force: a handful of dry days and that's what happens. Although, to be fair, it had been a very dry winter as well.

I had the impression he liked being in his garden: even from a distance his well-tended, bright flowers shone with colour and any weeds would have the life expectancy of one of Asa's pints. He straightened up from his tub of geraniums, laid down the watering can, and spoke first, looking skywards. 'It's a hot one right enough.'

'And more to come,' I said.

I would say he had been retired for a few years now: the time spent outdoors had turned his head and forearms the colour of a good cup of tea. His face was wrinkled, with some of the creases running vertically down his brow and cheeks, and his body had curved forward to help prop up all the years he had spent on earth: but he didn't appear to be carrying any excess weight. His hair was white, tidily combed, and his gardening clothes were neat, showing only a few dustings of soil. They

73

would be washed often. I was interested to see how much whiter his hands were – when the gloves came off. I imagined his nails would be as well tended as this patch of lawn.

'It's been a great spell,' I added: anything beyond one day of good weather more than amply satisfied the criteria. 'Mr Redditch, is it?'

'That's right. Do I know you?' It was a polite way of saying, 'how do you know my name?'

'I was hoping to ask you a few questions, if that's all right. My name's Johnstone...'

'I know who you are,' he said quickly, nodding, seemingly happy to be saying it. 'Are you on the case?'

'Well, I'm no Humphrey Bogart but Jackie Gittes was a friend of mine and I just want to do my bit. This is Chiara.'

Mr Redditch's eyes dwelt on her, lingering on her legs. Chiara had taken the precaution of not wearing too much today: a short, white dress with a pattern of very large poppies, and red sandals with a big cork wedge of a heel. Her chestnut hair was up, as usual, and her sunglasses were large, with red frames.

Mr Redditch asked, as he reluctantly turned back to me, 'So what can I do for you then, Mr Johnstone?'

'Call me Jin. Do you think we could talk inside – if that's okay?' I gave a glance both ways. There was no-one in sight but I've learnt to be cautious: voices can travel far in a still and tranquil air. It helps not to be in the open when you want someone to be open with you.

He nodded as though he understood and invited us in.

'Has the hosepipe ban started?' I asked, by way of filling in the time it took for him to ditch his shoes and gloves at the front door and to show us into the front sitting room.

'Not yet. But I like to do it that way, though. Keeps the muscles in order. A bit of a work-out for them.' He looked at Chiara. 'Like lifting weights. Shortcuts aren't always the best
74

answer.' He tugged on the rolled-up sleeve of his white cotton shirt, bending his arm with a tightened fist, giving her the full view of his pale but taut bicep – it was the same colour as his hands. A large grin spread across his face like butter on a piece of wholemeal bread. I reckoned his teeth were dentures: top and bottom.

When we sat down, he asked, 'How can I help you then?' There was a great deal of enthusiasm in his voice – which I found heartening – but the way he talked mostly to Chiara, with just the odd look in my direction, wasn't so.

Chiara sat forward, upright, on the edge of the seat, her hands clasped firmly on her lap. She made no reply. There was a creaking from the ceiling and the sound of footsteps pacing back and forward. I glanced up.

Mr Redditch turned his attention to me for an answer but when I said nothing either he explained, with a hint of reluctance, 'My wife. Getting ready for her spinners' group.'

'Spinners?' I said.

'Twice a week they meet. Goodness knows what they talk about. The meetings take forever. They even take minutes – so, I suppose, that can lead to hours.' He gave a hearty chuckle. He would use that line a lot.

Neither of us joined him in laughter so his face fell quickly as he went on, 'My wife's the secretary. Types them up when she returns – the minutes, I mean.' And to Chiara, 'I hardly ever see her these days. She's so busy.' He added, with a shrug, 'But then I'm busy as well – in the garden. Good exercise. Keeps one fit, you know, as I said.' His eyes ran down the lines of her dress as the tip of his tongue ran across his lips.

I raised my voice to grab his attention. 'I just want to get an idea of what happened yesterday, Mr Redditch, that's all. If you can talk me through it, with as much detail as you remember, that would be great. Take as long as you like. I know you've spoken to the police already – but it might help. Don't leave

75

anything out.'

'If that's the case,' he replied with relish, standing up, 'I'd better go and put the kettle on.' He asked Chiara, 'Would you like a biscuit, dear? They're chocolate ones.'

She declined with a shake of her head: her eyes were hidden in the sunglasses but her face was strained. He left and we sat in silence: I didn't know what to say.

'Seems like a nice man,' Chiara whispered at last, a weak smile pushing in. She turned to look out of the window. The scent from the flowers on the sideboard had combined with her perfume to bring a rich, potent fragrance to the room.

Mr Redditch returned eventually carrying a tray with three cups, a sugar bowl and milk jug, all in fine china. There were no biscuits; and he hadn't asked me if I'd wanted one. 'Now where were we?' he said, passing over the cups. 'Ah, yes. Let's see. I was in the back garden from about three o'clock onwards – and started on the lawn some time after four, I would think.'

He was about to go on when Chiara cut in, 'And did you see anyone in the field at any time?'

Mr Redditch formed his already open mouth into a slight grimace. 'Sadly, no. The hedge blocks out a lot of the view. I didn't see anyone – not until all the commotion started and Wallace was at my gate. I didn't notice him at first – busy with the grass – but when I turned round he was hanging onto the fence, waving his walking stick in the air, trying to shout above the noise of the mower.

I rushed down and helped him in. It was clear something bad had happened but it took him a while to catch his breath. He kept pointing with his stick towards the field. Eventually, though, he managed to tell me.

So I rushed into the house, called 999, and brought out a chair for him. Then I had a choice to make: stay with him or rush across the field to try and help. Fortunately, in no time at all, I heard a siren in the distance so I hurried out into the street, down the track, opened the gate for them, and told the ambulance where to go.' Mr Redditch took a sip of his tea. 'The first police car arrived shortly after that.'

He went on, 'My wife was upstairs the whole time, but at the front. She didn't realise something was wrong – not until she heard the noise going in the street.' He shrugged. 'And that's about it. Not much to go on. Sorry.'

'Do you know what time Mr Lemon arrived at your gate?' I asked.

'Around five, quarter past, maybe – might be a bit more. I should have looked at a clock, I know, but it all happened so quickly. I wasn't prepared for it, really. And I don't wear a watch either – not since I retired – but I'm sure the police will know exactly when I made the call.'

Chiara spoke again, 'And you're certain you saw no-one else from the moment you went into the back garden?' Her voice was a touch harsh, perhaps trapped in the obvious tension she was feeling – her tea remained untouched.

Mr Redditch looked a little perturbed. 'Again, I can assure you, no-one.' He went on the defensive. 'That's not to say that someone might have passed when I wasn't looking. I was busy as I said. I don't spend the time gawking.'

'No, I'm sure you have lots to do – big garden, and all,' I said, reassuringly.

'Yes, it is a big garden,' Mr Redditch agreed quickly, happy to be back on a familiar footing.

'Do you know your neighbours well, if you don't mind me asking?' I said.

'Well, we only moved here about eight years ago: I wanted this size of garden and my wife needed an extra bedroom for her loom. Most people do the opposite when they retire, I suppose – downsize, rather than upgrade.' He gave another shrug. 'Miss Welch at the end: she's been here for ever, I hear. Came with the house: they built it round her.' He gave a sudden
77

laugh. 'I don't see her much. Sometimes I'll be passing and stop for a chat if she's at the front door. She's nice enough – once you get to know her. I'm not sure how she passes her time.

Wallace, I probably see more – especially since his accident. When he was driving his lorry he would be away for weeks on end. Going to the far corners of Europe, apparently. Every Wednesday and Sunday night he's off to The Griffin pub, without fail. The rest of the time, I'm not sure. He watches a lot of films, I know that. Even on these grand nights he'll have his curtains drawn and be inside. In the winter that's fine but it wouldn't do for me in the summer. Not at all – I need to be out and about. Each to his own, I suppose.' He pulled a face before going on, 'I think it was his parents' house. It's a fair size for someone on their own. But why move? There'll be nothing to pay on it. He still has his lorry driver friends dropping in from time to time: sometimes staying over. So it's not too bad for him.'

'Do you know what happened to his leg?'

'Hurt it at work. Must have been four years ago now, maybe six, hard to tell: the time passes so quickly. To do with his lorry: something falling on him when he was unloading.'

There was the sound of footsteps on the stairs and the front door opening and slamming shut. Mr Redditch gave us the unnecessary explanation, 'That's my wife off.'

I was surprised she hadn't said goodbye to him or wondered who was in her house – if, in fact, she knew there were any visitors present.

'She does a lot of the old crafts – not just spinning. She produces felt as well. That's the latest thing,' Mr Redditch was saying to Chiara. 'It's quite a thing to watch – felt making, by hand. And becoming more and more popular as well. You place two pieces of fabric together, take this very sharp needle with small hooks on it, all at different angles, and push it through and back and through and the fibres get caught up and meshed together. In and out, in and out. And that's how it's done.'

I was becoming increasingly uncomfortable in this house and, although it sounded like Mr Redditch was giving a rendition of the Hokey Cokey, I wasn't too happy with the accompanying hand gestures. I might have been a wee bit too sensitive though: with Chiara here, and all.

'There's a big demand for it, apparently,' Mr Redditch went on. 'Lots of people wanting felt these days.'

I stood up immediately and ushered Chiara ahead of me, towards the front door. 'Thanks very much for all your help,' I threw over my shoulder, as I bundled her forward and away from the man.

I continued to talk as we made our swift exit, 'We'll be away now. Maybe have a word with Miss Welch first. Find out if she saw anything.'

We stopped on the other side of the front gate, back in the sunshine. Mr Redditch had remained on his doorstep. I couldn't resist a final question though, 'Oh, by the way, why do you think Mr Lemon went past Miss Welch's house and his own one – which were the closer – and came to yours?'

Mr Redditch paused for a moment in thought, seemingly unaware of the alarm he had generated in me. 'Probably heard the lawnmower. Knew he could get help straightaway rather than waiting for Miss Welch to answer her door. And, I think, he needed someone to help *him*: physically, I mean. He was a bit wobbly. Wouldn't you be after witnessing that? That's why he wanted me.'

I thanked him and we left.

'Could you let me ask the questions here, Chiara?' I said, in my least offensive tone, as we walked past Mr Lemon's house to the end one.

'No problem,' she said, walking with her arms folded stiffly across her middle.

I knocked and, after a while, the door opened – gingerly. A small woman peered round its edge. Her voice was sharp, but with an imbedded touch of frailty, 'Yes?'

'Miss Welch?' I asked.

'Yes.' The confirmation held a 70-30 blend of stand-offishness and interest.

'I was wondering if I might ask you some questions about what happened yesterday, if you don't mind.'

'Are you reporters?'

'No, we're not. My name is Johnstone. Jackie Gittes – the man murdered – was a friend of mine.'

Miss Welch came further forward and gave me a good look from head to toe, like a sparrow sizing up a piece of bread. I reckoned she was well into her eighties or beyond. Her blue-white hair had been permed recently and sat tightly on her scalp. Her eyes blazed with intelligence and annoyance. Although thin and slightly bent, she had a wiry determination about her.

'And who's your friend?' she demanded, with a nod of the head.

Chiara stepped forward, probably to shake her hand. 'My name is Preston.'

Miss Welch slunk back instinctively at the approach, using the door as a shield.

'We just want to ask a few questions, that's all,' I said, softly. 'We've just been talking to Mr Redditch.' I added comfortingly, 'He knows me.'

It took a while to make up her mind, as I stood patiently, smiling, trying out my best harmless expression. Miss Welch said, 'The police have been here. I told them all I saw. And the reporters as well. I thought I was going to get some peace now.'

I gave her a wounded look and she opened the door fully, still barring the way with her full five foot height. 'Will it take long? Only I have things planned, you know.'

I said it wouldn't.

Her mood relaxed a touch and she asked, 'Would you like a cup of tea?'

'If you're making one,' I replied, cheerily.

'And if I'm not,' she returned, sharply. 'Do you want one then?' She had me there. A hint of a smile played on her lips. I said nothing. One up to Miss Welch.

We trooped in behind her, following through to the tidy kitchen, sitting down at the table by the window while the kettle boiled. There was a view out to the field. The hedge on the right blotted out Mr Lemon's garden but the one on the left was lower and, from where I sat, I could make out the tops of the trees over on the far side.

'Terrible business,' she muttered, with a shake of the head, her eyes fixed on the table. 'Especially round here. You don't expect it.' She glared in my direction, daring me to contradict her.

When I gave an earnest nod in agreement, she spoke again, the tone easing back a notch, 'So you were friendly with the deceased, were you? I'm sorry to hear that.' Miss Welch peered out of the window for a while, and then turned back abruptly, giving me, once again, the full force of her stare. It lingered on my face much longer than was necessary. She said, testily, 'And what makes you think you'll be able to do a better job than the police? Surely *they* are the ones who should be seeing to such matters – not *other* people?'

It was clear I needed to be honest with her. 'That's true. But there's no harm in offering a little help, is there? I may, in some way, be involved – innocently, I must add – as I was speaking to Jackie only the other day. He asked me to look into one or two matters for him – a couple of jobs – and he was waving a lot of cash around. I would hate to think I had, in some way, been responsible for this happening to him. I need to put my mind at rest.'

81

She pondered for a moment. 'What is it you want to know?'

'Just what you told the police.'

She busied about making tea, bringing three cups and saucers over to the table. 'Okay, I'll go through it again.' She sighed to emphasise the favour she was doing. 'It's not very much and it's really very simple. I make a cup of tea at five o'clock on the dot – when I'm home.'

She stared into space, picturing her movements. Out of the corner of my eye I could see Chiara, arms staunchly folded, eyes straight ahead. At that instant I wanted to know exactly what she was thinking.

'I sit where you are sitting, Mr Johnstone, and listen to the radio. It's a habit. My father used to say habit is a peg to hang your hat on.'

'For me, it's a pivot to balance the day,' I replied.

Miss Welch pursed her lips, waited a moment, and then continued, 'I *had* sat down, not very long though when I saw a man running by...'

'You saw the jogger!?' I knew immediately it was the wrong thing to do. I coughed and edged back a little in my chair.

She gave me a stern look, making it clear I had disturbed her flow. After an overemphasised pause, she continued, 'As I was saying, he passed by my house, running in the field, in a tracksuit. And before you ask, I didn't see his face as the hood was up but the tracksuit was brown and had a white stripe down the side. Oh, and he had on white shoes, what do they call them?'

I hesitated before answering, 'Trainers?'

'Right. And fairly soon after that, maybe five minutes, maybe a bit more, I heard a rumble at the side of the house, down the track. The ambulance arrived, then police cars with all their lights flashing and sirens screaming – quite a racket. I could barely hear the radio. I think they should have cut the noise as soon as they entered the street, don't you? It's not as if

82

there's traffic to get in the way. They didn't even stop all their whooping until they were over on the far side – and there's no traffic in the field, is there? I think it was a touch overdone.

Eventually, I decided to go into the back garden, down to the fence, for a closer look and a policeman came over and we went inside and he took down my statement. I told him just what I've told you.'

'Thank you, thank you very much, Miss Welch. And the jogger ran past your garden?'

'That's what I said. There's another gate at the far end of the field. Perhaps he was heading there.'

'Do you think you could be more precise about when you saw this jogger? Was it a man or a woman?' I asked, glancing at the clock high on the wall to my right.

'I didn't look at the clock but I'm pretty sure I had taken a sip of my tea. And a bite of my biscuit. But, as for the gender, it would be a guess. I thought at the time it was a man – going by the size – but then you get a lot of big females nowadays, don't you?'

'And how much had you eaten or drunk when Mr Lemon came along, would you say?'

'Mr Lemon? Oh, I didn't see him.'

'But he must have passed by to get to Mr Redditch's house?'

'So the policeman said – but I didn't see him,' she replied, indignantly. 'I was probably feeding the cat by then. She comes in all hungry at precisely the same time every afternoon. Very regular in that respect, she is. If my clock was on the blink, I'm sure the cat would tell me when it was her tea-time. She always waits until I'm sitting down and started on my biscuit. Every day it happens. Every single day – when I'm here. I think she takes great fun in it: getting me back up onto my feet again. Clunk, and she's through the cat-flap, ready for her meal. And woe betide anyone who doesn't do as she wants – and immediately at that. Very bossy, indeed.'

83

I rose from my seat. 'Thank you very much, Miss Welch. We need to get going now.'

Chiara jumped to her feet and started for the door.

'How does she know, do you reckon – the cat?' Miss Welch went on, stopping us in mid-step. 'I think she hears the kettle and then waits just long enough for the tea to brew before she's in. What do you think? Every day it's the same. We all like fun, I suppose – so she must think it's fun. But I disagree with her there – although it makes no difference to her.'

There was an empty cat dish on the floor in the corner.

Miss Welch continued, 'Once, though, I thought I'd caught her out. Last year it was. I'd sat down, had my tea and biscuit and there was no sign of her. I waited and waited and still nothing. I checked the clock – and still nothing. So I was beginning to think something had happened to her: she's a nuisance but I wouldn't want anything bad happening.

It was a full hour later before she shows up, sauntering in, cool as a cucumber. And do you know what? She was right all along: I'd forgotten to change the clock. I'd forgotten to turn it back an hour. What do you make of that? Bang on time she was and there had been no kettle to guide her then.'

Chiara gave out a hoot. I gave her a look. She covered her mouth and turned away, her shoulders heaving.

'What's wrong with *her*?' Miss Welch demanded – a little offended.

'Oh, it's nothing. Hay fever.'

'Isn't there something she can take?'

I changed the subject. 'Tell me, Miss Welch, will you be in this afternoon?'

Her eyes turned back to me and she took time to think. 'Yes, I should be. Why?'

'And will you be following the same routine – with the radio and the tea?'

'I would imagine so. I usually do.'

'Do you think you could make a note of the times: when you sit down, when you start to eat, when the cat appears, when you feed it, the time when you are half-way through your cuppa – that sort of thing. And when you finish eating?'

She gave it a moment's thought before nodding excitedly. 'And you'll want me to match up the state of my biscuit to when I saw the jogger yesterday – so we know exactly when he passed by.'

'Right. It'll work if it's the same rhythm and the same type of biscuit.'

I heard more noise coming from Chiara.

'Oh, it's always the same type – Garibaldi.'

We headed for the front door. I wondered how reliable she was and if her timetable of events could in any way be accurate. After all, she did think that her cat was familiar with the intricacies of British Summer Time.

'I'm sorry,' Chiara said, on clearing the house. 'Despite everything, I couldn't help it. How do you keep a straight face?'

'You have to, Chiara. Nobody needs to speak to us and we have no right bothering them, but they do it because they want to help. People tell you things they believe to be true and you have to go with it.'

'But the bit with the biscuit...'

'It could work,' I shot back. 'And even if it doesn't, it might focus her mind: bring up some small detail that's been forgotten or didn't seem important at the time.'

We walked towards the middle house. It was getting late in the afternoon now and the tomato sandwiches had worn off; nevertheless it would be better to get this last visit over and done before going home.

There was no answer to the doorbell at the front so we wandered round the side of the house to the back garden. Mr Lemon was slumped on a dark green, plastic chair, half-way down his long, unkempt lawn, facing his house. His right leg was extended out in front, while the other remained tucked under the seat.

He was younger than I'd imagined and might even have been about my age but vanity told me I was maturing better. He was as tidy as his grass: his receding, greying hair stuck out at all angles and his long, yellowed face held about two days of uncultured growth. The eyes checking our arrival were red and watery. Maybe he was still in shock – I didn't know the signs.

He wore striped pyjamas under his faded, green dressing gown and he was quite thin except for a protruding beer belly, like a smuggled football, poking out from the loosely fastened middle. He had outdoor shoes on his feet, but no socks. The heel of his left shoe was worn more than the right, making me speculate that he carried his walking stick in his right hand and used it to take the pressure off his bad right leg. The stick lay propped against the chair. It was standard hospital issue: hollow metal tubing with a rubber stopper on the end and holes down each side for easy adjustment.

I introduced myself and Chiara. He didn't take any interest in her and I apologised for disturbing him, explaining why we were there, trying to keep my voice light in an attempt to nullify his surly expression. He nodded increasingly as I spoke as though his brain was steadily waking up.

'I've heard of you,' he said. I couldn't tell if it was in a good or bad way. 'I can talk to you,' he decided. 'I've nothing to hide. Why does it take two of you anyway? Why did you come in numbers? Are you scared to be on your own, Johnstone?'

I remained standing – there was nowhere to sit other than on the grass – and shuffled my feet. I thought about a reply but decided not to bother.

'So you were a friend of this Gittes fellow?' he went on. 'What do you want to ask me, then?'

I wouldn't be allowed to take up much of his valuable time,

so I started quickly, moving round to make sure my face wasn't shaded and that he didn't have to look up into the sun.

'At what time did you find the body?'

'Couldn't say. Somewhere around five, probably.' His stare held my face as he waited for the next question.

'Must have been terrible to come across something like that?'

'It was.' He looked to the grass, his eyes ticked back and forth, as though searching for something.

'Was there any sign of life?'

His head came up slowly. 'Not a movement. I thought it was just a bundle of clothes at first – but, when I got closer, I could see a body beyond them. There was so much blood. Like a river oozing out.' He closed his eyes and gave a slight shake of the head.

'Then you went for help – you didn't have your mobile with you?'

'I don't have one. Don't like them.'

I had to agree with him there. It was only after Asa's insistence that I bought mine and hauled the landline screaming from the house. 'How long would you say it took you to reach your neighbour's house?' I asked.

He paused for a moment. 'It wasn't easy getting back up from that hollow. Could have been ten minutes in all. Hard to say. I had to keep stopping to rest.' He lifted his stick and tapped his right foot.

'Must be difficult to get about?'

'You're right there.'

'And you might have seen someone running away?'

'Aye – at the far end of the field. Thought I caught sight of a runner – then they were gone.'

'Where were you – when you saw the jogger?'

'It was just as I reached the top of the rise, after coming up from the dip.'

'And you didn't see anyone before, in the field, when you were walking over?'

'Nope. But then I wasn't really looking.'

'How come you were over there in the first place – if you don't mind me asking?'

He gave me a long look and a growl crossed his face. 'Can't let it stop you, can you? Got to keep on the move – *and* I make sure I get my paper everyday. Up to the shop and back. The doctor said when it first happened to make sure I keep the muscles going. It would be daft to let them wither. I wander round the edge of the field, maybe two or three times a week.'

Chiara spoke for the first time. 'How is it then that you didn't see anyone when you were walking round the field? Where do you think they were?'

Lemon's eyes narrowed. 'I don't *know* where they were. Maybe they saw me and hid behind a tree. All I know is there was someone running at the bottom of the field when I climbed out of that hollow. I saw them for a second – but see them I *did*.' He wasn't quite shouting but his voice had become agitated.

'Miss Welch saw someone too,' I said, trying to placate him, giving Chiara, what I hoped was another critical stare.

He gave out a, 'hmm' sound and turned his head away from us. I had nothing more to ask and knew it wasn't worth trying – so we left.

Now I had a problem: how to tell Chiara she was getting in the way and I didn't want her help with the case.

She had my phone number and now Chiara was about to enter my home for the first time – things were moving quickly. We stood on the pavement as she sized up the building, taking in each floor with a steady stare of a climber about to tackle a mountain. Then she walked through the gate without comment.

I wasn't embarrassed by my home – as Asa had kidded – but

it isn't the kind of place she's used to, that's all. It is an old red sandstone building, built in the early 1900s, and has signs of wear and uncare in places. Chiara, on the other hand, stays in brand spanking new ones, done up in their finery, ready for selling on. I doubt if she becomes attached to any of them or has time to uncover or understand their quirks.

I opened the back door, watched her take in some air, before guiding her into the kitchen. It was a little cooler inside but not by much. Hoogah's bank statements were on the table. I gathered them up quickly.

'Secret, is it?' she asked.

'Something I've to work on – when I get the time. Can't really show you, sorry – not without his permission. It wouldn't be right.'

She gave a quick nod of the head. 'Don't worry. I was only joking.' She wasn't smiling.

I didn't want to have secrets from Chiara. I wanted to be open with her, everything to be clear – that way she might not keep anything from me.

We wandered through the rest of my apartment. She stared into the bathroom, bedroom and sitting room but didn't cross any of their thresholds. My area of the house *did* need some sprucing up. It was a bit shabby as I viewed it through her eyes.

'When was your birthday?' she asked, as we stood in the corridor, in front of the connecting door. 'When you bought yourself that sparkling wine from New Zealand?' There was no warmth to her words: her hands fidgeted with the sides of her dress as she rolled the toe of her sandal back and forward over the floor.

'The beginning of the month.'

'Why didn't you phone me?'

I had the impression she wasn't interested in the answer – just something to pass the time. I replied anyway, 'It's no big deal. I didn't want you to think you were obliged to buy me
89

anything.'

She shook her head absently.

'Do you want to see the rest of the house? Although I can't show you the top floor as Rodger the lodger has the run of it.'

She shrugged.

I went on, 'His real name's Will. But he doesn't mind Rodger.' I was chuntering on, making up for the uncertainty I was feeling.

I dashed to the kitchen, grabbed a set of keys from the drawer, rushed back, slid the bolt on the connecting door, and led her through into the large hall of the main house, unlocking the front sitting room. 'It's not that I don't trust Rodger, it's more of a habit – with the keys.'

She didn't venture in, standing by its doorway.

'My parents had them fitted. They liked to have the doors locked. Something to do with security.'

We climbed the wide staircase to the first floor. She was ahead of me. 'Did you have lodgers then?' She was starting to rush now – not waiting for the doors to be unlocked. Just as well: I didn't have the key for my parent's bedroom on me.

I shook my head. 'Only friends of the family stayed here.'

She'd had enough, charging down the stairs, back towards my apartment. I hurried after her. 'All my relations lived in this street.' I wasn't sure she was listening.

We arrived at the kitchen and she hesitated.

'Do you fancy some tea?' I pulled a chair out from the table and stood behind it, hoping she might sit down. She didn't.

I added, quietly, playing with the keys in my hand, 'Do you think you might be able to stay here rather than the hotel? It'll save you money.' I wasn't sure if it was likely though – not after I explained that I didn't want her help. What would be the point of her staying on then? She would just be hanging around. But I had to tell her.

She moved to the back door, pulled it open, and breathed
90

deeply before saying, 'You know you can always come down and stay – and meet my father?'

I didn't know what to make of that – I said nothing.

She stepped outside, into the brightness; I was on the other side of the kitchen table. She asked, through the open door, 'What will be the next move in the investigation?' This time a tremble of a smile lit her face.

'I'll go and speak to Jackie's wife. Then back to see Miss Welch. After that, I don't know. I don't tend to plan too far ahead. Just see what happens.'

Chiara was wringing her hands. 'Look, I need to say something and I don't want you getting upset. I have to go now. I can't stay – sorry.' She added, 'I hope you get the killer. But I must leave. It's a long drive down.'

She turned abruptly and walked away, the sunshine sparking across the flow of her hair. She sensed I was following and spoke over her shoulder, 'You've got plenty to do. I'm going to Dorset, early, tour round, see what it has to offer. Call me when you feel you need me.'

Stop her, grab her shoulders, talk her out of it. That's what she wants, isn't it?

We reached the pavement.

Plead with her to stay.

But what would be the point? I had to keep on with the case. I couldn't stop now. She would always be waiting, hanging about here. That isn't right.

She marched onto her car. Her luggage was in the boot. Last night she hadn't committed herself to staying in my house – but she'd packed her bag.

I caught up with her. We kissed goodbye at her open car door, and she was gone, her hand waving out of the window. I stood and waved absently back, long after her car was out of sight. A sudden sadness hit me – my happiness had been tied to the bumper of her car and dragged away.

91

My hand was still in the air.

A voice behind me said, 'What on earth are you doing, Jinky?' I turned round. It was Hoogah. 'I was just passing,' he added. 'Thought I'd pick up those bank statements.'

What had made her leave so suddenly? Was it something I said – or did? She'd wanted to see round my home: we'd talked about it last night. So what was wrong in showing her? I followed Hoogah to the back door, thinking over every word I'd uttered.

He stopped before going in. 'What's the matter with you, Jinky? Is the talk of a gin shortage actually true then?'

Maybe it was something I had to figure out myself. If I couldn't work out what had just happened, what hope would there be for the future?

'Something wrong, Hoogah?' I managed to say.

'I told you, Jinky, I'm after my bank statements. I was passing and thought I'd introduce myself to your woman – if she's about. Although, the fact that you were standing like a chookie, all alone on the pavement, leads me to think she's not.'

'How can you tell what a woman's thinking?' He's had two wives: he must have learned something.

He gave his head a violent shake. 'You can't. It's not possible. Women are like the moon. Man has been on it, of course, poked in the crevices, but mostly it's unknown territory.' He stepped into the kitchen, spotting the papers on the window shelf. 'Did you find anything?' A smile smeared across his face like a toddler with a jeely piece.

'What? Look, Hoogah, I'm really sorry, I haven't had time to go through them. Do you want a cup of tea?'

'Not for me. It's too warm as it is. That's what I don't understand: why they drink tea in these really hot countries – in the desert?'

'What should you do if there's a problem between a couple –
92

but you're not sure what it is and don't know how to fix it?'

Hoogah rubbed his chin. 'I take it things are not going so well with Chiara, eh? My advice is to take a step back and let her come to you on her own terms. It's a bit like bull fighting: stand firm and let the bull approach. I hope that helps.' He stuffed the statements into his backpack. 'I'll take these away: the problem's been solved. I know about the changes now so you don't have to do anything.' He checked his watch. 'Must dash.'

'What do you mean?' I shuffled to one side of the doorway to let him pass. 'You don't want me to do anything? What about the irregularities?'

'I've just told you – it's okay. You don't have to worry about any of them. It doesn't matter.' He gave another toothy grin.

I muttered, 'You need to be careful with your money, Hoogah. It's important.'

'Yeah, I know. Let's just say that I've succumbed to identity fraud. But not to worry, this is the good kind.' He gave a quick wave and left.

I chased after him. 'What…what are you talking about? What identity fraud? That's a serious matter. Why are you so happy? Are you losing it altogether?'

'More like, found it all together.' He stopped. 'Look, you're not quite with it, Jinky. I can see that. I'm in a hurry, so I'll explain later. Next time in the pub – okay?' And he was gone, his whistle cracking the bullish air like a whip.

I lingered on the pavement again. If I was to follow his advice it would mean taking a step back, whilst standing firm. It wouldn't be easy. I needed a diversion. I locked up and set off in the direction of Jill's home.

It may be wrong, but if Jackie's murder involved some sort of sexual liaison gone awry, then his estranged wife would surely know about his preferences. Whether she would want to

93

share anything like that with me was another matter.

I wandered through the town. The walls of every building exuded heat, keeping to their contract of topping up the air temperature. The Sunday afternoon shoppers had left a paper strewn High Street and, judging by the number of dribbles and spilt cones – with accompanying packs of frenzied feeding seagulls – ice cream sales had been extremely robust today.

I passed the Midsteeple and stopped abruptly, looking up at the tower. The plaque above the door gave the distance to London: 330 miles. Another reminder of what I had lost: Chiara was driving down that road and beyond. Why couldn't I have realised how badly I would feel in her absence? Why hadn't I stopped her from leaving?

I trudged on.

She had been fine and then her behaviour had changed the moment I pointed out where the body had been discovered. Did that closeness to death make such an impact? Perhaps it was only then that she understood the seriousness of our task. I should have been more considerate: we could have talked to the witnesses, nothing more. I should have eased her in. But what did that matter now?

As I walked on, I realised there was another shameful sensation lurking within me: there was relief that I wouldn't be sharing my own bed for the very first time.

I picked up speed, disregarding the temperature. Somehow I had to forget about Chiara and concentrate on the case – I owed it to Jackie.

Jill hadn't moved from the flat they'd shared throughout their years of marriage. I heard her footsteps approach before the door opened. She invited me in with a surprisingly hearty welcome. The door opened straight onto a flight of stairs and I followed her up; her flip-flops thwacking off the soles of her feet as she climbed. We entered into an open plan kitchen and sitting room. I turned down her offer of coffee so she made me a cup of tea instead – her half-full coffee mug sat on the table.

Jill had thickened a bit round the middle since her school days – well, in fact, thickened all over – but the neat features of her face were still there. She wore a short denim skirt and a white, very sheer sleeveless blouse. Her hair was shorter now, straight, with a curl in under the ears. She hadn't made up her mind on its colour and had plumped for vertical bands of differing hues, ranging from blond, through brown, to deep red. Actually, it was quite fetching and matched her lively nature. Jill is a hairdresser – has been since leaving school.

She regained her position on her chair at the kitchen table and put feet up on another – after kicking off her footwear. I sat facing her, trying not to notice the vast amount of thigh she was showing.

'I know what brings you here. It's been a long time since I last saw you, Jinky.' She was trying to be that jolly person.

'We were never all that close, were we? But I am really sorry about Jackie.'

'Thanks.' She took a sip from her mug, cradled in her hands as though it was a cold day outside, and sadness pooled in her eyes as she stared at the far wall. 'You know we separated?'

'I heard.'

'That's Dumfries for you. Nothing's secret, is it?'

It seemed best to get to the point. 'That's kind of why I'm here, Jill – secrets. I wondered if you had any idea why it happened.'

She shook her head. 'I told the police the same and I would tell you *more*, if I knew – but I don't. So you're looking into it?'

'Yes.'

'I can't pay you, Jinky...'

'There's no need, Jill.'

She broke the building silence, 'So this is what you do now? I saw you in the paper earlier in the year – and you decided to
95

keep at it?'

'Wouldn't know what else to do. In fact I was doing a couple of wee jobs for Jackie himself, recently: finding out some things for him.'

She raised both eyebrows. 'What sort of things?'

'Nothing much. Someone he'd bumped into in his car...'

'And you think they wanted revenge?'

'No, no, nothing like that. It's just...I'm not really sure. He had a lot of cash on him when we met – in the pub. And he was the worse for wear. I did manage to persuade him to go home...' I shrugged.

She paused for a moment. 'There's no need to beat yourself up about it, Jinky. You know what he was like: always in trouble.' She shook her head gently from side to side, fondly remembering something, then added, 'I don't know what he was up to recently – hadn't seen him much over the last few weeks, and then just in passing, in the street. He was in a hurry; I was with my new man. We probably wouldn't have stopped to chat anyway.'

She took another drink from the mug and added in a faraway voice, 'He got himself into bother from time to time, you know that – couldn't help himself – and sometimes that leads...'

'If you don't mind me asking, why did you finally split up? You must have been together for, what, twenty years?'

'Twenty-one years of living together, twenty-five since we started going out properly. It's a long time.' She looked intently at me, perhaps wondering if my other question was a shade too intrusive, and if she should answer it. 'There was nothing really, Jinky, nothing you could put your finger on. No big blazing rows or anything like that. We kind of drifted apart, I suppose. I'm kept busy. Did you know I own the business now?'

'No, I didn't. That's great. Do you still get to cut hair?'

She laughed. 'Of course. I can't afford to sit on my...my

96

backside all day.' It wasn't her first choice of word. She went on, 'I've two girls working for me – well, my daughter, part-time, and another.' There was a great deal of pride in her voice. 'Been there since I left school – and now I've bought it over.' She turned to me. 'Why do you want to know about the split anyway? It can't have anything to do with…the attack.'

'Look, Jill, it's this business with the kilt. I wondered if there was a connection.'

She shook her head. 'What do you mean?'

'Did you hear about the way he was found?'

'There's been rumours but the police never said anything to me.'

'He was naked, Jill, with a kilt thrown over him. I was wondering if it might have something to do with – how can I put this? That he might have been meeting someone in the woods for a bit of…' I gave a cough and took a drink of my tea before going on, 'Jill, did Jackie play for the other team?'

A frown formed on her face. 'D'you mean Gretna?' She shook her head. 'He was never all that interested in football, Jinky.'

I added, quickly, 'No, not that. I mean, I mean – was he straight?'

It took a wee while for her to catch my drift. 'Of course he was,' she replied, indignantly, a hand brushing down her skirt. Then she gave a laugh. 'He was as straight as a wee crook could be.'

I pushed on, 'What about a bit, a bit…'

She waited for me to finish but when I struggled for the words, she prompted, 'A bit of what, Jinky?'

'A bit on the side, you might say. Way on the other side, in fact. A fetish?'

'Are you serious?' Her brow creased, then relaxed, and she gave a hearty laugh.

'I'm talking about the kinkier side of things – what if he was
97

meeting a woman then? Anything like that?'

'I can assure you there was nothing along those lines. I'm not going into marital details, and, judging by your face right now, I doubt if you'd take any pleasure in it anyway either. You were never like that, were you? Still the same? Have you ever had a girl?'

It was direct: it took me by surprise. 'There's been one or two, Jill. But I'm happy on my own.' It came out without a thought: an automated response. 'To be honest, I don't think I'll ever have the same urges as most men.' I bowed my head and rubbed at my brow.

Why say that?

She misread my reaction. 'Okay, I've embarrassed you enough. Let's just say Jackie was straight up the middle, if you know what I mean. You're after secrets, Jinky, but I have to tell you we didn't keep any from each other. He was always honest with me.'

She saw me fidget in my chair and changed the subject. 'So you don't work now – you know, properly?'

'No. This is what I do. Usually nothing as serious as this – mostly missing bins and pets. One last thing, Jill, when I was with Jackie in the pub last Thursday he was already well oiled. He said it was a special occasion. Do you know what that might have been?'

She paused. 'Last Thursday? The 13th? Well, it wasn't his birthday, and it wasn't our anniversary – not that he would have been celebrating it anyway. No, I've no idea.'

There was noise from the downstairs door opening and closing, firmly. 'That'll be my new man,' Jill said, standing up, straightening her clothes, before opening her door.

A man appeared at the top of the stairs and gave a jolt of surprise to find her with company. 'Jinky, this is my new man.' She swelled in satisfaction. 'Jinky is an old school pal,' she explained.

98

The man extended his hand and we shook. 'Jinky, is it?' he asked.

He was tall but a touch hollow-chested: his shoulders in advance of his torso. He looked fit, though, with his flat stomach and crew cut – and probably about the same age as Jill. He was neatly turned out in jeans and a loose cotton shirt. There was a diamond stud in his left earlobe.

'Call me Jin. School friends call me Jinky,' I clarified.

'Gardiner,' he replied. 'Nice to meet you. Call me Don.'

I met Asa in the pub. He had started before me – he greets every beer like an old friend. If he had a full pint in his hand, held his usual thirst, but his foot was on fire, there would be some doubt as to which one he would douse first. I moved him away to a table in the corner. By the way he was dressed, he'd come straight from work.

'Any more news about Jackie?' I asked.

'I've heard you've been poking your nose in – even though I told you not to.'

'How did you know?'

'It gets about. I hear words like 'amateur' and 'nuisance' and my ears prick up.'

'I wasn't doing any harm: not forcing anyone to talk. So what's the latest?'

Asa leaned towards me, keeping his voice low. 'The knife found *was* the murder weapon – but we sort of knew that. No fingerprints, sad to say. There would have been a lot of blood spurting out, so whoever did it would have been sprayed. They reckon it was unavoidable. We're doing door to door enquiries in the area in the hope someone might have seen something suspicious – although you'd have thought they'd have come forward by now if they had.

One other thing: from the entry angle of the wound, it looks like the killer was right handed and perhaps slightly taller than

99

Jackie.'

'And the jogger? Two people saw him.'

'Or her. Nothing to stop it being a female.' He shook his head. 'There's still nothing. We can't say for sure if this jogger had anything to do with it. We've tried asking along the route he or she might have taken after leaving the field – but no luck yet.'

I said, 'If it *was* him who did it, then running through the streets covered in blood would surely make people take notice. You can't get more suspicious than that.' I thought for a moment before going on, 'What about CCTV? Was he picked up on that? It was on the radio recently: we're captured hundreds of times a day on those things.'

Asa gave out a patient sigh. 'Jinky, you seem to think we don't know what we are doing. Of course we've looked at footage – but there's nothing. Not surprising really as there aren't any in that area. It's quiet. The one further up the main road, towards town, had nothing of note.'

'So you think he turned left rather than right on Edinburgh Road? Heading away from the centre?'

'It's possible.'

'That's the way you would go if you were heading to Georgetown, isn't it?'

'What about it? And what's Georgetown got to do with it?'

'And the kilt?'

He paused and narrowed his eyes, before going on, 'It's still being tested for fibres. It was definitely thrown over Jackie after the attack.'

'Did he have his clothes on when he was stabbed?'

'He did: there's a cut in his shirt where the knife entered. Which knocks your fetish notion a bit.'

'Couldn't the killer have cut through the clothes later to make it look as though Jackie was wearing them?'

'You need to give up on that one. We found threads in the

wound, matching his shirt. He was clothed when it happened.'

'Then why strip him?'

Asa shook his head. 'Have you spoken to Jill?'

'Yeah, I saw her. She has a new boyfriend. Wait 'til you hear this – his name is Don Gardiner, from Georgetown.' I folded my arms.

Asa shook his head. 'What about it?'

'Doesn't that sound familiar?'

'Ah, the man Jackie asked you to investigate?' He stroked his rough chin. I could hear the friction. 'Interesting.'

'Has to be the same man,' I said. 'Jackie told me he lived in Georgetown. I think this Gardiner did it. Why else would Jackie want me to look into him unless he was worried? I think he came up with the story of the poker game just to keep me happy – but, really, he wanted to know about the man who took his wife away.

And that's the motive, Asa: Gardiner wanted Jackie out of the way for good. Perhaps they had a meeting, an argument, and one thing led to another. I suppose there's the chance it was an accident, a fight – maybe, even, Jackie was the one carrying the knife.'

'Hold on, Jinky, don't get too carried away with yourself. It doesn't fit.' Asa squinted down at his beer, and cast a hand behind his back. 'Jackie and Jill were separated. This Gardiner fellow didn't steal her away or anything. Although...' he hesitated, 'we should find out when she first met him – maybe there's an overlap.' He took on some ale, savouring it in his mouth before releasing it down his throat. 'But if it was an accident, why strip away the clothes? No, I still can't see it.'

I shrugged.

He went on, 'Did you tell Ed about this Gardiner fellow when you were up?'

'Only found out about him an hour ago.'

'You should do that, Jinky – just in case he slips through.
101

And remember to leave me out of it.'

Monday 17th July

By seven o'clock in the morning and after a muggy, restless, sticky sleep, I had parked in a street in Georgetown waiting for Don Gardiner to travel to work. There are no pubs in this part of town so why anyone would want to stay here is baffling.

It was a cloudless day again and the early air simmered with trepidation: another day hotter than the last, the radio had said.

This might be a complete waste of time for a number of reasons: they do shift work at the factory where he works, so he might not leave at a normal time, or it could be his day off, or, above all else, he might have nothing whatsoever to do with Jackie's death. Nonetheless, I reckoned there would be no harm in spending a couple of watchful hours here to see what he got up to.

Jackie thought he drove a blue Ford Mondeo and as I had found only three possible addresses for the name Gardiner in this area – even allowing for different spellings of his surname – it was easy to track down the house.

I sat on the opposite side of the road, a little higher up the hill, while the correct make of car sat in the driveway of this semi-detached modern villa. Strangely, though, there had been no Don or D. Gardiners listed in the phone book and this property was under the name of P. Gardiner. Who else was living there?

No-one parks in the streets round these parts – every car nestles into the front garden or sits on runners by their garage – so I was conspicuous. Anyone poking their nose out from their net curtains would soon become suspicious of the man sitting in his car, reading a newspaper for hours on end. I had considered pretending to be broken down but that would have brought out helpers, making the situation worse, so I had gone with wearing uncomfortably warm painting overalls, hoping to look like a workman waiting to start a job. In future, if this unlikely event had to be repeated, it would be a good idea to hire a van and sit out of sight in the back.

Finally, Gardiner came out of the front door of his house – it was twenty-five past seven. I turned the radio down and wormed into the seat.

He was wearing a tracksuit.

By a quarter past ten, I had showered and dressed, and was sitting at the kitchen table in my only suit, ready for the ordeal of Manfred's funeral, with a cup of tea in my hand – if it's good enough for folk in hot countries then it's good enough for me – when I remembered the library book from Manfred's house. The fine would be mounting up so I decided to drop it in on the way to the kirk.

I explained the situation to the woman behind the counter, thinking it would free me from any charges, but it wasn't going well: she merely made a few uncommitted 'mm' noises and stared doubtfully at my face. I had a quick glance to see if the boss was around and spied him in one of the display cabinets, lying flat out on top of some opened-out books, fast asleep. I didn't dare waken him – nobody does.

'Did you say it was taken out by a Mr Mann?' the library assistant asked, scanning the book and the screen.

I nodded.

'Actually,' she went on, 'it was borrowed by a Mr Menzies. There's 65p to pay.'

I stood still, waiting for her to go on with something like, 'but in this case we can forget about it.'

She didn't.

So I squirreled about in my pocket, muttering, 'I must remember to tell Charlie about this.'

'Oh, it wasn't taken out by Charlie Menzies.' Her familiar
104

tone suggested she knew him well enough. 'It was taken out by a Lionel Menzies.'

I paid the money and left. Charlie had said his nephew didn't know Manfred: so why would Lionel give him a loan of a library book.

I usually golf on a Monday morning, and having missed last Thursday game and my Friday night session at the pub as well, my routine was completely awry – and that's something I don't like. Hopefully, it would be back on track by Thursday – my next scheduled golfing day.

Asa was waiting patiently by the gate of the church. I had taken my time walking round, trying to postpone the start of the inevitable sweat from the stinging warmth of the day. The sun was also feeling the heat and had taken off its hat to fan its face, producing a sultry breeze. With my jacket on – it was only right and proper to be wearing it – I was, for once, welcoming the prospect of entering a cool church.

It was a very sombre occasion. There was a genuine, resolute sadness across all faces as they waited to go in. Sometimes it is difficult to tell if the deceased is liked or not – perhaps, at these times, we are forced, or need, to search out the best in people – but here it was obvious that Manfred was held in very high regard.

Charlie sat alone, slumped in the front row. No-one joined him, unsure if it was appropriate, and many remained standing at the back of the packed room rather than take the risk. Now I wished he had asked Lionel along for moral support, and, for one brief moment, I even considered moving down to place a consoling arm round his shoulders. I didn't.

We sang a couple of hymns, heard some prayers, and then Charlie was beckoned forward to say a few words. He squirmed his way out of the long pew like a stubborn cork easing from a bottle and stepped forward: a small and lonely
105

figure.

The minister had adjusted the microphone, sitting on the sturdy lectern, to point lower. Charlie arrived at it, rearranged his papers, his eyes firmly on them, before giving a cough and looking up. His clothes were solemn today: a kingfisher-blue suit with a matching handkerchief in the top pocket, a pale green shirt, and black tie. His hands shook horribly.

He sucked in a deep breath – and another. Then, realising the large lectern blocked out most of him, he stepped to one side, twisting the microphone round as though throttling a chicken. It gave back a screech: aghast at this vicious manhandling.

Although Charlie's voice wavered, it was strong enough to reach the whole room: his training as a radio football reporter returning. Just as well, as the microphone had spitefully decided to pick up nothing.

He started, 'Manfred would have been pleased to see so many people here. He would have thanked everyone individually. I'll be doing that instead, later, at The Cairndale. All are welcome.'

A faint smile broke round the room.

Charlie took another deep breath and looked away from his papers, picking a spot high in the air. 'I've known him since I was five – he was six. I don't remember this incident at all but Manfred told me about it, so it's bound to be true. It was our first meeting.' He cleared his throat.

'I had just started primary school. We had moved back to Dumfries that summer – apparently my mother couldn't settle in Glasgow – and this was the dreaded first day. I was standing by myself, didn't know anyone, kicking my heels against the wall in the corner of the playground, when Manfred came over. He asked me where I'd got the yellow shoes…'

A rustle of grins and a couple of nervous laughs scattered across the church. Charlie gave a shrug and a look to signify, 'yes, even in those days.'

106

He peered down towards his feet – although there was no way he could see them past his overhang – and went on, 'There was nothing malicious in the remark – just curious, that's all. Apparently, I answered him by saying that I didn't know: it was my mother who had bought them for me. We stayed friends from that time on.'

He added, 'In case anyone is wondering, these are not the same shoes.'

He went on to give a potted history of Manfred's life.

Asa and I followed the wheeled-out coffin, and a head-down Charlie, into the sunshine. No-one came near him as he entered the waiting car and set off for the cemetery. Tread, Hoogah and Chisel were all tied up in little bundles of work colleagues and I motioned to them about a drink later. They nodded back. Then Asa and I set off towards The Cairndale Hotel – deciding against attending the burial – and I mentioned the library book on the way.

'It could be nothing, Jinky, there could be a simple explanation. Lionel takes out the book, passes it on to Charlie, who likes it, and then hands it onto Manfred for a read – and that's how he ends up with it. Or…' Asa's right hand moved behind his back as he raised his chin thoughtfully, '…it's more likely that Manfred and Lionel *have* been in touch with each other. Think about it, if Manfred's heart condition was a big problem he would have been to see a specialist. That would be Lionel – from what you say. Manfred decides to keep it a secret from Charlie and asks Lionel to go along with it as well. In fact, Lionel wouldn't be able to tell Charlie as there's the doctor-patient confidentiality in place. So it was Manfred's decision to hold it back from Charlie.'

'I suppose you might be right.'

We were the first to arrive at the hotel, a free drink waiting in the room set aside upstairs. We stood by the window looking

107

out to English Street and St Mary's church. 'Have you seen Hoogah since Saturday?' I asked.

He shook his head.

I related yesterday's incident. 'It seems crazy: why wouldn't he be worried about identity fraud? Even *he* must know the seriousness of it.'

Asa gave a firm nod. 'We'll need to have a word and get it all sorted out. I think he really needs someone to look after him. He's always been like that, of course.'

Charlie arrived half an hour later and meandered round, shaking everyone's hand. There were about thirty of us in the room. The boys had gone back to work; although that didn't apply to Hoogah who was on his summer break – but he was nowhere to be seen.

I wouldn't be staying long either: the house clearing business was hanging over me and it needed a good going over today to be ready for the gutting tomorrow morning. From experience, this task always takes longer than expected. I hoped Charlie was prepared for a lengthy session.

I sought him out; his face had loosened a touch. 'I hardly recognised you,' I said, pointing at his suit.

Charlie, his lips pursed, glanced down at his clothes. 'Bought specially. Didn't have anything else suitable in the wardrobe – if you'll pardon the pun.'

'I'm going over to his house this afternoon. When do think you'll be along?'

Charlie nodded some thoughts at this, before finally saying, 'Sorry, Jin, but like I said, I have to be away right after I've finished here.' He waved his hand in the general direction of the room. 'It's just the way things have worked out. I'll be back by Wednesday, though. You'll manage, won't you?'

I was a wee bit disappointed but tried not to show it. 'Okay, I'll see to it all, Charlie. When can I drop off his documents for you to look over? I don't want to go through them. And is there anything you want me to hold back for you: an ornament or something, as a keep-sake?'

'No, there's nothing I want. I have it all up here.' He tapped his temple with his index finger. 'And, actually, I'd like you to take his papers to the solicitors. Give them the lot – they can sort through them. They're getting well paid to do it.'

He gave me the address on Buccleuch Street and didn't appear concerned about leaving all the decisions to me. Maybe I should have taken it as a compliment. 'No Lionel?' I asked.

'Operations all morning. He seems to be the only one up there who's qualified to do them. I didn't want him rescheduling, just for my sake – not with all those folk waiting to be seen. They need him more than I do – at this time.' He gave a heavy sigh. 'And that'll soon be me.'

'I didn't know you used to stay in Glasgow. You never picked up the accent.'

He shook his head. 'I don't remember anything much about it. I think we only stayed there for a couple of years or so. I couldn't have been much more than two when we moved up. It's better down here – that's what my mother always said.'

'She's not wrong. By the way, Charlie, did you lend Manfred a library book recently?'

He paused for a moment. 'No. Actually, I can't remember the last time I was in a library. Why?'

'Did anyone lend *you* a library book?'

'No. What's this about, Jin?'

'Oh, it's just that I found an overdue book in Manfred's house.'

Charlie gave me a puzzled stare and spoke as though I was simple, 'Then it must be his.' A smile twinkled across his face for the first time on this clawing day. 'Are you worried about having to pay the fine? Is that it?'

I returned home and changed out of my sticky-hot suit –

sadly realising money would have to be spent on dry-cleaning it. The clothes barometer indicated it was time for the rare appearance of shorts; and although the stroll over to Manfred's house brought a lovely fresh feeling of air around the legs, it made me aware that, since their last outing of a few years back, fashion had decided shorts should be considerably longer and that showing five inches of thigh was not the done thing anymore. Moreover, this expanse of leg exaggerated the knobbliness of my knees – not a good look – but as they were the only pair I had, I decided to push on rather than return to the cling of breeks.

And I was glad I'd rushed up to the police station this morning rather than wait until after the funeral – they might not have taken me as seriously dressed this way. Although my painting overalls did raise a few eyebrows.

When Gardiner had appeared earlier, his tracksuit had been blue. He'd emerged from his house with a backpack slung over his right shoulder. It was put to the ground while he undertook a stern routine of ferocious limb stretching, lasting a full ten minutes. The front fence came into play on several occasions: used to crank a straightened leg into some fearfully high positions, allowing further vicious, chin to knee, bends.

Then he was off: down the road at a brisk pace, without a glance in my direction. He looked awkward: a closed, shuffling jog with little back-lift. It reminded me of a crab – but it didn't stop him from covering the ground quickly.

I'd never tailed anyone before so I decided on caution: waiting until he was about to disappear from view before starting the car. When he took a left, up the slope of Gillbrae Road, I was at least fifty yards behind. His pace didn't falter on the climb; I pulled in at the bottom to watch, the phone to the ear as though taking a call.

As he reached the top, I moved off again, this time stopping in the bus bay on the brow of the hill to watch his descent. I pulled away as he neared the bottom of the road. Instead of turning right, as expected, Gardiner took a quick left, followed by an almost immediate right, into the narrow lane leading down to the Dock Park. I couldn't follow him in there. I had a choice to make.

In our short conversation at Jill's house, he had mentioned his job at the factory out at Cargenbridge, so, hoping he was heading there, I drove to top end of the park and waited for him to come out. There was no sign of him. He could still get to work via the Kirkpatrick Macmillan pedestrian bridge at the bottom of the park, but it was also possible he was simply out for a run along the riverside path to Kingholm, before circling back home. I decided on the factory, and in five minutes I had parked in the street across from its gates and its security guard.

Gardiner arrived nearly fifteen minutes later, his tracksuit top unzipped, showing a red t-shirt dark with sweat from the hot morning air – but he didn't appear to be too much out of breath. An idea came to me: with his unusual running style, it might be worth videoing him to show Ms Welch and Mr Lemon. They might recognise it. Other than that, what was my plan? I couldn't very well follow him every day – even if I did decide to take out my old rusty bike from the cellar to cover any pedestrianised sections. And what would it achieve anyway? No, the only thing I could do right now was gather information on the man and report anything of note to the police.

I had my camera at the ready and caught his wave to the security guard as he passed through the entrance but the quality of the video wasn't nearly good enough: too far away. I eased out of the stifling car and wandered over to the gate, making it look as though I was just passing by, but had time to spare for a chinwag.

The guard, standing in front of his box, in his peaked hat and smart grey uniform, cradled a clipboard in the crook of his left arm and held a pen, poised and ready, in his right. He kept the red and white striped wooden barrier raised, choosing to step out smartly in front of each approaching vehicle, blocking the way until satisfied enough to let it pass through – a note going on his sheet. He appeared as efficient as The Queens' offside trap.

Unusually young for the job, perhaps only in his mid-twenties, he must have been hot under his uniform, but he didn't show it as he strode around. Yet, some of his importance was diluted by the long hair running over of his stiff, starched collar, and by the two tufts of hair, pinched and splayed between cap and ears, wafting in the warm breeze like a pair of windsocks.

He was suspicious of me and didn't make me feel welcome – but then that probably goes with the job. We didn't know each other and my chatter made no progress. I was about to leave when a car arrived. It was someone I knew from the golf club. So the three of us yakked away for a moment and, during the next few minutes, I was able to wave to quite a number of familiar faces heading in. This appeared to ease the uniformed man's worries.

I found out that people and cars are logged in and out by him and that he knows everyone by sight. Gardiner – although I was careful not to mention him by name, merely to comment on seeing someone jogging in – runs to and from work about three times a week, usually every second day. Other employees do the same: there is a group of them, Gardiner included, training for the London marathon in April next year.

The gatekeeper didn't have Saturday's sheets handy – and, even if he had, I doubt if our short, tepid friendship would have stretched far enough to allow me to check if Gardiner was working at the time of Jackie's death. Jill would know more about her boyfriend's work schedule and would need to be questioned again.

112

I said goodbye to the guard and drove off in the direction of the police station. Although I was in my painting overalls, there was no point delaying going to the authorities: Gardiner's brown, blood-stained tracksuit might still be in his washing basket, sitting on the floor of his home.

Again, the visit didn't take too long. I spoke to Ed once more. He might have been interested in the information but it was difficult to tell: he kept his face straight. And just like the last time he said very little and was quite brisk. Nevertheless, I was left with the feeling that there were still no major developments in the case as yet.

I took a deep breath before entering Manfred's house and this time I *did* open the windows to release the stagnant air. There was a change to the house since my last visit: even though I had the nasty job of delving into someone's past life, I was a touch more settled. I had the right to reset this house. I tried to keep in mind that it was now merely a storage area of superfluous possessions; although soon to be a budding prospect to the next tenant.

Finding an empty cardboard box in a cupboard, I gathered all the documents from the filing cabinet upstairs and then collected jewellery, money and searched for any secreted cash or cards. When clearing out my Uncle James' house, I discovered a very large wad of £5 notes, hidden at the back of drawer and another stash under a carpet in one of the bedrooms – and if Manfred was anything like me, his credit cards would be stuffed in the back of a kitchen cabinet.

I spent close to an hour on the task: checking under furniture, behind drawers, tapping for loose floorboards, but didn't find anything. If there was something hidden, the next occupant might get lucky.

By the time I'd cleared out the fridge, emptied the food cupboards, and piled all the clothing into some black bags for

113

the charity shop, I'd had enough. Besides, there was the balancing act of leaving enough items of value to offset the cost of the clearing company. I'd left all the electrical equipment so, hopefully, we'd end up even.

A quick glance in the garden shed brought some extra bargaining – with a lawnmower, his power washer, a lot of tools and a set of ladders. Manfred's vegetable garden was in full swing and still tidy. I could have picked a few things and had them for my tea but I was becoming weary and needed a shower. Someone else could have a feast.

As I closed the shed door, the ladders reminded me that I hadn't checked the attic. I gave a sigh and hauled them upstairs to below the hatch in the ceiling. There was a light switch and first thing I saw was the water tank and decades of grime. Rolls of insulation had been placed between the joists and the space was empty except for an old mattress in one corner and a small suitcase lying within reach.

I pulled it nearer and clicked back the catches: it wasn't dusty . A quick look showed it to contain heaps of old family photos. They would be of no value to anyone other than Charlie. Despite saying he wanted nothing from the house, I decided to keep it – in the weeks and months to come he might regret not having any mementos.

I started to load up Manfred's car.

It was the plump wife of the next-door neighbour who came to have a word this time. 'A lot of stuff to be cleared?' she asked. Her hand slipped into the pocket of her grey, nylon housecoat, rustled around, and came out. She popped a white, hard-coated peppermint straight into her mouth. There was a click as it hit off a back tooth.

The woman wore bright red lipstick but little else on her face had received attention. Her short, straight grey hair was held back by black clasps on either side, like tied-back curtains, and I suspect she had given up smoking recently as most of her lines radiated from her mouth. Below her old, tweed skirt, her surprisingly skinny legs, and unseasonable calf length socks stood in fluffy but worn and grubby slippers.

I gave the briefest of shrugs as I closed the boot. She probably wasn't getting a good enough view from her sitting room window and needed a closer examination. Her tongue circled the sweet as she spoke again. 'You were round early this morning. Thought you'd have waited 'til after the funeral before starting.'

It was meant to be her lesson in decorum for me but I didn't quite follow. 'How do you mean?'

'I heard you shuffling about this morning. It's not easy sleeping in this weather, and the walls are thin – you can spit peas through them. Couldn't be bothered getting out of bed for a look, though.'

'You're saying someone was in Manfred's house early this morning?'

She straightened, sensing a story. It was exactly the same motion her husband had made when he thought there was a bargain to be had with the car. 'So it wasn't you,' she declared. She voiced my thoughts, 'So who would it have been, then?'

I drove back home and parked Manfred's car out on the road, behind my own. I have runners at the front of the house, but as the garden's not very deep I can't close the gates when the car's on them, so I prefer to leave it out on the street and keep the gates firmly shut.

On the way, I'd mulled over what the neighbour had said. I'd managed to free myself from her by explaining that it was probably Charlie wandering round – having a quick look before the clearing company arrived tomorrow. This snippet of information on the timetable for the house left her in good spirits, and with her job done, she had gone back inside.

Before leaving Manfred's house, though, I had another look

115

round, checking the locks and windows – but there was no sign of a forced entry and nothing looked disturbed. It could have been Charlie but then he would probably have mentioned it at the funeral. If it wasn't him, then who was it?

I wasn't entirely sure what to do about the incident either: I was hardly in a position to know if anything had been taken. Furthermore, by the time I met up with Charlie again, in a few days time, the contents of the house would be long gone, as well as any possible clues. I suppose if I had his mobile number I could have called him: but he hadn't offered it and I hadn't asked, as it would have meant handing mine over in return. Perhaps, there are times when I take this phone business a wee bit too far.

I decided to let the matter lie. Come tomorrow the house would be cleared and off my hands for good. I didn't want any delay in that process.

After a long cool shower, I pulled out another t-shirt from my dwindling supply – three changes per day was beginning to put a strain on my normal laundry routine – and slipped on a pair of lightweight trousers for a more elegant visit to the pub.

There was still the matter of videoing Gardiner but that would have to wait until I found out his running routine from Jill. Wait a minute! I needed to tell her about my suspicions: she might be a wee bit interested to hear that her boyfriend is a murderer. I would have to visit her later and hope she was alone.

I filled up the washing machine, setting it for a delayed start: timed to be freshly finished on my return. I don't like wet clothes sitting for too long in the drum and have a theory that, by hanging them up straightaway, the amount and degree of ironing required is greatly reduced.

Even though all the lads would be in the pub tonight – funerals have that effect – I wasn't planning on drinking much. It was only Monday after all, and neither the task of hanging
116

the washing on the line at night, ready for the morning rays, nor the chat with Jill, should be attempted when too squiffy.

My timing was good: Tread was at the bar and my drink was perched on the counter. Asa brandished a freshly poured pint, his tongue moving like a windscreen wiper across his lips. I gave a nod hello to Andy the barman, who was drying glasses with a tea towel – the pub was quiet – and the three of us made our way to a table by the door.

Unusually, Asa's eyes locked onto me rather than his drink. He started up, 'Why didn't you tell me you'd been up to the station *again*? Must have been early this morning, was it?'

It came before I had a chance to sit down and before I could appease my scorched throat. I shrugged. 'What does it matter? You don't have to know everything anyway.'

His hackles came up – something was wrong. I tried to ease him back down with, 'Anyway, I mentioned the library book to you – but you weren't much taken by it. I tell you most things.'

'What's going on?' Tread asked, keen to be brought in.

I started to explain about Gardiner but Asa talked over me. 'He's been checked out. You're wrong about him, Jinky.'

There was a bit too much force in that last comment for my liking.

He went on, 'Gardiner had nothing to do with the murder. He's got a solid alibi – working in his office when the attack happened.'

'Is someone going to tell me what this is about?' a frustrated Tread asked.

'That was quick work,' I replied. 'Does that mean there are only a few leads to be going on?'

'I can't discuss it.'

'But he could have sneaked out,' I continued.

Asa scoffed, 'And all this is based on the fact that he owns a tracksuit – is that it? That's what you said at the station, wasn't it?'

I took in a gulp of my gafoni: some of its pleasure had disappeared. 'It wasn't just that,' I returned meekly. 'He's Jill's new boyfriend, don't forget.'

Asa shook his head. 'Give it up, man. You'll need to look elsewhere. Gardiner was sending emails around the time of the killing. We've checked his computer and the ones receiving the messages – all work related. He was in his office at the time – no doubt about it. He's in the clear.'

I turned to Tread and explained. A couple of deliberately placed snorts from Asa didn't succeed in putting me off before I'd finished.

A thought came to me. 'Anyone else see him, Asa? In his office. It was Saturday, after all – not so many people about, you'd think.'

Asa pulled in a huge amount of air. When he exhaled I felt my hair move. 'What is it with you, Jinky? Can't you take a telling?' He was working himself up again: his voice raised. 'You're to leave it, d'you hear?'

I held my hands up. 'Whoa, there, Asa. It was just a simple question. No need to get so het up about it. What's wrong with you anyway?'

He continued in a determined tone, 'No-one saw him, okay? It was the weekend – but he *was* working. We have the proof.'

I paused for a minute, wondering what I had done to rile him so much – and to tell myself to keep calm. 'What if someone else sent the emails for him?'

Asa's beer glass clattered down onto the table, loud enough for Andy to glance over. 'Will you just leave it, Jinky,' he rasped. 'I keep telling you this but it's not getting through. Forget about it. Do you honestly think he had an accomplice to murder – at his work? I don't think so. Now, can't you just turn your attention to something else? Why don't you concentrate your efforts on the work you've to do for Charlie, eh? And there's Sanny as well.'

'Easy, Asa,' Tread whispered.

'What's bothering you?' I asked again, taking in some deep breaths. When he didn't reply, I added, 'The person who helped Gardiner might not have known anything – only doing it as a favour. I'm going to have to go back to the police station again.'

This time Asa's fist found the tabletop and my glass jumped.

'Steady.' It was Tread again but this time sterner. He laid a hand on Asa's arm.

Asa swallowed hard to suppress his anger, his face red. 'Look, Jinky, I know you mean well. I do. *I'm* the one sticking up for you – but there's a few against you. And they're not folk you should be crossing.'

'What are you talking about?' I said.

He paused. 'I've been told to tell you not go about poking your nose in. Ed for one doesn't like it.'

'Well, why didn't he say so when I saw him this morning? I spoke to him in person.'

'He probably did but you wouldn't be listening,' he muttered back.

Ed *had* told me that finding the murderer was solely a matter for the police – and he'd repeated it with a snarl on leaving. I wasn't going to mention this at the moment.

'But, Asa, this time I'm doing exactly what you say I should always do: inform the police at every turn.' I gave a few shakes of the head.

He continued, after a largish gulp to finish off his beer, 'People have complained.'

'Let me guess. When you say people, you mean Mr Lemon. Am I right?'

He nodded back. His tone was more reasonable this time, 'Look, I'm caught in the middle. And I don't like the atmosphere at work just now. So can you do as Ed wants and leave it be? He doesn't care for his main witness getting
119

harassed and annoyed. And I don't like being told off in front of everyone. You watch they don't come after you for wasting police time.'

'They wouldn't do that.'

'Oh, I think they would.'

I stared him straight in the face. 'I'm afraid I can't do that, Asa.'

He gave a shake of the head. 'You're a pig-headed so and so. You know that?' He made to lift his glass, only to realise, halfway through the manoeuvre, that it was empty. His ruby face turned to one of disgust as he raised the glass high enough to drip some remnants onto his lips. If he could have wrung it out, he would.

No doubt to ease the tension, Tread came in, 'So this Gardiner fellow's going in for the London marathon? I was thinking about doing the same.'

I turned to him, trying to wipe Asa's anger from my mind, 'Don't be daft. Since when did you go in for any exercise? Not even at school. Always trying to get out of PE if I remember rightly – forging notes from your mother.'

'Now that's not fair,' Tread replied.

I went on, 'You should never have signed them "yours faithfully, mum" – that's always a giveaway.'

He said, unperturbed, 'I've done my fair share of sporty stuff in my time. Remember I used to go to that trampoline club? My father took me there when I was eleven.'

I shook my head. I didn't bother looking to see if Asa was taking part in the conversation.

'Come on,' Tread went on, 'you must remember. The club was in that building on Brooms Road. As soon as you got any good you had to stop.'

'Why was that?'

'It had a low ceiling.'

I'd walked straight into that one, but at least it seemed to do
120

the trick: the mood round the table eased a touch.

Tread went on again, determined to keep the subject well and truly changed, 'When's Hoogah coming in? Asa told me about this identity fraud business. We'll have to make sure he's all right. You know what he's like with money, and that.'

'He seemed quite happy about it,' I replied.

Asa spoke at last, 'He texted to say he would be late – nothing more. I don't know what's happened to Chisel though. Ah, now, look who's just walked in.'

I saw Jill making straight for our table. It was funny, although she had thickened out considerably since her school days and was now rather square, I still saw her as a sculptor views a chunk of marble: seeing the figure lying within, the shape I used to know.

'Thought I'd catch you here,' she said to me as she approached. She was in the same denim skirt as yesterday but with a red patterned blouse on top. There was the addition of a leather strap with a white bead round her neck. Her earrings were incredibly large, round and golden.

'It was either here or your house,' she said quickly. 'Still staying in the same place – where your folks were?'

I nodded.

Jill gave a warm smile, along with a nod to Asa and Tread, as she twiddled with one of her earrings. They each returned a few kind words on her loss.

She came straight to the point, asking me, 'Do you think you could come along with me, over to his flat?' Her eyes picked out the glass in my hand. 'Unless, of course, you've something better on the go.'

It was obvious she was anxious about something. I laid my drink down, asking, 'You mean Jackie's flat?'

'Right.'

This suited me fine. I was keen to leave: the atmosphere round the table hadn't improved nearly enough, despite Tread's
121

efforts. A fiery Asa is as friendly as the terraces at a derby game. Nevertheless, I needed to show some etiquette first. 'Do you fancy a drink, Jill, before we head?' When she declined, I downed my gafoni. 'Okay, let's go then.'

She smiled goodbye to them and we left. I did feel a bit bad at not offering the lads a beer – but I had a point to make to Asa.

'You've saved me a trip round. I was coming to see you anyway,' I said without thinking as we broke into the balmy evening.

'Oh, why was that?'

I hesitated unsure of what to say. Did I still think Gardiner was the likely murderer? The police had dismissed him as a suspect – so what would be the purpose of mentioning it to her now? And why was I so determined to break his alibi anyway? Was it only because I didn't want to be shown to be wrong? There must be plenty of other suspects: it could easily be someone seeking revenge for an event in Jackie's dubious past.

We set out at a rapid pace, passing the Burns Statue in no time – and I could feel the sweat building on my brow.

Jill tried again, 'What did you want to see me about, Jinky?'

'Later.' I veered her away, 'What is it you want me to do – at his flat?'

The night I'd helped a drunken Jackie home came to me again. It wasn't so very long ago – a few days. The memory brought sadness: the death of a wastrel is still a waste.

I was struggling to keep up. Her speed hadn't faltered so far: it was probably set to maximum for flip-flops. 'I just needed someone with me that's all. I didn't fancy going there on my own. Silly, I suppose.' She offered over a feeble smile. 'But I thought you might like to have a look around the place as well. It could help – if you're still investigating that is. You never know, you might find something.'

I appreciated her confidence in me and I was certainly keen

122

to see inside, but I said, 'I'm not likely to come across anything, Jill. I'm sure the police will have given it a thorough going over by now.' Asa was back in the pub, yet I was still trying to appease him by saying all the right things.

Actually, the fact that he'd witnessed Jill searching me out might help ease the situation. She wanted me to keep searching – so how could I turn her down? Surely he must realise it's not always about letting the police get on with it. There are times when people need to be active and enlisting help may be seen as a way of increasing the chances of success. I might not be able to do all that much, I might not find this killer, but Asa has to realise, at the very least, it stops people feeling completely powerless.

In ten minutes we had reached the address. Jill pulled out a Yale key. I'd opened this door for Jackie – he'd made a few unsuccessful attempts at locating the slot, scraping the key round and round, before finally dropping it. The marks were still visible on the metal.

The door opened into a hallway. This was where I'd left him. Jill checked the table for mail – there was none. We climbed the stairs and she stopped in front of a door with a number 4 on it; there was another across the corridor with a 6. It was a house similar to my own, with each room turned into a bed-sit.

'Hold on, what's been going on here?' The door had been forced, with splinters of raw wood down the edge. There was a temporary black clasp and padlock locking it shut.

Jill looked at me, surprised, 'You didn't know?'

I shook my head.

'When the police came round to search, they found the door jemmied and lying wide open. The room was a mess: everything pulled out. Someone had been through his stuff. The police say they've tidied it up a bit though.'

'Any witnesses?' I asked, nodding in the direction of the other door.

123

'I don't think so. That one's empty.'

'How did they get in downstairs then?'

She shrugged. 'You'll have to ask the police that. They didn't tell me much – as usual.'

'I don't think you can go in, Jill. This has to be a crime scene.'

She held up a small key to face level. 'They're finished with it. Gave me this tonight. That's why I wanted to get over here as soon as possible.'

'Why the rush?'

She undid the padlock and stepped into the room. The open door to a tiny bathroom faced us. It had been added at a later date: its walls cutting into the fancy freeze circling the high ceiling. Jill moved slowly into the centre of the room, watching where she stepped. There was an immediate smell of paint, wallpaper paste, and cooking fat. It was dark enough to need the central light – but she didn't switch it on.

'His wedding ring,' she said, at last. 'It wasn't on him when he was found. I would like to have it. I think he stopped wearing it. It must be here – somewhere in all this mess.'

The drawn curtains didn't close properly and the large gap at the top, where a few of the curtain rings had broken free of the rail, allowed the orange sunlight of the evening access to spread a low glow throughout. My eyes adjusted to the gloom.

Jackie's home was one large room – and a tornado had passed through. Cascades of clothes spilled from the heavy wooden furniture, and drawers lay upside down, discarded. Newspapers, magazines, paperback books and shoes were scattered across every surface. If this was the police's idea of tidying things up then they wouldn't get a job as a maid in a hurry. But they had managed to scrape some of the jumble into heaps, like molehills, on the dark brown, worn carpet, leaving spaces to walk.

What could I hope to find in this chaos?

A green sofa straddled the middle of the floor, its cushions ripped and gaping, and in one corner, cordoned off by a large, dark wooden screen, was the kitchen area containing a sink, cooker and small table – its two chairs flipped onto their backs, lying on the floor like two drunks sleeping. The sink cradled a dirty mound of carryout trays.

As Jackie had told me in the pub, the room was in the middle of being decorated. Half of it had received fresh white wallpaper with a raised white pattern, while the remainder waited glumly in its dingy décor of ancient, grubby-brown florals. The decorating equipment sat, stacked neatly in one corner.

'Do the police know what the intruder was after?' I asked.

'I doubt it. Do you think it was his killer? It doesn't have to be.' She tugged back the curtains, allowing some more light to wander in.

I picked my way around, sizing it up, not touching anything. There was no bed: I assumed the sofa turned into one. Jill watched me, her back to the window, unwilling to move – perhaps unsure of a starting point.

'If you notice anything unusual, let me know, Jill. You'll have a better idea. Anything at all, no matter how silly it sounds.'

'How do you mean – unusual?'

I shrugged.

'I've only been here once – to help him move in.'

Well, at least their separation had been amicable.

Jill gave a series of nods, as if making up her mind. 'Right, I'll be honest with you, Jinky. I was worried about things being taken if I waited too long. The police found a will – a scrap of paper, really – and I'm left with everything of Jackie's...' She winced.

I had a sinking feeling: she was about to ask me to help clear out the bed-sit. It was becoming too much of a habit. 'Why

125

couldn't you wait? I doubt whoever did this will come back.'

'No, it's not that.'

'What is it then?'

She paced the room, watching her feet, treading on the spaces like stepping stones. 'He must have thought Jackie had something he wanted,' she went on, not answering my question. 'The police didn't find anything. No clues, at least that's what they said. Maybe there was nothing here in the first place.'

I tried again, 'So why are you in such a hurry, Jill?'

She stopped and sighed. 'There's someone else I don't want sticking his nose in – Jackie's brother. Do you know him?'

I paused. 'No, I don't think so.'

'Lucky. Very lucky. I probably shouldn't be saying this: but I never liked him. He's always been trouble.' She squinted at me: the corners of her mouth had tightened. 'I know, I know, Jackie was kind of like that – but his brother is much worse. Even Jackie didn't get on with him, not properly, didn't like what he got up to.' She started to fuss about the room, picking up some clothes, folding them, replacing drawers and filling them.

When she didn't continue, I said, 'Jackie told me his brother was decorating here.' I pointed towards the corner. 'And he obviously didn't finish.' There was a fold-up pasting table, a half-full bucket of wallpaper paste covered with cling film, five rolls of unused wallpaper, a couple of ends of rolls and a box with several paint-speckled items: a large brush, a trimming knife and scissors.

'That's just like him,' Jill said. 'Jackie would have been waiting long enough for it to be finished. I don't know why he bothered.'

'Brotherly loyalty?' I ventured.

'I suppose it came down to that. He's quite a bit younger than Jackie.' She picked up some paperbacks and began

126

stacking them along the mantelpiece above the two-bar electric fire. They were all cowboy books.

I wasn't really sure why Jill wanted everything back in its place if it was to be cleared out at some point. On top of that, most of the stuff looked like junk and could easily have gone straight to the bin. But, then, in my experience, that's always the case: there seems to be a huge divide of opinion between what the owner deemed essential and what the clearer-uperer finally decides.

Jill added, 'He was always at Jackie for something. Money, of course, when things were slow – and Jackie would try to make him earn it with a wee job here and there. The only thing the brother is any good at is decorating. He did our kitchen at one time – even though it didn't need it. It took him long enough to finish. Just like here. Jackie hoped it would lead to a proper job. He wanted him to become a painter/decorator.' She saw my puzzled expression. 'I know, once again Jackie wasn't one to talk about proper jobs: never had one in his life…' She'd begun to re-hang some jackets and jeans in the wardrobe by the window.

'And you think the brother would actually come in here and take his things?' I started checking for hiding places: the undersides of furniture, gaps in the skirting, the cistern. It was becoming a habit.

'Oh, he would take anything he could. No doubt about it. He probably thinks he has as much right to it as me. *He* might even have been the one who broke in. I didn't say that to the police, of course.'

'Why not take his decorating stuff then? *And*, wouldn't Jackie have given him a key if he was in decorating? No need to force the door.'

Jill gave a shake of the head. 'Jackie would never have given him one – that's for sure. He would have been here to let him in and then left him to work away. Jackie would have hidden

127

anything of value – or had it on him. That would be why he was carrying all that money in the pub: couldn't leave it behind, you see.' She added, 'Did you hear anything about the money? Has it been found?'

'Not that I know of.' I hesitated. 'If you don't mind me asking, Jill, why didn't your boyfriend come over with you – if you didn't want to be on your own?'

'Don? He didn't want to get involved. Said it was a family matter. Do you think he's scared of the brother?'

'How would he know him?'

She had bustled her way to the kitchen area now. 'I can't imagine Jackie would have hidden it away anywhere special – the wedding ring, I mean. It wasn't worth much. It's just sentimental on my part.' She peered into the back of the cutlery drawer and shook her head.

'With the way it ended, Jill, was it worth getting married?'

'Of course it was,' she returned sharply, straightening, staring at me. 'That's an odd thing to say. Why would you ask that, Jinky?'

I shrugged and moved away from her spotlight.

She found a black bin liner in a cupboard and began heaving the rubbish from the sink into it. I had stacked up the old newspapers and brought them over. Now we were getting somewhere.

There were tears in her eyes. 'I've been wondering...' she whispered. 'The police said it was a long bladed knife. Was it a black-handled kitchen knife?'

I thought for a moment. 'It *was* a kitchen knife but I'm sure it was brown-handled. Why do you ask?'

'Because Jackie's kitchen knife is missing.' She went on, 'When he left he didn't want to take anything with him – other than his clothes and personal things. He said I would need it all. But I gave him some stuff all the same: a can opener, frying pan, microwave, and a kitchen knife – long-bladed.' She smiled fondly. 'He was never one for cooking but he did like his salmon. He could manage that. He was good at it.' She took in a deep breath. 'The knife's not here – unless it's in the bathroom.'

There was no microwave either.

Was there a grim reason for the intruder taking another knife: he had a use for it?

After a few moments, Jill emerged from the bathroom carrying a pile of clothes. 'No knife,' she said, anxiously. Then, to lighten the mood, 'You'd think after our time together and all the training he got from me, he would have bought himself a laundry basket and not leave all his dirty stuff under the sink.' She gave a watery smile as she dumped them on the kitchen table and lifted the telephone, pressing some buttons. '1571,' she explained. 'To see if there's any messages.'

'The police would have checked.'

'You never know, there might be something since.'

She listened for a while, pressed a couple more buttons, before sliding the phone back into its holder. 'No, nothing. And nothing saved either.'

A thought suddenly hit me. 'What did you say, before, about him leaving his clothes lying? That's it, Jill.'

'What's it?'

'The murderer. The jogger. The blood. He must have been undressed. Don't you see?'

She looked back blankly.

'That way...' I tried to think of a gentle way of saying it but couldn't. 'That way when he's covered in blood, he can wipe himself down and put his tracksuit back on. No-one will notice him then – just another runner out on the streets. That has to be it.'

'Was there that amount?' she said, a hand going to her mouth.

I nodded.

129

She turned away. I didn't know what to add to make it better. I found another bag and started filling it.

She had her back to me. 'So you're saying this person walked up to Jackie, naked, and that wasn't suspicious?'

'That's not quite what I'm saying.'

She faced me, wiping away at her eyes. 'Jinky, I'm starting to wonder about you. First you're talking about playing for the other team and now you've got people meeting up naked…'

I shook my head and said quickly, 'I know, I know. Believe me I don't like any of this at all. But think about it, Jill, whatever the meeting was about, the killer strips off first…' I stopped. 'No, you're right, that can't be it.'

I banged a knuckle against my forehead. 'Wait, wait. The killer was sunbathing – it was a nice day. Why didn't I think of that before? He's there first, waiting for Jackie to arrive, and he's taken most of his things off, lying in the sun, by the trees. That way everything is relaxed and easy and friendly – so Jackie wouldn't be expecting anything. He would have been taken completely by surprise. The knife was probably hidden in the pile of clothes, under the tracksuit. That makes sense, Jill. What do you think?'

Her jaw quivered; she looked pale. I'd said too much – there was no need to go on like that. 'What age is she now – your daughter?' I tried.

Jill tugged on her blouse, straightening it for something to do. 'What? Oh, she's twenty. Amazing, isn't it?'

I gave a shake of the head. 'Incredible. Where does the time go, eh?'

She decided we'd done enough for now. If she was disappointed by my failure to find any clues, she didn't show it. I padlocked the door and we clumped down the stairs. When we reached the pavement, I stopped her by putting a hand on her arm and took a breath. 'I think you should know, Jill, about your boyfriend.' She sensed something in my voice. Her muscles tightened. 'I think he may have something to do with the murder – Jackie wanted me to investigate him.'

I thought she would dismiss my accusation immediately – like Asa – but she didn't. Her face remained blank.

'I could be completely wrong, Jill. The police have checked up on him and he appears to have been at work at the time of... the incident. In fact, maybe I shouldn't have mentioned it at all.'

'Well, there's one way to find out if he's involved, isn't there?'

'How do you mean?'

'I'll search his house.' She moved off. I tagged along. 'He stays over at my place usually. I've been to his house in Georgetown – but only for ten minutes or so, while he's picked up some things. Now, come to think on it, that seems a wee bit strange.'

I gave the merest of shrugs.

She said, resolutely, 'I'm going to stay over there tonight – I'll make sure I do – and when he goes to work in the morning I'll search his house. If I find anything belonging to Jackie, I'll know.'

I should have said something to dissuade her but I didn't. In fact, I asked her to look in the washing basket for any bloodstained underwear.

Asa had left the pub by the time I returned – which was very unusual. He normally follows the FILO training doctrine of most great sportsmen: First in, Last out. I wasn't disappointed though and his place had been filled by Chisel, along with the recent arrival of Hoogah, seconds before me.

Tread motioned me to sit down. 'Listen to this, Jinky.' And then to Hoogah, 'Tell us again about your identity fraud.'

Hoogah gave the look that implied 'do I have to?' and we all nodded. He started, 'All those changes to my bank account? I
131

found out my money has been transferred into another account. And there's quite a lot there – almost a thousand pounds.'

Tread emitted an involuntary whistle.

'And you didn't know about any of this?' I asked, incredulously.

He shook his head.

'Who has *this* account? You'll need to get it back,' I said. 'That's an awful lot of money to lose. Have you informed the bank?'

'I haven't lost any of it, Jinky. That's what I'm trying to tell you. The new account is in *my* name. It's mine. As well as that, all my utilities have been changed to other companies – with the savings skimmed off and into this account. Have any of you done that: changed your gas and electric suppliers? It's well worth it. And car insurance as well. I *could* go on.'

'I've thought about the gas,' Chisel answered, seriously. 'Never got round to it yet. It's still on the back burner.'

Wait, wait, wait,' I said. 'I'm still not following this.'

'And remember all those free offers I kept getting,' Hoogah continued, apparently struck with temporary hearing loss. 'Cinema tickets, vouchers, you name it. So that's all good and a saving as well. I gave you some a while back, Jinky, remember, £1 off your Sunday newspaper, wasn't it?'

I shook my head. 'There's something wrong here. Why aren't you worried about this? And how could it happen without you knowing?'

He said, 'It was my girlfriend's idea – Lucy. She's been doing it for months now. She knows I need help with these sorts of things. Probably heard it from my second ex.'

'Your second ex-wife being Lucy's best friend,' reminded Tread – again showing distaste at the idea.

I tried to clarify, 'So she's the one who's been moving your money around and you didn't know until now?'

'There, you've got it at last,' he replied, as though talking to
132

an infant. He rose to get some drinks in.

I was about to say that, for a teacher, he wasn't very good at explaining things, but then that wouldn't have been entirely true: he's had his moments.

One time stands out above all the others. It was when we broke the widow of the manse. We were just kids and after the conkers in the grounds of the house. A stray stick missed the chestnut tree completely and cracked the glass in one of the upstairs windows. Needless to say, the scary minister was out, otherwise we wouldn't have dared be there – and we had Asa posted on lookout duty to watch for his return.

Then the minister did show up and Asa had run off rather than give the alert. And we were caught. It was Hoogah who stepped forward and braved the wrath. In the end he managed to talk the minister round and we didn't have to pay for a replacement pane nor were our parents informed either. It's a story that's told many times: much to Asa's considerable discomfort.

When Hoogah returned from the bar, I asked, 'Why did Lucy do all this without telling you?'

'She wanted it as a surprise. Something nice for me. She was going to reveal everything on my birthday – but I rumbled and spoiled it.' He took a sip of beer and went on, 'It's one of these ISA accounts I've got now. You don't have to pay tax on the interest and you can save over £3000 each year in it – from the 6th April, the start of the fiscal year. Have you heard of them? You should think about it, Jinky, for some of those hundreds of thousands of pounds you've got stashed away under your mattress.'

Suddenly he's a financial expert. I didn't bother mentioning the different types available; nor the unit trusts and government bonds I hold also.

He was still spouting on, 'I'm into my second ISA now and aiming to use up my full quota this time round.'

133

I muttered, 'That's all very interesting, Hoogah. Thanks for sharing that.'

Tread and Chisel nodded, earnestly, apparently grateful for his monetary wisdom.

I said, 'But, Hoogah, for her to have done all this without you, means she's pretended to be you and used your details…'

'That's why I said it was identity fraud. Don't you see?' He gave a vigorous laugh.

'And you don't mind her doing all this behind your back?'

'Look, when I was married, I never knew about any of it either. I've never had an interest – you know that.'

'Tax free interest,' Tread reminded him, with a meaningful nod of the head.

Hoogah went on, 'So where's the harm? We're a couple now anyway. In fact it's our hundred day anniversary tomorrow. We're going out for a special meal.'

'I wish I was sixteen again,' Tread stated with a sigh, as he tried to flutter his eyelashes. He added, in a high, girlie voice, 'And a hundred days is, like, forever and ever.'

I tried a quick calculation before giving up, turning to Chisel instead. 'What do you know about Jackie Gittes' brother?'

Chisel, the newspaperman, is almost as good a source of information as Asa. He thought for a moment. 'Not a nice fellow. One to stay clear of, I would say. He's been in prison. Long time ago.'

'How come I'd never heard of him?'

'Oh, he's quite a bit younger than Jackie. We'd have left school by the time he came on the scene. And we don't mix in the same circles – of that I'm glad.'

Chisel is well aware of the affairs of many people in town but it's not something he ever talks about. 'My advice is to stay clear,' he added.

'Even if he's a possible suspect?'

'Surely he couldn't have stabbed his own brother?'

'It's been known to happen,' Tread offered. 'There's those two from The Bible – Willing and Able.'

I went on, 'Just at this moment he's not top of my list, but you never know. If he's as bad as you say he is – and Jill doesn't like him – then I might have to consider him.'

Chisel replied, 'Well, I know his alibi's been checked – he was one of the first they looked at – and it almost stands up. He was playing cards with his friends at the time Jackie was murdered. Poker, no less. Although the kind of people we're talking about would probably say anything anyway.'

Where *does* Chisel get his information?

I asked, 'If I wanted to find him, though, where would be the best place?'

I didn't stay much longer in the pub: there was still the washing to be hung out and a quick detour before that. I called in at The Whitesands Bar, buying a drink, and asking the barman if he'd seen Jackie Gittes' brother recently. He told me, with a straight face, that he'd never heard of him.

The place was grimy and grimly quiet with a scattering of men, no women, with each one holding and staring into their pint as though it was a crystal ball – and it was giving them a prediction of a futile future. Unfortunately, no-one matched the description given by Chisel.

I polished off my gafoni and visited the toilet. It wasn't hard to find: I followed my nose. I was standing, minding my own business, when the door squeaked opened behind me. Immediately, a hand grabbed my left shoulder, while a foot simultaneously kicked the back of my right knee, buckling it. I was whipped round. When I gave out a yell, a tight hand clamped over my mouth and the shake of a head, inches from mine, ordered me to hush. The man had been drinking something with coconut in it.

He was slightly smaller than me. His head was tilted back:
135

our noses almost touching. I was staring into unblinking, ruthless eyes. I could tell instantly that this person held no boundaries, had no grasp of limits. He eased his hands away, as he took a step back, holding them out by his sides, palms out, as though signalling a cricketing wide, peering down at the space between us. He rose to my height: he'd been standing with his legs splayed like a drinking giraffe. There was a hint of a wry smile on his thin lips.

I squeezed hard and fastened myself up; there were no splashes on him.

'I hear you're prying into my affairs. I don't like that. I don't like anyone meddling in my business.' The threat of his words was diffused a tad by his fulsome lisp.

He would be in his mid-thirties, and wore a taut, white t-shirt tucked tidily into leg-hugging jeans. His hair was dark and slicked tightly back: unquestionably to a pony tail. His beard was no more than a ribbon of hair running along the jaw-line, ending in a triangle beneath his bottom lip. It must take a great deal of care and time to manicure it into such a precise line. There was no excess fat on him and his wrinkle-free face was shiny and firm.

He went on, 'But you see I'm in two minds about you, Mr Johnstone. I don't like the idea of you asking about me but I *do* like the idea of you finding Jackie's killer.' He looked away, at a spot just below the ceiling. 'What's that called: when you're in two minds?'

I shook my head, nervously.

He went on, 'There's a word for it – you must know it.' He saw me give a quick shrug and continued, 'So I'm not sure what I want to do about you.' The menace in his unblinking eyes was as real as the growing damp patch down the front of my trousers.

'Bivouac, that's it, isn't it? Am I right?'

'I... I think that's something to do with camping,' I stuttered.
136

My chest was tight and breathing had become quick and shallow.

He went on, ignoring my comment, 'That's right. I am bivouac about what to do about you. *But*, for now, I'm going to let it go, let you off this once and hope that you find the murderer. Bring him to justice, Mr Johnstone.' He nodded resolutely and when he turned sharply to open the door, his ponytail flicked out. I was left alone, standing still, my back to the urinal. I waited a couple of minutes before leaving. I didn't bother to mop up the floor.

He'd implied he had nothing to do with Jackie's death but I wasn't so sure: it might have been a ploy, a big performance, to make me keep my distance. I hadn't enjoyed meeting Jackie's brother for the first time but it wouldn't keep me away from him.

By the time I'd marched past Burns Statue, some of my fear had turned to anger; I was sure both sensations would be present the next time we met.

I turned my attention to other matters: Jill's safety. Her sudden insistence on staying at Gardiner's home tonight might make him suspicious – and that could make things dangerous. I had tried to persuade her against it as we'd walked away from Jackie's flat, but she couldn't be swayed. Once she gets going, it seems, she is quite a strong-willed character and not someone to be messed with. And now she was about to search my suspect's home. Having lost Chiara as an investigating partner, it seemed I had a replacement – all within a matter of hours. The bad news was that I had to surrender my phone number to her: just in case she hit a problem.

As I hung out my recently completed laundry on the line, in my back lawn, in the near-dark, I had a flash of light: my washing machine has a delay. So it *has* to be possible to set a computer to do the same. That was how Gardiner set up his alibi: it would have been rigged to send out emails at precisely the moment he met with Jackie.

There were three questions. How did he get out without the guard on the gate noticing? How long would it take him to run there and back? And, after Asa's earlier comments, should I inform the police?

Tuesday 18th July

I woke after a couple of hours, dripping in sweat, and dozed intermittently through the rest of the night, the covers pushed away. The iced water beside my bed had turned lukewarm: the house was a firebrick, sucking in the heat of the day, brutally releasing it through the night. The open window made no difference, it simply funnelled in scatterings of normally unheard sounds: shouts, thuds and clanks, punctuated by the occasional bark of a distant dog. When the dawn chorus arrived, it was magnificent but maddening loud.

My phone, on the bedside table, had stayed silent. It was Jill's lifeline. I worried about her and, increasingly, felt the need to be closer at hand. At a quarter past five, I dragged my drained body from the damp sheets, showered in cold water, and drove over to Georgetown once again.

I waited in the same spot, wearing the same painting overalls, a newspaper sprawled over the steering wheel, with the phone resting on the dashboard. I tried to settle down into a comfortable position; at least, for the time being, the car was in the shade.

It was a frustrating vigil: every passing minute ticked up my anxiety. Studying the front of Gardiner's house only emphasised its unknown interior: like the narrow beam of a torch on a black night accentuates the unseen darkness. What if she was in trouble and I was sitting idly by? What if she needed my help now?

I could walk up to the front door and ring the bell for an answer, but what possible reason could I give for being on his doorstep at this ridiculous hour? Gardiner knew me, he had seen me at her flat, and she would have told him about what I do. It could only alert him and make matters worse. But, maybe, I was getting it out of proportion. Although there had to be sufficient doubt in Jill's mind – why else would she choose

139

to be here?

Time moved on. There was a sharp rap on the half-open window beside my head. I leapt into the air, instinctively twisting away. A police uniform filled the glass. He bent forward and an unfamiliar face stared in at me. He motioned to wind down the window further. I did.

'Can I ask why you are parked here, sir?'

'I...I'm waiting for a friend,' I stammered.

'And who might that be? Only we've been told that you've been here for quite a while – hours, in fact.'

'I'm not doing any harm.' I don't like challenging the police. I never do – normally. It was the wrong thing to say and in the wrong tone. I felt it immediately.

Can I have you name, sir?' His voice strengthening with annoyance. He moved to the front of the car before I could answer, noting down my number plate with great deliberation. Then he returned and asked the question again. I gave my name.

'I'll ask you it again, sir. What are you doing here?'

'Waiting for a friend.' It sounded pathetic.

'Can I ask you to move on, sir?'

'Tell me where to and I'll park there.' It was far too disrespectful. I could see his increased irritation. 'Sorry, officer,' I said, quickly. 'Not been sleeping well. It's this heat. I arrived too early and didn't want to waken her up. So I thought I'd just sit and wait. I can't see I'm doing anything wrong. How does anyone sleep in this?' My dismal attempt at sweetening the situation was as successful as muscle rub on a broken leg.

'I would like you out of the area, sir. We'll be in touch if there's anything else we want to talk to you about. We'll find you.'

What could I do? I wasn't sure if he had the right to force me to leave: but to stay would be to challenge him. In the long run, that might not be a good thing. Was it possible that Gardiner had phoned? I tried, 'I spoke to Ed yesterday and reported my findings. He's the detective leading the murder investigation at the moment. You know who I mean, don't you?' It was worth a shot: it might make him change his mind.

The policeman paused. 'I'll check up on this, sir. Wait here.' With that, he returned to his car, parked behind me: he must have coasted down the hill, creeping into position.

I watched him in the rear view mirror as he contacted the station. He returned in a matter of seconds, apparently more annoyed than before. He said, sharply, 'I'm asking you again to move on – and you need to do it right now!'

I gave a sigh, started up the engine, and pulled away sharply, hoping he wouldn't have time to follow. I drove on, turning to the right and the left, working my way round the labyrinth of Georgetown. He wasn't behind. I stopped and waited for ten minutes, before circling round, back into Gardiner's street, parking at the top of the hill. His house wasn't visible – and there was no police car in sight either. I eased forward until I could see the first edges of the house. It would have to do.

It wasn't long before Gardiner's car backed out and drove off. I gave him a head start before tagging on. If Gardiner was in my sight, Jill was safe to search – if she was all right. I tried her phone. There was no answer.

His car slipped through a set of traffic lights on amber and was gone. I came to a stop. My phone buzzed. It was a call from Jill. She was fine. I breathed a sigh of relief. She had started her search. I decided to check on Gardiner and we arranged to meet up later.

I continued over to Cargenbridge, parking, and jogging over to the gateman. It was the same guy. He was curious as to why I was here again: I asked if he knew of any painting jobs needing done round the factory. He didn't. It took an annoying long time but I finally managed to sneak a look at his sheet and noted Gardiner's registration on it. That was good. But I couldn't stay to watch the gate though: Manfred's house had to be cleared, and I was late. I had to hope Gardiner remained at his work and didn't suddenly decide to return home.

The gutting was quick – insensitively so. Decades of living were wiped away, obliterated, in the blink of an eye.

Three burly, grubby t-shirted fellows were waiting for me in front of the house – leaning against a big, brown lorry, kicking their heels against its wheels. One of them lazily checked his watched as I pulled in: it wasn't much after eight o'clock. Yet the moment the key turned in the lock, the men turned into an efficient, well-oiled machine.

Within minutes of the front door opening, the house was empty, leaving only an echoing shell, retaining nothing but the smell of the sweat from their extra-large sodden t-shirts.

In the end we ended up all square – the new settee, new TV, furniture and shed equipment wiping out the cost of their efforts. But I gave each of them a tenner – for their wait.

During the frantic disembowelment I managed to salvage a few things missed on my last visit: framed photos from the sideboard and a couple of other personal items for Charlie to decide on. The sort of things I'd kept from my uncles' houses.

When I swung the door shut for the last time and turned the key, I was sorry Charlie wasn't here to do it. It would have been better if he had been the one closing down this chapter. I was an interloper.

'Nothing,' Jill said, as she dropped into the car seat beside me. 'There was nothing unusual. I searched everywhere – even out in the garden shed.'

I drove off. 'You were careful? He wouldn't know you'd been poking about his things?'

'I took out the furniture polish and dusted as I went. He'll smell it when he gets home. And I did an ironing and put the
142

stuff away, and tidied up, that way there's a good reason for any disturbed drawers. I think he should be pleased.'

'You're good at this Jill.' I dropped her off at her hairdresser shop.

So what did that mean?

I was home when the phoned buzzed. It was a call from Chisel. It wasn't good news: there had been another attack. It had happened last night, just before half past nine. A man called William Bones had been accosted in the toilet of a hotel – where he had been attending a wedding reception. The description of the attacker was hazy but one thing was certain: it had been someone in a brown tracksuit.

The jogger had interrupted Bones at his business at the urinal but he'd caught a reflection of the attacker in a mirror and had turned, fending off the assault, spinning the knife from the assailant's hand. Bones had ended up with a nasty stab wound to his shoulder, but not thought to be too serious. The jogger had run off.

'It may only be a coincidence,' Chisel ended with, 'but Bones was at a wedding and was in a kilt, of course, when he was set upon.'

That wasn't the only coincidence: I had been attacked in a toilet as well. I raced off to Jill's hairdressing salon, abandoning my cup of tea.

She was in the middle of sticking strips of tin foil to a woman's head, using a gooey, greeny paste on a big brush. She saw me standing at the door, beckoned me to come in, but when I didn't, she told a girl to take over, and we took a stroll outside, seeking the shade like a tightrope walker seeks balance. We paused under a large tree.

'Was that your daughter there?'

'No, I gave her the rest of the morning off – to make up for

143

her opening up for me. She should be in soon. Do you want to meet her?' She gave off a mystified look.

'No, it's not that.'

'What is it you want then, Jinky?'

'You were with your boyfriend last night?'

Her expression had no reason to change. 'What is this? You know I was.'

'Could you tell me what happened yesterday after you met up with him. Please.'

She gave a shrug to show it was no big deal. 'Don arrived at my place close to seven, I think it was. I wasn't long in. I said to him, you know, about wanting to stay at his place and he didn't seem too bothered – which was a good sign.' She gave me an intense stare and explained, 'If he'd been at all agitated, I might have decided against going to bed with a possible murderer – I'm not that daft.' She continued, 'So we picked up a carry-out pizza on the way over. And that was it. Watched some telly. Nothing very exciting. That's not to say I wasn't nervous. I still was – all night, but I tried not to show it. It was a long wait before I could search the house. I kept thinking: what if I find something? It wasn't a good feeling having that uncertainty. I didn't sleep well – and he'd been quite amorous, more than normal. Although you probably don't want to hear about that...'

'I know the feeling.' I added quickly, 'About the not sleeping, I mean.' I turned away to emit a cough, before going on, 'He didn't go out at all?'

'No. Why?'

'Are you sure? Around nine o'clock?'

'Of course I'm sure.'

I told her about the latest attack as we wound our way back to her shop, the pavement singing in the rays of the sun.

'Do they have any clues to the attacker?' she asked.

'None. The knife had no fingerprints on it. Bye Jill.'

144

'Bye, Jinky.'

Well, that had to be that: Gardiner had nothing to do with it right enough. Now I had the miserable task of apologising to Asa. And I needed to find a way of having a word with the fellow who was attacked – William Bones.

I had started the day on low batteries and now I was running on empty. I longed to put my feet up and rest, but before that delicious moment, it would be better to get the visit to Miss Welch out of the way.

I drove over and knocked on her door. There was no reply. I knocked again. It took a wee while before she answered, peering, as before, round the door, like an anxious tortoise out from its shell. 'You're a bit impatient, aren't you?' Miss Welch snapped, recognising me.

'Sorry. Thought you were out.'

'I've a visitor coming. There's no time to go out. What is it you want?'

'I was round on Sunday. Do you remember?'

'Of course I remember. I'm not senile, you know. I thought if you were keen you'd have been here yesterday or this morning at the latest. The early bird catches the worm, you know.'

'Yes, but it's the early worm that gets caught,' I returned promptly. I think you'll find that's one-all, Miss Welch.

She stalled for a moment by taking in my attire, toe to head. She didn't appear to like the shorts, and came back with bite, 'So what is it you want?'

I offered my friendliest smile. 'You said you might help with the murder. Give me a better idea of when it happened.'

'And do you think all I've got to do is to make notes for the likes of you?' She paused. 'You'd better come in, I suppose, but I've a visitor coming. I want you out before she arrives.' She opened the door wider and signalled me to enter. We
145

walked through the house to the kitchen again.

She glanced at the clock on the wall. 'I've time to make you a cup of tea.'

I thanked her and sat down at the table, looking out of the window, onto the field. 'Is your cat still as punctual?' I asked.

'Oh, yes. Quite a nuisance, she is, at times.'

I gave a nod. 'I know another cat just like it. In the library. He's the boss of the place. Do you know the one? His name is Blue. He was sleeping in one of the display cabinets the last time I was in. The time before that, he was sprawled out across the checking-in desk. They didn't dare move him – he's got quite a temper – so they worked round him.'

'That's all very interesting,' she replied in a tone suggesting it wasn't in the slightest bit interesting. Then she shook her head. 'I haven't been to the library in ages.'

When the tea was produced she said, 'I made a list. I thought you'd have been round sooner to get it. I put it in this drawer.' She opened it and handed the note over.

5.00pm: Pressed button on kettle.

5.01: Poured water into cup.

5.04: Sat down with tea and biscuit.

5.05: Had first sip of tea.

5.06: First bite of biscuit

5.08: Second bite of biscuit – jogger appears in field and runs past.

5.09: Cat flap sounds.

5.12: Sat down again to drink tea and take third bite.

5.19: Tea and biscuit finished. Continue to listen to radio.

'Is that any good to you?'

'Excellent,' I replied and stuffed the paper into my pocket. 'This means the murder must have happened before 8 minutes past 5 – if the jogger had a hand in it.'
146

'That sounds about right. Now if you don't mind going, I've a visitor coming.'

I left my three-sipped tea and started towards the front door, then stopped. 'If it's not too much trouble, Miss Welch, do you think you could go through the same routine this afternoon just to check the timings are the same? If you're in, of course.'

'And if I'm out? Do you want me to do it then, eh?' she replied, with a narrowing of the eyes.

Sorry, Miss Welch, I can't let you have that one – repetition – at best it's off the post.

'Did I mention,' she went on, 'that the jogger in the field had a bag over his shoulders? Why would he have that if he was running? It would get in the way, don't you think?'

That was interesting. 'A rucksack, would you say? With a wide strap over each shoulder?'

'Yes, that would be it – a rucksack.'

I thought of Gardiner and his one. 'Do you remember the colour?'

'Black.'

Gardiner's had been blue – but then there's not much between them, colour-wise, especially to older eyes.

'You haven't said why they do it,' she said.

'Do what?'

'Carry a bag, of course,' she replied, as though talking to a child.

I was fed up with people treating me like this. 'I...I'm not sure,' I stuttered, but went on, trying to show I was smarter than a kid. 'It's something to do with carrying a weight around, making it easier the next time – when there's no weight.'

The answer seemed to satisfy her.

I gave a wave as I left her standing on the doorstep. She wasn't looking at me but peering into the distance, on the lookout for her visitor.

147

I knocked on Mr Lemon's front door. It wasn't a good move – I knew that. It might rile him enough to call the police again, but the piece of paper in my pocket required some further information. There was no reply to the front door so I walked round the side of the house. Mr Lemon appeared at the back door, a mug of tea on a saucer in his left hand, at the precise moment I turned the corner. He stopped in mid, awkward, step when he saw me.

'You again?' he said, his mouth suggested a bout of wind was on its way.

I flashed a smile across my face and jollily replied, 'Nice day. I was passing. Just one or two things occurred to me. Do you mind if I ask you, Mr Lemon?'

He eased down the two steps to his garden, his stick moving in time with his right leg. He hadn't shaved since the last time we'd spoken but, at least, this time he was dressed in day clothes: an unironed grey t shirt and black trousers, although still in his slippers, no socks. He said nothing more as he hobbled on to the waiting plastic chair and sat down with a groan and a thump. Some tea splashed into the saucer, saving his clothes, thus explaining its presence. The soles of his slippers were worn, both with large patches of dark rubber poking through.

'What is it you want?' he barked. But he hadn't told me to leave.

'Sorry,' I said. 'It's just something I needed to ask. When you walked round the field on Saturday, did you go clockwise or anti-clockwise?'

Mr Lemon's eyes moved back and forth, perhaps trying to work out the answer. It would have been easier if he'd been facing the field. I have the same problem with maps, always turning them to point the way I'm going. He might not give me the answer, but his mind was curious enough to try and work it out.

148

I offered some help. 'Did you turn left or right after going through your garden gate?'

'To the right.' As soon as he'd said it, it was obvious he was annoyed: as though he'd been tricked into a reply.

'And at what time would that have been?'

He gave a shrug. 'It might have been half four, five. I don't know.'

'And you didn't see Jackie at any time on your walk? Only he must have cut across the field at some point.'

Mr Lemon didn't reply. He gaped at me for a while then nodded in the direction of the road. I left on that same course.

Mr Redditch was in his front garden. I strolled over. I had nothing to ask him but there seemed no harm in having a word – and maybe my reading of him might change. Everyone should be given a second chance: sometimes.

He looked up from his rose-bed as my footsteps approached – I thought he would. He had a spray gun in his hand. His smile appeared genuine enough: as if glad to have an excuse to stop working and shoot the time.

'Aye,' he said, with a sharp twitch of his head. The word held a considerable weight of foreboding.

'You're not wrong there, Mr Redditch,' I replied. 'Getting hotter every day. How long's it to last?'

'No-one's saying, but the fly seem to like it: playing havoc with the roses. And there's all the watering to be done. I might need to get the hose back out before they ban it. The can takes too much time.'

'Do you think they'll allow hoses to be sold when the ban's on?'

'Any luck on the investigation front?' Rightly, he'd dismissed my question as not worthy of an answer and had moved on.

'Nothing yet.'

'You been visiting Miss Welch?'

'Lucky to get a word with her. She's always busy with visitors and the like.'

Mr Redditch shook his head. 'Sadly, that's not quite the case. She doesn't do anything. Never leaves the house. What day is it? Tuesday? That's right, it'll be her cleaner. She comes on a Tuesday and a Friday. Then there's the gardener: he's in on a Wednesday. Her nephew brings her the shopping at the weekend and a hairdresser calls every second week on a Thursday. I don't know what she does with the rest of her time – but she's never out.'

'I'm sorry to hear that.'

'Still, at least she can afford a cleaner. D'you have one?'

I shook my head.

'Me neither – not any more, anyway. It's funny, I can work outside all day, no problem, but ask me to do housework and I hate it, absolutely loath it. Still, it has to be done from time to time. And with the wife being so busy…'

I agreed, offering a crumpled face and a couple of short nods, by way of saying, 'it's the way of the world.'

I was about to leave when Mr Redditch piped up, 'My advice is not to load the dishwasher with unnecessary things: give the barely dirty plates a quick dicht under the tap and set them on the tray to dry. Use it for the really greasy stuff only. And don't hoover too much either: that just creates more work by kicking up the dust. Then the polish and cloth have to come out, and so it goes on. And don't get me started on the things that don't need ironing – like underpants.'

I had the urge to mention my theory about wet clothes lingering in the washing machine – and I think it would have fallen on a friendly ear – but, if I had, the conversation might have gone on at considerable length. I put in an affable goodbye wave and turned towards the car. Mr Redditch wasn't such a bad soul, after all.

Then it hit me. The suitcase I'd taken down from Manfred's

loft – it wasn't dusty.

I rushed back home, raced round the side of the house, and into the kitchen to fetch the key for Manfred's car. He had a heart complaint, yet some time, not so long ago, he'd gone to his shed to lug heavy ladders up the stairs. It was an awful lot of effort to put one small suitcase in the loft. So why had he gone to all that trouble when he had plenty of cupboard space?

I pulled the case out of the boot, returned to the house, and placed it on the kitchen table, flicking back the catches. I towelled myself down to lose some of the sweat and sat. Once more I saw the photographs: old ones, mostly small, some in black and white. There was one taken from the front of a house, looking very much like Manfred's house – but, then, most council houses look the same.

In the picture a young woman was holding a baby. At first I assumed it was Mrs Mann with a very young Manfred. But, as I studied it, with the aid of my specs, I realised it wasn't her but another woman altogether – and I recognised her from another photo I'd seen recently. One that Charlie had shown me: his parent's wedding picture.

Manfred was a year older than Charlie; they were both born in Dumfries and might even have lived close to each other at one time. It was quite possible for Charlie's mother to know Mrs Mann, visit her, and have her photo taken with the new baby. And judging by the size of Manfred, Charlie's mother would have been pregnant herself by this time: although she didn't look it in the picture.

It wasn't until I reached the bottom of the case that I found the hand-written letter. It was folded. I flattened it out and read it through. Then I read it again – and again.

It explained so many things – but left a mass of questions.

The note had been sitting in front of me for a long time and

I'd surrounded it with photos. I'd been staring at them. They'd made me cry. My phone buzzed. It startled me from my trance. I checked the screen. It was a call from Chiara. I replaced everything into the case, except the note, putting it in my pocket.

'Hello.'

'It's me, Chiara. How are you?'

Her voice fizzed through me. Images of her wonderful face blazed into my mind. Instantly, I could remember how smooth her skin felt, how soft her hair was.

'I'm fine.'

Tell her you miss her. Right now, tell her.

'How's Dorset?'

'It's nice. And hot. I'm booked into a hotel with a pool. So that's good.'

I pictured her in that black bikini, lying on a recliner. Was there anyone beside her?

My heart thumped.

'I wanted to apologise for leaving so abruptly on Sunday,' she said.

'There's no need.'

Tell her the truth. Tell her how you thought she was getting in the way. You have to own up. She deserves to know.

'It was probably for the best,' I replied.

Tell her.

'Have you found the killer yet?'

'Not yet.' I hesitated. 'Chiara?'

'Yes.'

'I should have told you it wasn't working out: you and me together. I should have said at the time.' I took in a deep breath. 'I *miss* you, Chiara.'

Silence.

'What are you saying?' she said. 'I don't follow what you're saying. It's not working out? What d'you mean? Do you want
152

us to finish? Do you want us to stop?'

'No, I don't want that. I never want that.' I could feel the tears building again. 'I'm trying to be honest. I have my work, Chiara, and I need to do it on my own, in my own way. It's better like that. That's what I mean. I should have said.'

There was a laugh – a slightly nervous laugh – then a hesitant voice. 'I think I understand. You're like me. I need to be on my own as well – some of the time.'

'But, Chiara, I had my phone switched off,' I blurted out. 'When I was in the pub, with the boys, on Saturday, I had switched it off. You couldn't have called me from your hotel room. I was late and you couldn't have got in touch. I didn't tell you about it. What does that say?'

'I don't understand.'

I remained quiet.

She asked, 'Do you *want* to see me again?'

'Of course I do.' I paused, before adding, 'But I don't see how. You live so far away. And I'm busy right now. I can't stop this, Chiara. I've just found something important. If you came up here, it wouldn't work. You'd be hanging around.'

'We can go on holiday. When it's finished,' she said.

The line died.

I tried to compose myself on the eleven mile drive out of town on the road to Moffat. I felt stupid. What had sparked that outburst? I put it down to the heat and lack of sleep. So much for taking a step back, or, at least, standing firm, as Hoogah had said.

But there was nothing I could do about it now: it had been said, it couldn't be returned to the bottle. I had told her I missed her. Then, suddenly, I felt proud of the words. I rolled them round my mouth again and enjoyed the sensation. I could have been clearer – with a wee bit of planning – but I had told Chiara, shown her – and myself – my feelings. I had uttered the
153

words. I had actually said them. I felt a surge of excitement. I wanted to shout out the window, yell at every passing car, tell them that I'd never felt this way before in my life, explain that I now had a passion other than football and it was for this one, special woman. I danced behind the wheel of my car. I danced as though Queens had just won the Scottish Cup.

Yet, if I hadn't spouted on she might have told me why she had left. I should stop the car right now and phone her back. No, give her space – that's what she'd said. Let the dust lie for a wee while. Maybe that was the reason all along: she needed to be alone. We had been visiting witnesses most of the morning – it must have been too much. I would have given her room if only she'd said.

I reached the nursing home, dragged my limbs from the car, and met with the large nurse again, asking her about Mrs Mann.

'I can't help you, sorry, none of that comes to mind,' she said. 'I doubt it would be worth asking her either: she's not so good. She hasn't spoken for days – and hasn't eaten much. We don't like forcing them, but it may come to that. Why don't you try Margaret over there? She has long chats with a lot of them.'

She pointed into a room where a small, white-haired woman in slippers was busy tidying magazines into a rack. I went over. I would have taken her for a resident except that her sunken face held bright, kind eyes and she was wearing the regulatory blue, nylon overall.

'Hello,' I said. 'Can I have a word?' Her look told me she required some information before she would answer. I added, 'I was a friend of Mrs Mann's son and I need to find out something important.' I was willing to say more but it seemed enough.

'What do you want to know?' Her voice was quiet and husky.

'Did you know her son, Jimmy – or Manfred, as we called him?'

154

'Yes, yes. I met him many times. It was very sad to hear about him. Such a nice man. I thought about going to the funeral but couldn't get off. Someone from the home was there, though, representing Mrs Mann. That was only right.'

'He came to visit often?'

'Oh, yes. Every Sunday.'

Last Sunday he was in a coffin.

'Do you remember Mrs Mann ever having something for him recently – like a small suitcase?'

Margaret took her time before answering. 'No, I don't think so. In the past they used to be able to talk together. She was lucid then. It was always about the olden days though – that's what she could remember best. Ask her what she'd had for breakfast that morning and she wouldn't be able to tell you.'

'I know the feeling,' I joked.

The nurse gave me a disciplining stare, meaning, 'it's not the sort of thing we laugh about here.' I took no offence.

She said, 'Now where was I? Oh, yes. For Mrs Mann it was getting less and less every time – her conversations with Manfred. This last month or two he'd sit holding her hand for most of his visit – and they'd be quiet. But there was still comfort in that.'

Margaret shook a sad head, then looked up suddenly, pointing a sharp finger at me. 'But now you ask, wait. Yes, there *was* one time when she wanted me to phone him. That's right. That was unusual. It must have been about May time, earlier this year. That's right, we were outside and I was pushing her in her wheelchair – I like to take them outside if they're willing. The cherry blossom was out. Yes, that's right. There's some great trees round here.

Anyway, she hadn't been saying much, but then, right out of the blue, she says, 'Phone Jimmy. I need to see him. Right away. Phone Jimmy, Margaret...' and that was all she said.

Of course I did: it had to be important. I think she was

155

worried she would forget if she delayed. So he came out that afternoon, and I'm sure she gave him something but I couldn't say what.'

'That's great, thanks. You've been most helpful. One last question – what's Mrs Mann's first name?'

I wandered through the room and over to Mrs Mann. She was in the same chair, but unwilling or unable to rock back and forward today. She appeared much more slumped, and very fragile. I wasn't sure how to start. I crouched beside her and touched her arm. There was no reaction: her dull eyes staring towards the window.

'Mrs Mann. Do you remember me? I was here a couple of days ago. With Charlie…wee Charlie.'

She didn't turn to locate the sound – and she didn't answer. I moved in front of her: there was no change in focus. I spoke again but without any reaction. I gave up. It appeared the news of Manfred's death had sunk in and she was sinking fast.

As I stood in the grounds, looking up at the cherry trees, I was close to working out what had happened. Margaret, a few minutes ago, had used the word 'lucid', but I wasn't sure what she'd meant. I hadn't come across it at school, although that's not really surprising: my body might have had an almost perfect attendance but my mind was rarely there. Yet, at a guess, I would say my thoughts on Manfred's death were becoming lucid.

Charlie had said he wouldn't be back from his trip until tomorrow. I needed to see him urgently. I didn't like the way things were shaping. It was making me nervous.

The call to Chisel lasted five minutes.

I made a deliberate effort to be in the pub before Asa tonight: it's never easy, yet I'd managed to fit in a twenty minute soak in a cool bath back home before coming out. His beer was ready on the bar – along with an extravagant packet of crisps as an added softener. I wasn't sure of the greeting I would get or how he would take my apology.

He sloped in, spied the beer, and stopped in his tracks. His eyes flickered in thought and, reluctantly, moved away from the glass, to target my face. But it wasn't long before the draw of the liquid took over and his eyes were tugged back. Then he wiped the back of his hand across his brow, finished his walk to the bar, and gave a flash of welcoming teeth to the ale as he lifted it up.

So far so good.

'Asa,' I started. 'I'm sorry about what happened the other day. You were right: Gardiner had nothing to do with Jackie's death. And I'm sorry it put you in bother at work. There, I've said it.'

He replaced the half-empty glass on the counter. 'You must have been up to something *else* this morning. I didn't like to ask. What was it?'

It could have been a few things. I went with a rather sheepish, 'Watching Gardiner's place – again? But I had a good reason this time,' I added quickly.

Here it comes – the latest tirade.

He gave a weary shake of the head, and a friendly, 'When will you learn, Jinky?' Then he clapped a hand against my shoulder. Weird. There was no anger in his voice – it had been replaced by, what appeared to be, resigned amusement.

'How come you're taking this so well, Asa?'

He shrugged and reached for his drink.

'Come on – out with it.'

He finished off the beer whilst summoning Andy the barman – Asa can multi-task like a woman. He said, 'Ed wanted you arrested – or, at the very least, brought into the station. No doubt thought he could threaten you with wasting police time, or some such thing. He was really quite annoyed – which was

157

why I stayed as far away as possible. From what I heard, he went to High-Heid-Yin-Harris this afternoon about you, and do you know what?'

I thought for a moment. 'The fact that you're sharing this, and you're not, em, grumpy, would lead me to suppose that Harris denied Ed's request.'

'Not bad. I'll make a detective of you yet. But it went further than that. Harris actually backed you up. He said you were to be left alone and allowed to do what you do – if you know what I mean. At least that's the word going round. Now why would The-High-Heid-Yin do that? Normally he's a stickler for the rules.'

It was surprising, that's for sure. I knew the Chief Constable, but not all that well. We'd crossed paths in the past. The only possible thing is that he's a close friend of one of my golfing buddies, Doc Halliday. Still, I couldn't see that being a good enough reason for this benevolence.

'So it looks like you're back on the case – as far as I'm concerned, at least,' Asa went on.

'Thanks.'

Fresh drinks arrived and we took them for a walk. It was reassuring to have Asa back on my side – I felt calmer. 'Well,' I said, lowering into a chair, 'you'll be at liberty to tell me a few things, then. The weapon used on this fellow Bones, for a start? Was it a black-handled kitchen knife by any chance?' I gave him a quick account of Jill's concerns about the knife missing from Jackie's flat.

'Naw, this was a short bladed affair. It was found on the toilet floor beside Bones. He'd been standing at the urinal – in full flow, if you know what I mean – when the attack happened. But he'd caught a glimpse, a reflection, of someone approaching quickly. As he turned, to protect himself, the knife dug into his shoulder and must have sprung out of the attacker's hand. That movement probably saved him. He shouted, and then fell to the floor after the attacker ran off. The knife had traces of paint on the handle but no fingerprints.'

I didn't dare tell him I'd heard most of that from Chisel. 'What do we know about this Bones fellow?'

Asa shook his head. 'Not very much. He's fairly new to the area. Has some relations down here. And is out of work at the moment. His wife does cleaning. No kids. That's about it.'

'And the fact he had a kilt on?'

'Too early to tell if that's the connection.'

'Did he, eh, spray his attacker, by any chance?' I asked, innocently.

'How do you mean? Oh, I get it – at the urinal, when he turned. Why do you ask?'

'It might make it more noticeable – someone rushing away and dripping.'

'And you don't think a jogger at a wedding, wearing a tracksuit, when everyone else is in kilts, would make him stand out? I doubt if the dripping aspect would make all that much of a difference, Jinky.'

'Well, there might be a trail to follow then – at least give an idea of the direction he took?'

Asa produced a sigh. 'Even if he'd been hosed down by the good souls of the Dumfries Fire Brigade I doubt if that would work, Jinky.'

Was this starting up again: this constant shooting down of my ideas?

He went on, 'The wedding was held in the extension at the back. There's a corridor with windows linking the two buildings so anyone can watch from outside and see people coming and going to the toilet. The attacker must have waited and then followed Bones in.'

'No smokers outside?'

Asa gave me that familiar look. I knew what it meant. 'Yes, we did think of that,' he muttered, adding, 'To put your mind at rest, as far as I understood it, Mr Bones' tap shut off and only opened up again after the attack, as he fell to the floor. There was quite a puddle: that mixed with blood.'

'It doesn't always shut off straightaway, Asa. I can tell you that for sure.'

'What are you talking about?'

I decided to keep my meeting with Jackie's brother to myself. I went with, 'How's he doing anyway?'

'Bones? Apart from needing to give his kilt a good wash, he'll be fine. Should get out of hospital quite soon. He was lucky. It was never life threatening. But he didn't get the chance to see his attacker.'

'Anything from the kilt covering Jackie?' I asked.

'Nothing so far. It had a Made In Scotland label on it but there are doubts about that. We'll know more when it comes back from analysis.'

We each had thoughtful sips of our drinks.

Asa said, 'Jinky, *I* overreacted as well.'

And that was it: we were officially back on a normal footing. I gave a quick explanation of why I was up at Gardiner's house this morning and we moved onto more important matters.

'How about that bet then, Asa: Gretna finishing above the mighty Queen of the South in the league?'

'Wash your mouth out.'

For some reason I always end up taking on wagers I never want to win. Although, the fact that Asa would rather drink lager than bet against The Queens probably has something to do with it. So it was decided: as before, I would win a year's supply of kippers if Gretna ended up higher in the league, while Asa gained a year's supply of beer if he won. But, as supertankers can't get up The River Nith, it was scaled down to a reasonable and affordable one beer a month for twelve months.

As I was about to leave the pub at the end of a good evening, Andy waved me over. 'This guy here's been asking about you,' he said, pointing to the far end of the bar.

I walked over. Don Gardiner was standing, no drink in front of him. 'I hear you've been asking about me,' he said.

Wednesday 19th July

Mondays and Thursdays are my golf days but Doc Halliday goes out every weekday and the fact that the weather was supposed to hit a staggering thirty degrees today wouldn't be enough to stop him.

I drove over to the club and watched him heave his golf clubs out of his boot. He had attempted to nullify the sun's rays by donning a faded-blue floppy cotton hat: its small brim providing very little shade for his big, round face. And he had gone for khaki, belted, shorts, as old as mine, and just as untrendily short. The ensemble was finished off by a tucked-in blue striped, short-sleeved shirt, ruthlessly unbuttoned down to the navel, offering the unwary onlooker a wiry display of grey chest-hair. Out in the open, Doc's white legs seemed precariously spindly compared to the bulk of his middle and they had seen less sunlight than Dracula: the knees bulging like large, white walnuts.

He saw me leaning against my car. His power trolley trundled in front of him as he came over, checking his watch as he spoke, 'Funny, this says it's Wednesday on the dial.' He gave his wrist a sharp shake, held it to one ear, and allowed his mouth to part with a grin. 'Must have stopped. Didn't realise it was time for our usual game already.' At close quarters, Doc's legs were unnaturally hairless: although it is said brown corduroy can be as good as an epilator.

'Would you mind if I caddied for you, Doc – for a hole or two?'

He didn't show any surprise at my unique request. 'Good idea. Learn from the master, my boy. Watch and learn.'

We play off the same handicap – high.

He went on, 'And we don't often get the chance to speak these days when out playing: always seem to be heading in different directions. They say the rough's quite dreadful this

162

year. Is that the case?'

I was introduced to two other, similarly attired, retired doctors, both fielding broods of expensive clubs. And we set off.

It wasn't until the second fairway – after his normal very short, but safe drive – that I had the chance to catch him alone. 'Know anything about a Lionel Menzies?' I asked. It was the same question I had put to Chisel when I'd phoned yesterday.

Doc, who used to be one of the bosses at the hospital, pondered this for a while as he selected his next club. 'Not a lot. He's reasonably new to the area. I've only met him the once. He seems to be a very competent surgeon, from what I hear. And he's Charlie Menzies' nephew – I daresay you knew that. What about him?'

Most of that would be the party line: professional manners. I needed something behind it but I doubted he would oblige unless I was more forthcoming. 'You remember Manfred dying last week?'

He nodded back, slowly.

'I think Lionel Menzies was involved in his death.'

Doc's club selection froze for a brief moment; then he flicked a club to one side to allow access to his seven wood. He said nothing more, taking up his stance as normal, and, after checking six times to see that the green hadn't moved, finally swung at his ball. It came up short, with a bunker blocking his approach to the flag. He gave off a little sigh before walking on jauntily: it was as though I had said nothing more than it was a nice day and he suited shorts.

We had walked for thirty yards before he spoke. 'That's quite a statement to make, Jin.' He stopped and stared gravely at me. 'You need to be very careful about making such accusations.'

'I know. I don't say it lightly. Do you know anything about him?'

163

Doc weighed up his response as deliberately as the selection of his last club. 'He's not particularly well liked by the staff – that much I've heard. He can be quite dismissive, arrogant – but then that's nothing out of the ordinary for surgeons, is it? I've had to deal with plenty of *them*, in my time. Par for the course.'

'Nothing more?'

He shook his head.

We arrived at his ball. Doc stood behind it, hands on hips, legs apart. I gave him my phone number to show how serious I was, asking him to contact me if anything arose. I had dropped a very large bolt from the blue: I hoped he would ask around.

Before he, inevitably, dumped his ball into the sand, I made to leave. When I turned back for one last question, his eyes were still on me. I said, 'Oh, by the way, Doc, do you think you can get me a walking stick?'

From the golf course, I drove round by Charlie's house. I wasn't expecting him to be back this early – nearly half past ten – but it wasn't much out of my way. Surprisingly his car was there, sitting behind his closed gates.

Charlie's face looked much better and cheerier today: as though he had returned from a good, restful spa holiday. His clothes showed he was still in mourning: deep blue trousers, a dark green shirt, topped off by a purple, silk cravat and burgundy slippers. He showed me into his cool home, with a wave of his arm.

I spoke for a minute or two on how the house clearing had gone, to fill in the time it took him to make the offered smoothie: the robust blender dealing easily with a moundful of fresh exotic fruit and large crackle of ice. The outcome was extremely good and chilling.

I handed over the key of Manfred's house and we stood, turning our attention to the weather, each appraising the day through the window. Soon, though, we'd reached the end of natural topics and I knew he was waiting for me to get to the point.

'How are you feeling?' I asked.

'Not bad. I'll be glad to get this operation over with though. Still a few days to go though.'

I returned a 'that's understandable' nod, and asked, 'Have you been unwell before – only I never heard?'

'No, I've been fine, all things considered. Ah, you're wondering why the op?'

'It's not like you would have it done if it wasn't necessary.'

'Very true. No, it was just one of those routine visits to the Well-Man clinic. Do you go?' I shook my head, he went on, 'Probably too young. It's a good system. They call you up every year for all sorts of tests. My blood pressure needs an eye kept on it, of course, and they spotted something else – and I *had* been feeling a bit ropey from time to time, but hadn't done anything about it. My doctor decided I should go for more tests. Luckily Lionel was down here by then and took over. He was very thorough, explained it all. I know there are risks, but it needs to be done.'

'Isn't there something about doctors not treating family – or have I got that wrong?'

Charlie shrugged. 'I don't know about that. I would have insisted he did it anyway: he's by far the best down here, if not in the whole country. It would be crazy to go with a lesser surgeon. Don't you think?'

He was becoming anxious about the lingering length of my visit, and my hesitation didn't help. When I didn't reply, he went on, 'Sorry again, Jin, about you having to do all that work with the house. Just the way things worked out. I'm very appreciative of what you have done – really. Sound's like you did a great job. Don't forget half the car's yours – that's what I promised.'

165

'Charlie, were you in Manfred's house on the morning of the funeral, early on?'

'No, no. I haven't been in at all. Sorry. That's why I'm grateful to you.'

So it wasn't Charlie the neighbour had heard. It was time to get things moving. 'Can I ask you a few questions?'

He sensed something and sat down purposefully at the kitchen table, glad I was finally coming to the point. In his unease, he had put the empty glass to his lips on three, separate occasions: each time the lack of liquid had forced out a snort of derision. He nodded for me to start.

'You showed me a picture of your parents on their wedding day...'

'Yes?' he replied, deliberately dragging the word out into a question.

'Your father was in the army?'

'That's right. They married during the war. Must have been near the end though. What about it?'

'Did he come back especially for the wedding?'

Charlie started to fidget. 'I don't know all that much about it, Jin. It's not something you ask when you're young. All I know is he was stationed in the south of England for a while and then abroad.'

'They knew each other for a long time?'

'What is this, Jin? I don't know – really. I supposed they must have been together before he was sent away. Maybe even from before the war. But I'm not sure.' He gave a shrug and tried again, 'What's all this about?'

I chose not to answer, following up quickly with, 'I take it your mother passed away before your father?'

'Yes, that's right. What's...'

I didn't let him finish. 'Did Manfred seem different recently? I mean, was he acting in a slightly odd way? Anything – no matter how small. Did he seem preoccupied?'

166

Charlie took his time: his brain split between answering my questions and wondering where they were leading. Finally, he said, 'No, I can't think of anything.' He produced a sad shake of his head and looked down. 'I hate to say it but I think most of the time I was only concerned about *my* health problems. I never enquired about his. That's not right, is it? It's not what friends are supposed to do. I should have been looking out for him as well. I suppose I just thought he would have told me about any troubles. *This* is what gets me.' His face folded.

I pulled the photograph from my pocket. 'I think this is your mother with Mrs Mann.'

After a struggle to his feet, Charlie located his specs on the window sill and sat down again, studying it closely.

'Have you seen this before?'

He shook his head.

'And that's probably Manfred your mum's holding.'

He nodded. 'Yes, yes, it could be. Not very big, is he?'

I slipped the piece of paper out and flattened it on the table before him.

He said, sadly, 'Quite a coincidence: both of us ending up with heart problems, isn't it?'

'Not as much as you might think. I found this letter as well.' I explained where – and Charlie's eyes went wide.

The suitcase was in the boot of my car, parked in front of his house.

He started to read.

> *Dear Emily,*
> *I don't know how I can ever repay you.*
> *I know you will be a good mother.*
> *I couldn't have done it otherwise.*
> *I will help whenever I can.*
> *And I will be able to see him*
> *almost every day.*

But I know it will be
from a distance mostly.
There is one thing I can do though
and that's make sure
he'll always be able to spot
a brother or sister.
And then you never know...
      All my love to you.
      Celia xx

Charlie must have read through it five or six times before looking up. When he shook his head, his cheeks flapped. 'I don't get it,' he said.

'They told me at the nursing home that Mrs Mann's first name is Emily. Your mother's name was Celia, wasn't it? It says it on the plaque on the piano.'

He nodded; then came the instant dismissal, 'There are plenty of Celias. It doesn't have to be my mother who wrote this.'

I shook my head.

He looked down and, I assumed, read it again. This time his eyes were watery when they returned to stare at me. 'You think he was my brother? Is that what you are saying? You think Manfred was my brother? Mrs Mann was...was looking after him for my mother? Adopting him?'

I nodded and said, gently, 'I'm sure of it. Remember what Mrs Mann said? "You should tell his *real* mother."'

In his kitchen, as he sits at the table, trying to take it in, this, other, Visitation races through my head. It's Celia, Charlie's mother. Her husband-to-be is away at war, and she learns she is pregnant – but not by her fiancé.

Distraught, she visits someone she can trust, Mrs Mann, and confides in her. If her fiancé finds out, she says, there will be no wedding and no happy life together. She will have let him down. But most of all, she will have let her baby down: her life and its future will be difficult. A single mother: she will be shunned.

For whatever reason, Mrs Mann decides to secretly adopt the baby. Does she start to dress in a way that implies she is pregnant? Does she tell her husband immediately or wait until the baby is brought to their home? I don't know.

Celia hands over the child but she is never far away, watching him grow. Perhaps Mrs Mann takes wee Jimmy round from time to time. Celia definitely visits: there is the photograph.

Charlie's father returns from war, unaware of what has happened in his absence. They wed and soon Charlie is on the way. Celia dresses her new baby brightly, a beacon for her other child to see. Perhaps Mrs Mann takes wee Jimmy out and they meet Celia on the way.

Mrs Mann: Look at that wee baby, Jimmy.
    Isn't he great?
    And look at all the
    wonderful colourful clothes he's wearing.
Wee Jimmy nods.
Mrs Mann: Wouldn't he make a great friend?
    And he'll be so easy to spot.
Wee Jimmy nods again.
A seed is sown: to be followed up on the first day of primary school.

Charlie's family move to Glasgow but Celia can't settle. They return. There must have been enormous delight when Charlie and Jimmy become best friends and play together. Jimmy is round her house almost daily. She might even be able to believe that he never really left.

169

All that might be fanciful on my part. I might be altering the past. And if I hadn't taken Chiara to see The Visitation statue, then I doubt I would have thought about it in the same way.

I glanced back at Charlie and said, 'It explains why you've always liked…' I wasn't sure how to say it, '…nice, bright clothes. Your mother did it deliberately, right from when you were young. Think back to when you were kids – when Manfred came round to your house to play. How did your mother act towards him?'

'She fussed over him – as she did me. But she would be like that to anyone.'

'Are you sure?'

Something – a distant memory – must have flashed before him. He started shaking his head frantically, perhaps in the hope that this unearthed information could be dispelled. He wasn't ready for it but whatever it was. But it made him certain. 'He was my brother.' He nodded and repeated the statement several times, trying it out for size.

Then it dawned on him. 'He knew about this? Manfred *knew* we were brothers. He had the note but he didn't say? *Again*, he didn't say.' His face contorted beyond despair. There was pain through his next words, 'Why would he do that? Why would he keep quiet about this? I don't understand.'

I told him about my visit to Mrs Mann yesterday. 'I think he found out some time in May.'

'He knew all that time, two months, and said nothing to me? Why would he do that?'

I had a few thoughts on the matter – and they were tied into why he never mentioned his heart problem either – but I decided to keep them to myself for the moment. I needed more information. I chose to shrug instead.

'Did you know Manfred never reversed?' I asked.

The question caught him off-guard. His mind was still
170

whirling. 'What?'

I repeated it.

'I knew. A lot of people did. Why do you ask?'

'I didn't know until recently. Why, then, do you think he drove up a dead-end road?'

Any other time, he might have come up with an answer – but his brain was saturated. He didn't reply.

'Look, I'm sorry about bringing you this…this news – but I thought you'd want to know, Charlie. Mrs Mann must have thought Manfred needed to know the truth as well.'

Charlie's head sunk into his hands, and he made no reply.

I went on, 'I think there's something suspicious about Manfred's death – and I think it is linked to this letter.'

He wasn't listening: it was better to leave it for now, until I had the evidence. He wouldn't believe me otherwise. I fetched the suitcase from the car and handed it over without a word. I didn't like leaving him in such a state but I had to go: I had arranged Sanny's flitting for this afternoon and he wouldn't appreciate me arriving beyond the scheduled time.

Anytime ago, I would have had difficulty containing my excitement at the prospect of setting foot in Sanny's caravan, his lair, and having the chance to examine and pack his things; perhaps the first to witness the treasures lying within. After all, as a youngster, when I'd heard my first story about him, I built a large cardboard pyramid and placed a razor blade, on a cotton reel, underneath. It was said that if the blade was at the same, relative height to the burial chamber of the Great Pyramid in Egypt, it would, not only stay sharp, but *sharpen* itself. Today, I should be feeling like an explorer, like Howard Carter on his way to break into Tutankhmun's tomb, but, sadly, having left a desolate Charlie, the prospect of helping Onion Sanny on this day did not fill me with any thrill at all.

Really, I wanted to postpone the move, but I couldn't: the
171

hotel was scheduled for demolition tomorrow, its grounds to be flattened, ready for building. Sanny had to move. Furthermore, he was expecting me.

I returned home to change into an old t-shirt, leaving the shorts on. I would need to buy another pair: these were getting grubby, but I couldn't bear to return to trousers in the daytime, not in this fiery weather.

I picked up the van. It was on a four-hour hire to keep the cost down, and having seen how quickly a house could be gutted, I figured Sanny's small caravan wouldn't take very long either. I parked on the torn driveway of the old hotel, as close to his path as possible. After a few deep breaths, I made my way between the bushes. It was going to be a trek back and forward in the beating sun but I couldn't see any way round it: it would be too big a job to cut back the undergrowth to allow the van closer.

As I approached, I was pleased to feel the first tremors of curiosity rising within: I *had* been waiting most of my life for this moment. My pace quickened, each eager stride taking me to discovery. It's said that it is better to travel with expectation than to arrive: and one step into the clearing proved it. The sight awaiting me punctured all excitement.

Spread on the ground, in the front of his caravan, sat fifteen large tea chests with lids. I sensed the entire contents of the caravan were in them. As I neared, it was obvious that the tops had been nailed down.

Sanny was sitting on the wooden steps, head down, carving irregular patterns in the earth with the end of a large twig. His head lifted and cocked to an angle to show his dismay at my ten-minute-late appearance. He was still in hefty black trousers, with a pair of unlaced boots sitting hotly on his feet, but, this time he had tucked his white shirt neatly into the waistband. He might even have tried to tidy up his hair by employing a comb – but with limited success.

172

'Didn't realise you'd be packed up and ready,' I said, trying not to show my disappointment, attempting to lift one of the boxes. I couldn't get it off the ground. Where on earth do you get tea chests nowadays anyway? And how did he get them here in the first place?

'Whit did ye think?'

'I think I can't lift any of these boxes, Sanny, that's what I think. They're much too heavy for me. You'll need to give me a hand?' I didn't like to ask.

'A cannae dae that, son. A cannae lift noo. Ye should hav brought sumyin with ye. Whit were ye thinking?'

I gave Sanny one of my fiercest stares. 'Okay, I'll see what I can do.' I squeezed my phone out. It needed to be someone right away: there was the van's short hire to be considered, and, also, more importantly, I had another task later – one requiring picking up the walking stick from Doc.

Sanny gave a, 'it's not really good enough' grunt, before adding, 'A wanted in this efternin, ye ken, an git settled.'

'I can understand that, Sanny. I'll try my best.'

I stepped to one side and started to text. Asa would have been the best, with his brute strength, but he would be at work. The same with Chisel and Tread. It was down to Hoogah – still on holiday. Perhaps the work he'd put in at the gym earlier in the year could now be put to use, if it remained in his slender frame.

I waited for a reply – unsure of what to say to Sanny in the meantime. 'You managed to pack okay?' was my effort. 'I thought I was going to lend a hand. Looks like a big job.'

'A can manage. A cannae drive an' a cannae lift owt heavy – other than that, A could hae done it mesel. Am no fur the scrapheap yet, ye ken.'

Hoogah returned the text, stating he was busy. The situation had to be classified as vital. I phoned. He took a fair bit of persuading but I finally managed it: my point about witnessing

173

history probably tipping the balance.

I left a huffy Sanny sitting, and dashed off to pick up my new removal colleague from his home.

We heaved the boxes into the van. Sanny had shown no interest in Hoogah when introduced, giving him the briefest of glances, whilst making a noise in his throat – perhaps attempting to dislodge a stuck crumb.

It was devilishly hard, hot work. We were sodden within the first few minutes and nastily scratched by the undergrowth.

'I always thought history was boring – and this proves it,' my co-worker grumbled, as we stumbled our way along the path, a chest between us, out of ear-shot of Sanny. 'This had better be worth it. I'll expect nothing less than a couple of bottles of that liqueur from him.'

'Don't bank on it, Hoogah. You can never tell with him. But, as I said, I'll make it up to you – if he doesn't. And don't forget you can always tell people, "I was there."'

With rests between each box, it took us close to an hour to fill the van. Sanny hadn't moved from his perch on the stairs the whole time, an eagle-eye on the proceedings. But when we returned for one last look at the empty site, he rose to his feet and wheeled out his big black bike out from round the back of the caravan. I offered to stow it in the van: he turned it down.

'You sure you don't want a lift over?'

'Al make it there mesel, if ye don't mind. Al get ye over there.'

He gave us the directions, locked the caravan door, threw a leg over his machine and pedalled away, his head high and without a backward glance. We both stood, staring at the abandoned caravan, showing it a great deal more reverence than its last occupant.

'Funny, you'd have thought he'd be more bothered about going. He's just taking it all in his stride,' I said. 'And Hoogah,
174

why would he lock the door when it's completely empty and probably going to be demolished anyway?'

He shrugged and we set off for the van, heads down.

It wasn't far to the new site – out on the Moffat Road, in a field, at the edge of town, near to the turn-off for the village of Mouswald. Sanny was waiting for us, sitting on the steps to his new home. It was no great surprise he'd beaten us as we'd been held up at every set of traffic lights and he would have been able to take the cycle path along the disused railway some of the way.

It was a brand new caravan – more a mobile home, really – and a great deal bigger than his last abode. This time we were able to bring the van right up to its door.

'You'll have plenty of space for all your stuff in there,' I joked as we unloaded, leaving everything spread out on the ground in front of the caravan, as instructed.

'Aye,' Sanny said, 'There's at least one extra room in it. All bought for by the housing company.'

Sweat and grazes combined to nip, and arms, back and legs ached, Hoogah whinged, and Sanny remained tetchy. It was great fun. I grumbled under my breath, 'I need this kind of work like a hermit needs a guest bedroom.'

'Whit are ye saying?' Sanny shouted across.

'Nothing,' I replied quickly, making a note to polish up the line for future use with the lads.

Sanny watched on intently and cringed every time we let a chest slip. 'Careful. Ye'll need tae be careful,' he repeated, his voice seeping anger.

There had been no pleasure in this job, no peek into the workings of his life. It was like being asked to go to the Grand Canyon only to find out that viewing was in the blackness of night.

When the last packing case found the dry earth, I gave it one

175

last try, asking Sanny if he would like us to make a start at putting his things inside – but he was having none of it.

'Al dae it in ma own time,' he said, looking skywards. 'Doesnae look like it's gonna rain for a while. Av plenty o time.'

And with that I made a show of leaving, lingering with the van door open, waiting expectantly for reimbursement. Sanny didn't move from his seat nor offer any words of gratitude, so we drove off.

'Where was his hammer, Hoogah?'

'What?'

'Everything was nailed down – so where was his hammer? He wasn't carrying one.'

'I don't know Jinky, and I don't care. All I can think of right now is a cold shower.'

Turning onto the road, I noticed an elderly man with tidy white hair walking towards us. He gave a wave as we passed, and we both nodded back.

'Who was that?' I asked.

'No idea. I thought he was waving at you.'

'He looks familiar, right enough,' I added. 'Is he heading into Sanny's? He might be, you know.'

'That's not likely, is it? Probably just out for a stroll.'

I slowed down to keep a check in the rear-view mirror – but when we turned a corner, the man was lost from sight.

Hoogah asked, as we neared his home, 'Do you think Sanny'll pay you the money? You should have got it up front, you know. Sometimes you can be a soft touch.'

I had the walking stick, thanks to Doc Halliday: it was waiting at the out-patients department for me. It was the standard hospital issue: hollow metal, with holes down the side, and a grey plastic handle. Asa and I left my house at eight in the evening, my shorts replaced with trousers. The hug of the cloth made me walk like a cowboy: as though my legs had been dipped in warm treacle. We inched into my car and drove off, seeking out a different pub.

'What's all this about, Jinky?'

'No matter what happens, Asa, say nothing. Can you do that?'

He presented a pained expression rather than a reply. A few seconds later, he asked, 'And what's with the walking stick in the back seat?'

'I'll tell you about it later.' I didn't want to hear the sound of his scoff at this latest idea, and I had no doubt he would have objected strongly to our destination.

'I'm not sure you deserve it, treating a pal this way,' he said, 'but you might want to know that the man attacked at the hotel, William Bones, was released from hospital this afternoon.'

'Thanks, Asa. Where can I find him?' I turned my attention away from the road to see him shaking his head vigorously.

'No, no, I'm having nothing more to do with it,' he said. '*You* should be able to find out where he lives easily enough. I still want to be left out of this as much as possible. And I don't think *you* should be getting involved either – despite what happened with High-Heid-Yin-Harris yesterday.'

'Fine. I take it Mr Bones hasn't been able to tell the police anything much about his attacker? You would have told me, wouldn't you?'

He gave a tremendous sigh. 'It's hard work being with you. The most I want to say is that there's been no progress. Okay? And seeing how I'm in this car, can't you at least tell me where we're headed?'

'Surely the fact that it's a pub is enough. A thirsty man doesn't need to know the source of the water: all that matters is to have it pouring into his glass. Isn't that one of your sayings?'

'No, my one's much better than that. And I'll be expecting a bit more than just water tonight.' He turned to look out the side

177

of the car, where his trailing hand dangled, tilted to deflect some cooling air onto his face.

The Griffin Bar, with its corrugated tin roof, is little more than a shed tacked onto the end of a row of houses like an afterthought. The weathered wooden frontage has two iron-barred windows, sitting like eyes, on either side of the paint-flaked brown nose of a door.

I parked the car, eased from its sweaty confines, grasped the stick, and started to limp towards the pub, making full use of my prop. Asa's eyes skied to the heavens in disbelief – but he did rush past me, and with an overblown bowing action, opened the door fully, allowing me to enter ahead of him. It was my first visit into the depths of this hostelry.

I shuffled on into a rectangular room, heading directly for the bar, straight ahead, positioned against the back wall. It wasn't a big place but it was busy, hot, and sticky, with the heavy clatter of dominoes sounding above the clammer of voices. The air was of beer and sweat, with hints of beef gravy. By the time we reached halfway across the floor, the door, on a hinge-spring, closed with a loud click.

Compared to The Bruce, this was like stepping into someone's front room – albeit a tacky, old, smoke-stained, wooden-panelled one. It would be a place where everyone knew each other. The type of pub where the customers held hands with friendship and animosity: depending on the time of day.

Plastic seats, with their plastic tables, lined both sides of the room. They were filled with men in short sleeved shirts, crowding over their games. The floor was covered in brown, unshiny linoleum – and it was sticky, making my sliding limp awkward.

I wouldn't have been entirely surprised if the talking had stopped abruptly, the piano player had paused in mid-chord,
178

and every head had turned in unison to watch the entrance of a pair of strangers. It didn't happen: there was no let-up in their play, and there was no piano player. We reached the bar unobserved by the punters entwined in their serious games.

Only the barman had studied our arrival: apparently he had nothing else to do for the moment. He waited, cross-armed, and, probably, legs akimbo, behind his tall, chest-high bar, waiting for us to reach the focus of his work. I bought a beer for Asa – their selection on draft wasn't to his liking so he chose a bottle – and I took a plain orange juice. It was going to be a long night and I needed to stay sharp.

We stayed at the bar and surveyed the scene. Sweat had gathered dramatically in the baffled creases of Asa's brow. He was quiet and viewed me from time to time in the hope that it would encourage the surrender of the reason for the visit.

Wallace Lemon was there. I watched him as he sat, concentrating hard, a black pint at his elbow. He was side-on to us and his walking stick sat hanked over the back of his chair. This was his pub night – as his neighbour, Mr Redditch, had said.

Asa noted my stare and gave a quick, nervous clear of his throat. He tugged my shoulder and turned me back to the bar. 'Is that who I think it is?'

'It depends on who you think it is.'

'This is not a good idea, Jinky,' he said, using a whisper that could rasp rust from scrap metal. He shielded his mouth with his hand. 'That *is* Mr Lemon over there, isn't it? You knew he'd be here, didn't you? That's why we're *here*. He's complained about you, Jinky. You shouldn't be doing this. Even with High-Heid-Yin-Harris' supposed backing, you shouldn't be here. And what's with the stick anyway? What do you hope to get from that, eh? Are you trying to goad him into something? It's not right, d'you hear?'

'Remember what I said – say nothing.' I took a mouthful of

my drink, indicating he should do the same.

Five minutes later, as I watched on beside an increasingly squirmy, but silent, Asa, Lemon stood up stiffly, pushing himself upright with one hand on the table, the other on the back of his chair, before spying me, his eyes tightening as he processed my face. His expression was decidedly dour as he gathered his stick and hobbled over, shouting his order to the barman on the way, his stare never leaving the stick in my hand.

'Following me, are you?' he said, gruffly. His face came close to my own, there was stout on his breath. He had shaved today – and his hair was flat.

I noticed the others at his table look up. I put on my most charming voice. 'Oh, hello, didn't see you there. Do you know Asa?' I motioned to my friend beside me and noted, as he took in Asa's hulk, the quills of Lemon's aggression retreat a touch.

'No, we just dropped in,' I continued. 'Been a long time since I was here.' I gave the room a thorough going-over. 'It hasn't changed much,' I added happily.

'Bit of a coincidence,' Lemon muttered, with meaning.

'And here's another.' I lifted up the walking stick.

'Is this some kind of joke,' he snorted back. 'Only I don't think it's funny. You trying to take the piss – is that it?' His grip on the handle tightened, producing white knuckles.

'Don't be daft,' I chuckled back. 'I'm just back from the hospital.' I lifted the leg of my black breeks to show the thick bandage round my ankle, disappearing into the over-sized trainers I'd fortunately kept from earlier on in the year. I didn't look at Asa but hoped he wasn't emitting any disbelieving looks.

'A car ran over it,' I said. 'Don't ask. Someone not looking where they were reversing.' I gave a withering look towards Asa – who, much to his credit, continued to stare back with barely a flinch, and with monkly silence to boot.
180

'I can appreciate a little what you have to put up with,' I added.

'I would doubt that. Come back in six years from now and maybe we can talk about it then.'

His drinks were ready. Lemon handed over a note and turned back to his table without another word. The barman, carrying the full tray, dutifully tagged on behind.

We emptied our glasses and I moved towards the domino players, inviting Asa to follow, and stood behind the now-seated Mr Lemon. 'Having much luck?' I asked, still cheery, smiling at the faces opposite peering up at me.

Mr Lemon didn't turn, but shuffled the doms round the table. 'Luck doesn't come into it,' he mumbled back. Each of the players reached for a fresh rack and clacked their selection into a line in front of them.

I motioned to Asa to leave and took time shuffling across the floor to the door, hoping Lemon had turned to watch. 'Do you think anyone saw?' I asked when we were outside.

'Saw what?'

That was good enough for me: and the wide cover provided by Asa must have been enough. We reached the car and his voice thundered, 'What the hell was that all about, Jinky?' He was a champagne cork of frustration, fuelled by lack of information, and about to blow. I put a finger to my lips. He paid it no attention.

'Were you just trying to rile the guy? Was that the plan? What was the point in that?'

I repositioned my finger to the front of his lips. He didn't find it funny, knocking it away with the ferocious swat.

He went on, 'Why on earth would you think that would help? I don't get it. I've had it with you this time, Jinky.'

I ignored him, told myself to stay tranquil, and said, 'I don't know how long I'm going to be here, Asa. I need to wait for Lemon to leave.'

181

'I'll make my own way back then.' He stomped away without a further word.

I called after him, 'I can give you a quick lift somewhere else, if you like.'

He continued walking and didn't reply.

Maybe I'd been a bit hard on him: dragging him over here, exploiting his size, without offering a good reason in return. But, in a way, I still felt he owed me something after his outburst the other day, and his unwillingness to take any of my ideas seriously. He was far too quick to dismiss them. He was a friend, after all. He should give more. It was as if I had nothing to offer this investigation – or any other, for that matter. If our roles were reversed I hope I would be a bit more encouraging.

I waited inside the car – the door of The Griffin pub visible. It was the third time in three days: I should be getting good at this surveillance lark.

It took another hour and a half before Lemon dragged himself home, foo as a whelk. I watched him limp and stagger his way back, keeping to my strategy of moving the car onto each corner, always keeping him in full, swaying view. I shot a text off to Ron. He had helped me before and I'd helped him – so I wasn't sure who was due the next favour. It wouldn't matter to Ron anyway: he didn't mind breaking into houses.

As Lemon unlocked the front door of his home, I slipped out of the car: no need for the stick now. His hall light flashed on as the door closed and, after a long time, an upstairs light blazed, which, judging by the different type of glass, was the bathroom.

I crept down the lane beside Miss Welch's house, and into the field to watch. Nearing the longest day of the year, it wouldn't get completely dark tonight and even though I had dressed in black I needed to be careful not to be spotted. Lemon's curtains were closed as usual so the chances of him seeing me were slight, but a call to the police from one of his neighbours would leave me with a rather tricky explanation. Neither Mr Redditch nor Miss Welch's lights were on: hopefully, they were in bed already.

Another upstairs light snapped on: the curtains were heavy but there was a glow round the edges. A few minutes later more downstairs lights came into life, brightening each curtain. If Lemon's set-up was the same as Miss Welch's, he was in the kitchen now. This one stayed on for a long time, most likely preparing a snack: the natural thing to do after a night in the pub. I had to hope he was the right kind of drunk: enough to sleep soundly but not to much to end up collapsed downstairs in a chair.

It might only have been half an hour but the time stretched uncomfortably. My legs became heavy from standing still – moving would have made me more noticeable – and the earlier efforts at Sanny's had left many aching muscles.

Moisture gathered under the star-freckled, dark-blue sky. The grass dampened. It was almost chilly: I liked the feeling. It brought a memory from a distant age: a time when we had the luxury of adding garments to become comfortably warm.

Lemon's lights disappeared, one by one, leaving only one upstairs: it had to be his bedroom.

Give him time to sleep.

I sent another text, shading the illuminated phone-pad in the cup of my palms, before returning to the car to wait for the reply.

At 1:10am Ron rolled his van in behind my car. We both got out and nodded to each other. He noted the walking stick in my hand. I led the way: I wasn't limping. We stopped in front of Lemon's gate and I allowed the expert housebreaker to take over.

Ron checked the street and eased the gate open slowly, guarding against squeaks: it hadn't when Lemon had returned, it didn't now. We moved round to the back door. He had it open in about ten seconds and gave a shake of the head. I knew what he was thinking. Why no bolt? Why make it so easy? Security is always high on Ron's mind: it annoys him when others don't take it seriously.

We shook hands, he gave his customary thumbs up, and left, as silently as always. He hadn't questioned my reason for the break-in. He didn't need one.

I took a deep breath and stepped into the house, quickly closing the door behind. Lemon should be far away in the sozzled land of nod. If he was anything like Asa it would take a charging buffalo to waken him.

Thursday 20th July

Despite the state of the investigation, the clammy weather, and the lack of sleep, I was desperate for a game of golf to make up for the missed ones on Monday and last Thursday. I expected my swing would be cranked up a few notches beyond its customary tightness, but hoped, eventually, for some release from the tension coiled up from last night. I needed a wee bit of calm to settle through my body.

However, this wasn't the only reason for the visit to the golf course: Doc hadn't been in touch with any further information on Lionel Menzies, and I needed some soon.

He was the first to arrive. His shirt was different but the rest of the outfit was much the same. I wandered across the golf course's car park towards him, spinning the walking stick like a drum major.

'That was quick. Most people don't tend to heal quite so rapidly,' he remarked, and waited for my explanation.

When I offered nothing but the stick, he chucked it in through the open window, onto the back seat of his car. I could have returned it myself – the Crichton Golf Club is opposite the hospital, after all – but I try to avoid the place as much as possible.

Doc began the awkward effort of pulling his golf clubs from the boot while I stood and watched. 'Anything on Lionel?' I said, finally.

He straightened and studied me for a second or two, his mouth forming a tight line. 'There *is* one thing but I'm not sure I should be telling you this. It's only a rumour.' He paused for a moment, before continuing, 'I've known you for a few years. I think you can be trusted...'

It was an odd comment: almost as though he was speaking to a third party, explaining his decision.

He went on, 'It's said Lionel does a lot of gambling, and is
185

heavily in debt. That was one reason I was given for his moving down here – the money. He sold his house in Edinburgh and bought a cheaper one.'

'That fits,' I replied. I hesitated, unsure. Five seconds later I had blurted it out. 'I think Lionel is going to try to kill his uncle.'

It caught his attention. I thought it might. I waited to see what reaction it would get. Would it be an Asa-type dismissive one? Did Doc's scoff have the same annoying tone?

'Charlie Menzies?' he clarified: his face solemn.

He was about to say something further but I pushed in ahead of him, 'And I think he killed Manfred. I can't prove it – but there are too many things pointing that way. What I need to do now is convince Charlie not to go ahead with this operation. He's having heart surgery in three days from now and Lionel's the surgeon. I can't let that happen. It's too big a risk. I need to find a way to prove Lionel's guilt – and I need to keep Charlie safe. If Lionel doesn't find out I'm onto him, Charlie should be okay for now – but I don't have much time.'

I suppose, deep down, I expected Doc to burst out laughing, asking what pills I'd been popping, whilst summoning an ambulance to take me away. He didn't. He rubbed his chin instead. 'Those are very serious claims to be making, Jin – especially when you have no evidence. If I was you I wouldn't go about saying that kind of thing.'

A red car, containing two of our golfing buddies, turned into the car park – there can be as many as six of us in all. My phone sprang into life. No wonder I hate them: it's as though they can sense when it's inappropriate. I should have left it alone, but I checked the screen. It was a call from Jill.

I wanted to talk things out with Doc. Try to explain everything to him but the other buddies had burst from their car, their laughter ringing out. Suddenly I felt alone, as though in the middle of wasteland, and I was miserable. It was foolish
186

to have spouted out like that to Doc. I golfed with him –
nothing more. We didn't frequent the pub together or invite
each other to dinner parties or go to the opera. Our lives were
separate – except here. In a matter of seconds I'd built a wall
between us: one that could never be pulled down. I'd
disparaged one of his kind. It should have been Asa – I should
have spoken to *him*. It wouldn't have mattered then. He's used
to my rants. He would have taken no offence in the long term.
He'd be telling me how daft it sounded.

But it was too late now.

Doc motioned to the phone in my hand – perhaps stalling for
time, trying to gauge a reply. It was still vibrating.

I took the call. It wasn't Jill.

'Who's this?'

The man's earthy voice said, 'Let's just say I'm a friend.'

I turned away from Doc and started walking. 'Where's Jill?'

'She's here.'

'What do you want?'

'She'll tell you.'

There was a heavy rustling sound then Jill's voice sounded.
She was urgent, scared, near hysterical. 'Do as he says, Jinky,
and I won't get hurt. He's given me his word I won't get hurt!'
The phone must have been snatched away. I heard a thud.

The man's voice came back on. 'That's right. You have to do
as I say. Do anything else and she gets hurt. Properly hurt.
There'll be no second chance. Do you understand?'

'What do I have to do?'

'Get to your car and start driving.'

I left Doc standing, staring at me. I watched him in my rear-
view mirror, mouth open. I saw one of the buddies come over
and clap a friendly hand on his back. It made him jump. I
hadn't said anything before leaving. I'd only shaken my head
and shrugged and raced for the car.

Sweat ran from my brow, seeped down my back, and more

gathered behind the knees. I was sticking to the seat. The
windows were open. The car wouldn't cool. I turned towards
the town centre. I didn't know which way to go. It seemed the
best direction.

The phone buzzed. I don't have a hands-free system. I put it
to my ear – not liking it. I didn't want to get caught.

'Gretna, go to Gretna.' It was Jill. 'I'll phone you back in ten
minutes and tell you what to do next. He'll hurt me, Jinky.
Don't get the police involved. Promise me you won't call the
police.'

There was a pause.

She added, 'I don't know what he wants you to do yet.'

The phone went dead.

'There's a package waiting to be picked up,' she said. 'You
have to fetch it and bring it back to my salon.'

I had five miles to go to Gretna.

The phone was snatched away again. The man gave me
instructions.

'How do I know you'll not harm her? How do I know you'll
keep your word on that?'

'You don't.'

I had two choices: follow his instructions or contact the
police.

Gretna is twenty-two miles to the south-east of Dumfries. It's
not a big place and, unsurprisingly, I rarely visit. I don't know
it well. I stopped and asked for directions. The town sits beside
the border with England so maybe this is why they have a
distinctly different accent to us doonhamers.

Before I could drive off my phone buzzed again. The screen
said it was from Doc. I didn't have time for this right now.

'Jin?'

I tried to send out my calmest voice. 'Can I call you back?

I'm a wee bit busy right now, Doc. Maybe in an hour?'

I shouldn't have given him my number.

'Jin, don't hang up. You'll want to know Charlie's in hospital.'

'What?'

'He's in hospital for his surgery.'

'It's not for another few days, Doc. You've made a mistake.'

'There's no mistake. He's having his operation right at this very moment. I only found out seconds ago.'

'But it can't be.'

'Must have been pushed forward. He must have come in last night.'

'But I saw him yesterday. He said nothing about it. Why didn't he say something to me?'

'It's happening. That's all that matters, Jin.'

'You have to stop it, Doc! Remember what I told you!'

'I can't. I'm not in charge anymore. And even if I was…'

'He's going to murder Charlie. I know it. Lionel's going to do it.'

'There's nothing I can do Jin.' He hesitated. 'Do you *really* know?'

'Call the police, Doc.'

'You know I can't do that. Take a breath, Jin. Steady yourself down.'

I tried. It didn't work. I burst out, 'This is wasting time.'

'Think about it. What can the police do – really? There's no evidence. They have no authority.'

'You *have* to do something, Doc. I'm not in town right now. I won't be back for…for an hour, at least. Maybe more, I don't know. There's something I have to do here. Even if I left now it would take twenty minutes to get to the hospital. We can't stand aside and let this happen. Where are you?'

'Look, I doubt if anything's going to happen in the surgery…'

189

This was taking too long. I needed to get moving. I had to help Jill. 'It's his chance, don't you see, Doc. It's Lionel's chance. A slip with the knife and it's over. That's what he wants. I *told* you. He won't be suspected. It'll just be one of those things.'

'It doesn't work like that, Jin. There are too many people there – monitoring the procedure. If it's a routine operation, Charlie will be safe for the moment. It might even be finished by now. He might be safely back in the ward.'

'You have to do something to protect him. I *will* when I get there.'

'I don't see what I can do.'

'You think he is safe in surgery, Doc?'

'Yes, I do.'

'Then we have to make sure he is safe afterwards.' I thought of something. 'Doc, how well do you know the maintenance man at the hospital...?'

I found the house in Gretna: it was a bungalow. There was a line of them. I parked on the same side of the street, out of sight of its windows, but able to see the car on the runners at the side. It was a red Astra with the correct registration. It was headfirst against the house. That made it easier. I slipped from my car and crept forward.

The street was clear. If I kept low enough, the car would keep me out of view of the house – but it would look suspicious to anyone watching elsewhere. There were no other options. The car had a 'if you can read this you're too close' sticker on the back window and an Ecosse badge beneath it. I crouched in behind and fumbled underneath its bumper, the opposite side to the exhaust – as I'd been told. There *was* something. It was plasticy. I yanked at it. It wouldn't budge. What now? It was taped in place – I felt the strands, tried to pick them loose. It was taking too long.

190

Keep at it!

I took out my penknife and jabbed away. I tugged it free and ran, hiding the package at my side like a rugby player with the ball. I thought of Jackie in Tesco's car park, doing exactly the same thing.

Sweat poured from my brow into my eyes.

I drove off hurriedly and stopped a mile further on, calling Jill's number. 'I have the package.'

She answered, 'You've to bring it to my salon. Call again when you get there – and wait in the car.'

I headed back to Dumfries.

'I thought you'd want to know – Charlie's out of surgery. It went well, they say.'

'Thanks, Doc. I'll be there in half an hour, I hope. I'm on the A75, back to Dumfries.'

'This would be the time, Jin, if anyone wanted to…to do anything.'

Why was this happening? Had Charlie contacted Lionel about the note, after I left, wanting to discuss it with him? And Lionel had rearranged to bring Charlie in early? I should have told Charlie about my fears yesterday. I thought I had more time to prove Lionel's guilt.

'I'm outside the salon.'

Jill's voice. 'I'll call you back.'

I watched as a young woman – might have been Jill's daughter – stuck her head out of the open door and waved to me. I waved back. It was foolish and light. She scanned the street both ways and disappeared back in.

My phone buzzed.

'Bring the package to my flat, Jinky.' It hung up.

I didn't have time for this. I rang back. It kept ringing. What
191

are they playing at?

I drove over to Jill's flat. The downstairs door was open. I climbed the stairs, the package under my arm. Her door was slightly ajar. I pushed it.

A middle-aged man with thinning hair stood in the middle of the floor. His high-patterned shirt showed snakes and parrots in the jungle, his trousers failed to reach his ankles, showing a fully exposed pair of white socks and brown sandals. *And* there was the long-bladed knife in his outstretched fist. I couldn't see the colour of its handle. His other arm lay cradled in a blue sling.

'Put the package on the floor,' he grumbled, and his grimace showed discoloured, larger-than-normal, tombstone front teeth. A coffee-drinking rabbit came to mind.

He added, 'She's in there.' The knife flicked towards a door.

I hesitated. I thought about rushing him – taking him. The knife flashed again. I dropped the parcel and moved towards the door. He watched me.

I opened it. Jill was sitting on a chair in the middle of her bedroom, her hands and feet taped. There was another strip across her mouth.

I turned back to the room. The man had gone – along with the package.

'I'll go after him,' I said.

Jill shook her head frantically: her eyes wide. I tugged away the tape round her mouth.

'Let him go,' she shouted.

I was inches away from her face. I pulled back. 'We can't let him away with it, Jill.'

'He'll torch my salon – that's what he said. I'll lose everything. I can't let that happen. It's all I have. You *must* let him go.'

I thought of Charlie Menzies being wheeled away to a ward.

The tape was wound several times round her wrists and

ankles. It was taking too long. I needed to move. I took out my penknife once more. 'This isn't finished, Jill, we'll go to the police...'

She broke in immediately, 'No police, Jinky. I can't lose my business.'

'I have to go, Jill. I need to be somewhere else. Will you be all right?' What could I expect her to say?

She nodded. 'Go then, go. I'll be fine. He has what he wanted – he won't be back.'

I reached the door and turned. 'Who was he?'

I knew what she'd say.

'William Bones.'

'Where are you, Jin? We've seen him.'

'I'm just coming through the hospital front door, Doc. I had to dump the car. Where's Lionel?'

'He's already *in* Charlie's ward. He must be checking up on him.'

'Can't you stop him?'

'I'm too far away. You're closer.'

'I need to put my phone off, Doc. It says so on the signs.'

'Go straight there, Jin. Ward 7. Do you hear? Ward 7. Right at the far end of the corridor, last room. You can get there before us.'

I charged up the stairs, two at a time. I couldn't let this happen. No-one was going to stop me. I reached the second floor and sprinted down the corridor of the ward. Beds on either side held patients too sick or too drugged to notice me. It wasn't visiting time. They were alone. There were no nurses at the nurse station. Where was everyone?

I could see a room at the far end: its door facing me. It was closed. A black shape moved across the circular window in the door. My footsteps clattered against the walls and ceiling: my lungs were heaving now. The muscles in my legs complained, and my chest was aching, my shirt sticking to my skin.

I burst into the room – the door smacking against the wall with the force. Immediately I saw a big man. He was hunched over an unconscious, large body, lying flat on the bed. The man straightened, pulled away: the tube of the drip feeding into Charlie's right hand moved. He turned, his hands rose in mock surrender. I recognised Lionel's face from the photograph: although it had widened out over the years from his graduation. His black suit looked expensive. A suit in this heat?

He backed away from the bed. I froze. I saw the hypodermic needle in his right hand. It was empty – pushed all the way in. He had injected straight into the catheter feeding into Charlie's wrist.

'Don't. Don't do that,' I shouted. My hand shook as I pointed. I knew it was stupid. I knew it was too late.

There was a smile playing on Lionel's face. 'It's been done,' he said, calmly.

I turned for help. The room was large and empty except for a sink and an impressive machine rigged up to the patient. It sat on a trolley to his left and gave off a ping like sonar. I couldn't see an alarm. There was a curtain behind the bed. It could be behind there.

The sun shone in. The window was big. I rushed to it. I screamed at it. I shouted for help through the glass. Two stories up, I shouted for help.

The door had closed, its window showing an empty corridor outside. I charged to the side of the bed and shook Charlie. 'Wake up, wake up.'

The machine, with its light blue metallic front, monitored his heart. If I switched it off, someone would come running.

Or was it keeping his heart beating?

I wiped the sweat from my eyes and turned to Lionel. He was by the sink. 'How could you do this to him? You're a doctor, for God's sake.'

194

'Do what?' His tone was indignant. He thrust his shoulders back and his chest out as he spoke. 'I'm giving him post-op care. Complications can set in. I'm making sure. It wouldn't be too surprising, would it, though? Look at the state of his body. Look at his size.'

'What can I do to save him? Tell me what to do,' I pleaded.

Stupid question again. He's not going to help.

He shook his head. His black hair was glossy and moved freely. 'There's nothing.' He grinned.

I ran to the door, opened it, and yelled along the corridor for a nurse, for a doctor. I shouted for help again.

'I sent them away on errands,' Lionel said.

I glared back. 'What have you done to him?' I should grab him. He was bigger but maybe I could beat out an answer.

Lionel let his smile fall. He talked gently. 'There is no need to worry. It's over now. He's finished. There is nothing to be done, I can assure you. And I'll do my best to make certain he doesn't feel anything.'

Suddenly, I felt exhausted, weak – my legs faltering. The sweat ran down my skin – every surface covered and flowing. I had no energy in my body. I couldn't fight him. What good would it do anyway?

Lionel said, 'He got what he deserved.' A harsh smile broke across his face.

At the far end of the corridor, through the window in the door, I saw Doc Halliday. He was still in his golfing gear, his bare legs the colour of the walls. He had a nurse beside him. They were walking towards me, towards the room, but they weren't hurrying. Their steps were in unison. It gave me a surge of hope. I shouted and waved my hands, cajoling them to move faster. They would be able to see me through the window. They didn't speed up.

Lionel spoke, 'No-one will believe what you say. No-one will take your word over mine. They won't find what's in the
195

injection. You need to know precisely what you are looking for. Once in the bloodstream it becomes virtually undetectable. You need very sophisticated machinery to test for it. We don't have anything like that here. They won't even look – it'll seem like a natural reaction to the surgery. We'll go through the motions, of course. We'll try to resuscitate him. It won't work. Listen for the monitor. Any second now.' Another cruel grin twisted in his face.

'It's your word against mine. Johnstone, isn't it? He mentioned you last night. I know who you are and I know who they'll believe. He has no chance. Let it go.'

I glanced back again. They were halfway along the corridor. They weren't rushing: they were moving slowly, one deliberate step after the other, walking together, side by side. I shouted again. The machine in the corner beeped.

What can I do? Give Charlie mouth to mouth? What good would that do?

'You want to know why?' Lionel asked, suddenly, peering through the window in the door. He could see along the corridor.

'It's obvious – for the money. You needed the money,' I spat out.

'That's only the half of it.'

I could seize the syringe from his hand. There might still be liquid inside. It wouldn't help Charlie but it might be enough for the police.

Lionel was saying. 'He killed my parents.' He noted my shock. 'Yes, that's right – my kindly Uncle Charles.' His eyes went back to watching the door.

'I thought they died in a car crash.'

'They did. They were in *his* car when it happened.' Lionel motioned to the bed. 'It wasn't in a fit state to be driven. The report said that. The brakes were faulty. *He* deserves to die – it's as simple as that. My parents would be alive if he hadn't
196

given them his car to drive.'

'And what about Manfred? Did he deserve to die?'

'That was unfortunate. He got in the way. His timing was out. If his mother hadn't passed on that suitcase... Where was it?'

'In the loft. He put it all the way up in the loft. He was never going to mention it.'

The door opened. Doc and the nurse strode into the room: they could have been of the same age. They stopped, and coolly sized up the situation.

Anger, frustration, tension – they all burst from me. I couldn't keep still. I took a couple of quick steps and was in front of Doc's face, pointing, shouting, 'He's poisoned him. Lionel's poisoned Charlie. You have to do something. It's in his bloodstream. I saw him inject something into that tube there. You have to do something, Doc. I *told* you this would happen.'

Doc Halliday raised his hands to calm me. He laid a hand on my shoulder. I shoved it away with force. 'Do something!' I roared.

He stood still. The nurse remained beside him.

I moved beside the bed, motioning frantically at the lying figure. They wouldn't budge: standing stock still. I glimpsed Lionel pulling a wet syringe from the sink. 'Look at this,' he said. 'Shocking. Someone has left a used syringe in this sink. Nurse, come over here and dispose of it, will you?'

'Don't do that,' I shouted at her. 'It's the evidence.'

'Looks to me as though it's been washed,' Lionel answered, smugly, holding the syringe up to eye-level.

'Doc,' I begged. 'Don't let him get away with this.'

Why wouldn't he move?

The monitor beeped steadily.

Doc looked on. 'Why don't we wait until the police arrive?' he said.

197

Lionel piped up, nodding towards me, 'Quite right. Get this lunatic out of my hospital.'

I shouted, 'Doc, you have to do something for Charlie. Pump his stomach, or whatever you do. Why are you just standing there? Get rid of the poison in his body.'

Doc, again, held his hands up to quieten me.

'Just do anything,' I implored. 'He's going to die. Charlie will die. Why can't you understand that? What do I have to say?'

He didn't move. The nurse didn't move.

The next thought made me feel sick. 'Oh, no. Don't tell me. Oh, no. You're in this as well. You're all in this together. How much did he say he'd pay you, Doc?'

Doc bridled and shouted back, his finger pointing straight at me. 'Don't say another word, Jin.'

'Or is this something else?' I went on. 'Is this doctors keeping together, is that it? Avoiding a scandal? You wouldn't want that, would you? Not in your precious hospital. *But it's not yours anymore, Doc!* Don't you know that?'

'You need to calm yourself down,' he shouted back.

'And why are you here anyway, Halliday?' Lionel asked, huffily.

Doc said, 'I'm doing a favour. The police will be soon. I phoned Chief Constable Harris.'

We stood. No-one shifted. No-one spoke. I looked at Charlie in his bed. He seemed to be breathing well – for now. The sheet curved high over his vast belly. The machine gave another beep. The room was quiet. Lionel checked his watch.

Another beep.

Charlie's heart was beating. We stood.

Beep.

What was the point in waiting?

Beep.

Lionel shuffled his feet. Beep. Charlie's breathing was
198

comfortable.

Beep. Were we supposed to wait, beep, until the poison took effect? Beep. Was that all there was to do? Beep. Lionel glanced over to the bed. Beep. He was looking edgy now. Beep. Something should have happened. Beep. Sweat formed on his brow. Beep. Doc dragged out a smile. Beep. He was staring at Lionel. Beep. The nurse was grinning. Beep. Lionel's eyes flicked to his watch. Beep. I let out a long-held breath. Another beep.

The door burst open. Ed stormed in, a uniformed officer beside him. He saw me and gave off a foul look. 'What's this about? What's *he* been doing now?'

Doc stepped forward. Charlie's monitor beeped steadily on.

Lionel said, 'If you'll excuse me I need to attend to other patients.'

'Stay where you are,' barked Doc. He started to move towards the bed. 'Nice, regular beat. Sounds like you've done a good job, Lionel.' He turned and spoke to Ed. 'This patient has just undergone a routine heart operation. As you can see from the monitor everything is just as it should be, thanks to the surgeon over there, Lionel Menzies.'

A smile, no more than a twitch, flickered over Lionel's face.

Doc tapped the patient's chart. 'Supra ventricular tachycardia,' he said to the policeman. 'Charlie must have been experiencing palpitations: worrying, uncomfortable, but not too serious. Normally this operation can be done by local anaesthetic, but Lionel would have argued that, with Charlie's size, it was safer to go for general anaesthesia in case complications set in and the patient needed to be intubated. Of course, Lionel wasn't expecting his patient to waken up at all.'

Doc pulled away at the curtain behind the bed with all the flourish of a magician. It revealed a second drip. 'But what Lionel didn't know,' he continued, 'is that I had Charlie rigged up to a drip on *this* side as well. It feeds down behind the bed,
199

through the cannular, and into the *left* hand side of the patient.' He tugged on the sleeve of the gown, exposing the left wrist where the tubes entered the arm.

Ed stepped in for a look.

Doc said, 'The drip in full view, over on that side, is a dummy – nothing more than that.' His eyes were lit by excitement as he paced round the bed quickly, forcing Ed to take a sudden backward step to avoid a collision.

Doc went on in flamboyant mode, his hand running up and down the decoy drip-line. 'It looks like the real thing – it's supposed to. I had the nurse, an old friend of mine, put in what we call a double blind.'

The nurse, standing by herself, returned his smile.

Doc directed the next comment towards Lionel. 'We used to have these as a training mechanism: long before you were a student. It was stopped when it was deemed to be too cruel – to the doctors.

It allowed genuine practice on patients. I can't tell you how many times trainee doctors have issued a lethal dose: injecting patients with ten times, sometimes as much as a hundred times the required strength of drug. And when it's pointed out to them, when they actually believe they have administered this deadly dose...' He shrugged emphatically. 'It is a lesson they never forgot. One minute they think they have killed their patient, the next there is relief. They have been given a second chance. It makes them check and double check everything. It made them better doctors. And then they banned it, of course.'

Doc glanced round the room before going on, 'This drip-line from the bag does not enter the body, as it appears. In fact it is made up of two, parallel tubes. Anything injected into the catheter is gathered in the second tube.' He held it up and twisted it. We saw a colourless liquid wash back and forth.

Lionel made a burst for the bed. Doc was too quick, blocking his way, a defensive elbow catching Lionel across his cheek.
200

The uniformed officer leapt forward and grabbed Lionel by the arm.

Doc held the tube in both hands and rocked the liquid within. 'What you will find in here, inspector, is, well, I don't know what it is, but we can safely say it is a poison of some sort. Something to induce myocardial infarction – a heart attack.'

The machine on the trolley beeped again.

I was interviewed in a bare room at the police station with High-Heid-Yin-Harris in attendance. I told them everything I knew: from the first meeting with Mrs Mann, to the finding of the note. I gave the order of events, as I saw them.

Manfred goes to his doctor, or maybe has a routine examination at the Well Man Clinic. A heart problem is detected and it leads to a meeting with a consultant – Lionel.

Perhaps around that time Mrs Mann summons Manfred to her care home and shows him the note. She has decided to tell him about his birth mother while she can remember: she realises it can't be put off any longer. Manfred has the same mother as his life-long friend. It should have been the most obvious thing to tell his newfound brother. But something stopped him.

Over one of their many drinks together, it plays on Manfred's mind, it lingers, a secret. He doesn't want to have secrets from his friend – but, then, he hasn't mentioned his heart condition either. He hesitates. We know he hesitates.

Why doesn't he say?

He may have promised Mrs Mann, his mother, as he thought at the time, not to divulge what she was about to tell him. It's possible. It may be something else.

As time wears on, Manfred's desire to share the information increases unbearably. He talks it through with Lionel: someone he trusts, the specialist, the expert, the man who's dealing with

201

his heart, his life. It is perfect. Lionel can give a family viewpoint on the matter and the doctor-patient confidentiality stops him revealing anything to his uncle.

At this point, Lionel has already decided to murder Charlie. Coming back to Dumfries has only highlighted the harsh facts of his life: his parents are dead and Charlie has flourished. Lionel needs to level things up – and, of course, he needs the money. He's the heir. It's his right. He might even have convinced himself that Charlie's murder was justified: it is revenge for the man to blame for his parents' death.

Suddenly, in one conversation, in one sentence, Manfred's disclosure alters his plan. Manfred must die first. Lionel can't take the risk of leaving him alive. Charlie must not know he has a brother, or the will might change. Lionel needs the money: he has debts. It is his by right.

Initially, though, Lionel manages to take a step back. He thinks better of it: an innocent man should not die. He convinces Manfred to keep the secret, and Manfred, resolutely, goes to the bother of placing the suitcase in the loft – well out of the way. But the letter cannot be destroyed: it is too precious.

However, as days pass, Lionel becomes increasingly worried. He cannot take a chance on Manfred's silence – especially after Charlie's death. He doesn't want Manfred laying claim to anything, so Manfred has to die. There is no other way.

They become friendly but Lionel forgets to take the library book back and it is left in the house. Lionel drives the car out to the countryside, to the dead-end lane, and injects Manfred with the same substance he tried to give Charlie – and then walks back to town. It is simple: no-one will suspect.

What was it that stopped Manfred from telling Charlie? Maybe he thought it might produce complications. He didn't want their friendship to alter in any way: he was more than happy with their relationship. It can't be bettered: and they have been brothers anyway in everything but name. Charlie is a very wealthy man and money is a danger. It can twist trust, sense, and reason round its finger. Why risk a change if there is chance, albeit a faint one, that it will make things worse?

Whether the police believed any part of this, I don't know. They sat and listened and said nothing. When I finished, I asked them how much had matched Lionel's statement.

'He's not talking. Completely silent,' Ed replied. He was more civil towards me – perhaps the presence of High-Heid-Yin-Harris had something to do with it. 'He may stay that way. We might never know the full story. But, at least, we have the liquid. It will take a while for it to be analysed. And we have the film of him injecting it as well – thanks to you.' The last part was said with a glance over to his superior.

'Is the use of video evidence allowed in Scotland?' I asked.

'It all helps.'

Doc Halliday, still in his golfing gear, was waiting for me, leaning against the gate, when I left the police station. I reckoned he had been contacted: his timing was too good. We walked slowly for a while, towards my car. I told him, sheepishly, that I was sorry for what I had said in the hospital.

He put an arm round my shoulder as we lumbered on. 'It was understandable. A heated time. You don't need to worry about it.' He withdrew his arm to allow another of his generous shrugs. 'Perhaps I should have said something to you.'

I kept quiet and he went on, 'When I stepped into that room, I needed to assess the situation, figure out what, exactly, had happened. And I didn't want to start explaining there and then: not until the police arrived to restrain him: I didn't want Lionel running off. *And*, to be completely honest, Jin, I wanted to observe his reaction. Once I knew you were right, I wanted to see that smug expression dissolve from his face. It was priceless. It will live with me for a very long time – thanks to you, my boy. How much did the Chief Constable tell you?'

'Harris? Tell me what?'

'Ah, he can be a bit like that.' He coughed. 'I think, then, it falls upon me to explain things further. I think we owe you that.'

'Owe me?'

'Yes, you see there's a little bit more behind Lionel leaving Edinburgh than I said. I was about to mention it earlier, at the golf course – but then you rushed away. What happened there? What was the hurry?'

I dismissed it. 'Nothing... nothing to do with Charlie, at least. Another problem.'

'And it's fixed? Do you need help with it?'

'Thanks, Doc, but I should be able to sort it out soon enough. I've friends who'll help if needs be.'

'Good, well, getting back Lionel Menzies, there *was* his gambling – I told you about that – but there was something else. It was suspected he may have obtained money from an elderly, wealthy patient. Nothing could be proved, mind you: they were only flimsy suspicions. But, it was decided, by mutual agreement, that he should leave the hospital in Edinburgh.'

'What about the patient? What did they have to say?'

'Nothing – she died.'

I gave a nod.

'Natural causes. Well, that's what was thought at the time. In the light of today, I imagine it'll need to be re-examined now.' He paused to allow me time to say something. I kept walking, so he went on, 'The authorities put a word in our ear down here to keep a look out for any irregularities in relation to Lionel – not that we were thinking of his relations, if you know what I mean. As I say, nothing could be proved in Edinburgh and, as Lionel is an excellent surgeon, he was a boon to the area. With
204

my contacts at the hospital, I was asked to keep an ear to the ground and a nose to the wind – no mention of what to do with the throat, though.' He gave a laugh. 'Medical joke,' he explained to my stony face, turning out another brief chortle.

'And it was your friend, High-Heid-Yin-Harris, who asked you to do this?'

Doc nodded back. 'But I'd heard nothing. Then you started asking about Lionel yesterday, so we had to decide how much to tell you. And then you dropped that bombshell today. Well, I didn't know what to do.'

'What *did* you do after I drove away?'

'I played golf,' he replied, as though it was obvious. 'In fact, I was just lining up a birdie putt when the call came through from the hospital about Charlie's operation.'

'Unusual for you, Doc.'

'I know, I know, not the done thing, having the phone on – and I've always said that people using them on the golf course should be buried up to their necks in the ninth hole pot bunker...'

'No, I meant putting for a birdie.'

He scrunched up his mouth and produced a short hum, before going on, 'Anyway, I needed it on in case anyone wanted to contact me: delicate times, of course. I didn't like the way things were shaping up. And, naturally, after that call, I knew I needed to act quickly. Even if your accusations weren't correct, it wasn't the time to take chances.'

We walked on in silence for a few moments. It reminded me that I hadn't switched my phone on since the hospital. There was a text waiting from Hoogah – it couldn't be too important – I let it lie.

'Why didn't someone phone you last night – when Charlie was admitted?' I asked.

'Well, for a start, Lionel had managed to do it on the quiet. He did the organising himself. And, also, my, eh, contacts at the hospital don't work nights. It was only when they turned up this morning that they saw Charlie was first in.'

We'd reached my car now. Fortunately, it hadn't been clamped up at the hospital despite being abandoned at the front door. I'd left the keys in the ignition and its door open and someone had thoughtfully moved it round the corner into the car park. I'd followed the police car holding Lionel back down to the station. As I opened its door, a burst of heat sprang out: glad to be released into the open.

'What made you think of the maintenance man?' Doc's thumb and forefinger stroked his chin as he asked.

I rested an elbow on the roof – it was too hot. I jumped away as though stung, walking round the outside of the car, opening the doors, winding down the windows. 'The boys had been talking about web-cams: the one at the Robert Burns Centre and the other one at the hospital. Chisel said they have a live feed now, so it seemed like a good way to monitor and record the situation – as long as you could get Charlie into a room where the camera could pick him up. Was there any problem changing things round?'

'It wasn't *too* difficult, once we'd figured out which part of the building we could zoom in on. Then we arranged for Charlie's bed to be in clear view of the window, as you said. That was it: we only had to move two beds into another ward. It was a small effort to make if there was a chance it would save a life.

I'll need to give the maintenance man something for all his efforts though: up the ladder, turning and adjusting the camera.'

'I imagine Charlie will want to show his gratitude to him as well, Doc.' I took in a breath – it had been gnawing away at me. 'What I don't understand, though, was the length of time it took you to get to the ward and along it. You didn't seem to be in much of a hurry.'

He gave a nod. 'Well, for a start, I was downstairs in the
206

room controlling the camera, which happens to be in the basement *but*, I have to say, I still didn't really think Charlie *was* in any danger. You have to understand I was in some doubt. Well, actually, quite a lot of doubt about your accusation – despite that Edinburgh business. It's not the sort of thing that goes on round here normally. I couldn't contact the police until I was sure, until I saw him do it, until I saw him give the injection – and now it's on film.' He paused and then held my stare. 'I'm sorry.'

I shrugged it away.

He had an afterthought, 'Is this what it's like for you all the time – when you're not golfing?'

'Not in the slightest, Doc. This was just another one-off.'

'There was one other thing,' Doc added, 'and I know I'm no expert in these kinds of matters, but I thought that if the two of you were left alone for a wee while, he might start talking. Isn't that what usually happens? Murderers have a desire to explain, boast, seek the audience of one? It's your word against theirs and nothing can be proved. Isn't that the way it goes?'

I nodded back. 'It's been known to happen.' I couldn't put it off any longer: I sidled in behind the steering wheel, closed the door, and looked up at him. 'How could you be so sure Lionel wouldn't just inject straight into Charlie's body?'

'I couldn't. But that's the funny part, you could say. In a weird way, Charlie's obesity saved him: it's not easy finding a vein on a large person, so the catheter is the easiest, and, just as importantly, the quickest way. And, also, Lionel wouldn't want to leave a mark on the skin, just in case suspicions were aroused.'

I gave him a smile, and asked, 'Did you make it?'

'Make what?'

'The birdie putt – when your phone went off.'

He grimaced. 'What do you think?'

I drove off, thinking I knew how hunting dogs must feel: the ones used to flush out game. And I wondered if it would be possible to have my screaming through the window at the web-cam edited out. It wouldn't be a pretty picture.

I stopped by my home for a change of clothes, something to eat, and to find a number in Glasgow. Half an hour later, as I locked my back door, and walked round to my car, it dawned on me: there was something Doc had said didn't make sense. I had spoken to him about Lionel yesterday, Wednesday. If he and Harris were waiting to see what I would find out, how was it that Harris backed me up on Tuesday, the day *before* I spoke to Doc?

There was only one answer.

I returned to Gretna. This time it was by choice but it still felt like operating behind enemy lines. I parked in Woodside Road and knocked at the door – the red Astra wasn't there this time. A woman, probably about my age, answered, her hair was pitch black and awry. She was in a large, white lace summer dress with frills round the bottom – the sort they wear in Spain, if the TV's to be believed. Her sturdy form, on the raised doorstep, swelled over me. Unfortunately, the fat round her bulky waist threatened a breakout, making the middle of her dress bumfle like a squashed top hat. She held a pleasant enough expression on her face and her bare feet and legs were just as deeply tanned.

'Would you mind if I asked you a few questions?' I said.

Her eyes scrutinised me but showed no alarm at the stranger confronting her. 'I thought you were the postman: they're getting later and later every week. What's it about?'

I could tell, by the persistent stare, that she saw something familiar in me and was attempting to nail it down. They get newspapers in Gretna so it was possible she might have seen my photo at one time.

208

'My name is Johnstone,' I said, offering her memory a kick-start. 'You know there was a murder the other day in Dumfries?'

Her face registered shock. 'No, I didn't. Who was it?'

It was unlikely she would be acquainted with every person in town, but you never know, so I gave her Jackie's name.

She shook her head, slowly at first, then more firmly with relief. 'No, can't say I've heard of him.' She added, 'I work in Dumfries. You're not a reporter, are you?'

'No, but I am trying to find out who killed my friend.'

That tipped the balance. 'Oh, I know you,' she said, in a friendly way. 'So what happened? We've been away on holiday. Not long back.' Then it dawned on her and she became suspicious. 'What makes you think *I* can help you?'

I flicked a thumb towards the distance – to allow her time to decide on whether to invite me in or not. 'Is that Gretna's stadium?'

Her eyes beamed. 'Yes, it is. It's great, isn't it? Raydale Park. We can hear the cheers every time they score. It's a great place to stay: property prices have shot up because of it.'

'Right enough, it must be nice and quiet.'

She offered me a cup of tea.

They – her husband and two kids – had returned from camping in the North of France late last night. It had been a great holiday, and, on my insistence, she brought out the brochure to show me. A few minutes later, I had said goodbye. It was another step in the right direction.

This time I left my car in the correct spot at the hospital and glanced up. The web-cam had been re-positioned; it was now assessing the success of my parallel parking. The earlier text from Hoogah told me that the hotel up by Sanny's old caravan was going to be demolished this afternoon, and he wanted to know if I fancied going up to watch. 'Another slice of history' he had added in sarcastic quotation marks.

I didn't reply. I wasn't sure. I couldn't make up my mind: I was getting tired. It had been a long day and it had only just turned one o'clock.

I spoke to the nurse on duty. She allowed me in for a few minutes, even though it wasn't visiting hours. Charlie was awake, but still lying flat on his back. His heart monitor beeped merrily and now there was only one drip feeding into his left hand. I found a chair from the hallway and pulled it up to the bedside. His head turned towards me.

'How are you doing Charlie?'

His skin was pale and his voice was weak and husky, 'Don't bother to sit down.'

'The nurse says you're doing fine. But I won't stay long: I know you'll be exhausted. Just wanted to see how you were.'

'Get out of here,' he rasped back, using all the venom he could muster.

'It's me. Jin.'

'I know who you are. Get out.' His hand struggled to lift itself from the bed, his finger pointed in the general direction of the door. 'I'll have the nurse throw you out.' He was becoming weaker by the second. 'Leave me alone. I don't want to see you.' He turned his head away.

I stood up and bent over the bed to get his attention. 'What's wrong, Charlie? Didn't you hear what happened?'

He whispered back in a hushed, forlorn sigh, his face turning from anger to sadness in a flash. 'I heard. Now go.'

I remained, not sure what to do.

When he spoke again, his eyes were closed. 'I have no-one left. And it's down to you.' A tear escaped out the corner of his eye and over the bridge of his nose. The red button was lying on his bed this time. He must have pressed it. The nurse hurried in.

I said to her, 'It's okay. He wants me to leave. I'm going.' I turned back. 'I hope you improve quickly, Charlie, I do. I'll come and see you when you're better.'

I heard a 'don't bother' from him as I left the room.

The nurse walked along the corridor with me. 'Sometimes there's a reaction to the drugs,' she said. 'Some people vomit, others have been known to hallucinate. It might be that.'

It didn't seem to be the case here.

I returned home, threw my clothes off, and collapsed onto my bed, worn-out and bewildered.

I heard the noise of the text coming through, travelling along a corridor to reach me. It took an age to understand what it was and to pull myself awake. The pillow under my head was damp and my hair was wringing wet. I'd been asleep for more than an hour but didn't feel any better.

The message was from Hoogah again – he was up at the old hotel and the demolition was underway. Was I coming to seeing it?

I wandered through to the kitchen, pulled the calendar down from the wall, and took out a pen. A few moments later I had the answer – yes, I *did* want to go over to the hotel, but it was more to see Hoogah, not the destruction. He wasn't going to be at all happy: I had some very bad news for him.

I sipped at a glass of water. The sleep had ordered my brain, organised the facts. The plan was clear, obvious. I sent a text to Hoogah telling him I'd be there soon and then sent more messages to the rest of the boys inviting them to a meeting in the pub tonight. If they were willing, I would ask them to help me catch Jackie's killer. As a group, we could do it.

After a cool shower, I tugged on my new shorts and t-shirt, bought earlier on a quick visit to the Gretna Outlet Village – although that had felt like giving funds to the foe – and drove out to the Lockerbie Road.

Sanny's old caravan had gone. There was nothing to indicate it had ever been there except a bare rectangle of dried earth. There was no blue plaque, nothing to remind the world of what once had been. I turned away – at least the weeds would be glad of a new space to be conquered, but only until the new houses appeared.

Halfway up the old drive, a mesh of wire barriers blocked the way. I skirted round. At the top of the hill, at the back of the hotel, some people had gathered to witness the fall of the great building. I saw Hoogah, gave him a wave, and wandered over. We gave each other a nod but said nothing. The demolition was in full swing.

I had expected a wrecking ball at the very least, or a controlled explosion, at best, but, instead, we were offered the sight of a slow-chugging bulldozer with an extendable arm and a small claw at the end. It wasn't too bad though. The roof was bashed away – the tiles cracking like fireworks – then it was the turn of the walls, and they caved in with clouds of dust.

An elderly man approached us – he might have been the same person we'd seen yesterday near to Sanny's new caravan – the one I couldn't quite place. I nudged Hoogah. The man's white hair had been the victim of a recent and brutal haircut but, splendidly, he hadn't fallen foul of the current hot weather fashion and had stuck to his guns with a smart pair of light grey trousers and a loose white shirt. His sprightly walk was unhindered by his sturdy sandals – no socks.

'Hello there,' he said to me. He looked well cared for and well nourished, and without any sign of fat.

As was traditional, I gave him a sharp, 'Aye.' As did Hoogah. We were both surprised when he stopped to talk, since our response was designed purely for passing recognition.

'You don't remember me,' he stated, obviously aware of the Dumfries greeting code.

I gave his face a quick once-over again, but without resorting to a stare. 'You're familiar, right enough – but can't think from where.'

'It was *here,*' he said. 'We met *here.*' He shot out an arm in the direction of the doomed hotel. His face tried to smile but his eyes wouldn't allow it.

Then it dawned on me: I remembered the night, I remembered him. But he had continued offering more clues. 'I was dancing. In there.' This time his head nodded in the building's direction. 'It wasn't a very good light,' he added, in an attempt to stop my memory feeling too bad. 'And I was a bit more formally dressed as well when we met.'

He was the Waltzing Man. The man I'd happened upon one windy night in April. Splendid in his evening suit, he'd been dancing sublimely round and round in one of the broken-down rooms of this old hotel, in an attempt to recapture the feel of the first dance with the woman who would become his wife.

Suddenly I felt sad for him. 'It must be heartbreaking for you to see the fall of this place? Where will you dance?' I sensed a confused look from Hoogah. He would have to wait for an explanation.

The man gave a shrug back. 'I can't complain. I've had plenty of dances. I can go to a place in town now, if I want. It's fairly new. It's all the rage again – this dancing. It's even back on the TV. Imagine that.'

He stared at the demolition for a while as we shuffled our feet in preparation for walking. He went on, as expected, 'Although, it *is* a shame to see the old building going to the ground – but that's the way of things.' He gave a 'that's life' gesture. 'In some ways I'm glad it's going.'

What is it with these people? First, Sanny, and now the Waltzing Man: taking everything in their stride, unbothered, able to move, positively, on.

'I used to live here as well, you know,' he said. 'I don't think I told you that. It was a while ago.'

213

'Really? You lived here? Was Sanny's caravan around then?' I didn't realise, not until after I'd said it, that the question might be construed as being a wee bit cheeky: suggesting he predated Sanny's arrival to the grounds.

'Oh, yes, of course, he was here.'

'So that's how you know him: you were neighbours.' He *was* going to meet up with Sanny earlier. 'So you actually lived in this hotel?'

He nodded. 'I was the proprietor. That was after the war.'

Hoogah suddenly came to life. 'Wow. It must have been a grand place in its day.'

'It was. It was. And it was still doing well when I left. We moved onto another part of the country, my wife and I. I only returned recently – after she died. I had this urge to return to where it all started.' He looked at me. 'But then you know all that.'

This was interesting. I might even be able to find out some useful information. Mentally I was rubbing my hands. I started with, 'And you didn't mind Sanny staying near-by in his caravan? Weren't the guests bothered?'

'Not at all. Probably didn't even know he was there. He was never noisy: kept himself to himself.'

'Did you charge him for rent?' I asked, nonchalantly.

His face remained serious. 'No, I didn't charge him rent. Wouldn't have been allowed to.' And with that he started to leave. I wanted to stop him, there were many more questions, but he walked on, without a backward glance at the flattened hotel.

I followed Hoogah's car back to his home – it was surprising he hadn't walked over. We got out and stood in the shade of the tree in his front garden: I had turned down his offer of some tea.

'You and Lucy still together?' I asked.

'Yeah, of course. That's a strange thing to start with.'

'Maybe so. And here's something else that's strange...'

'Go on.'

'You said you'd been dating for a hundred days. You had a celebration a couple of days ago, on Tuesday, wasn't it?'

He went on the defensive. 'Right, but there's no law against that. You don't just have to be sixteen to do it.'

I went on, 'And you say she's done all these financial things to help you out – kind of as a present?'

'Yes. What's your point, Jinky?'

'How could she be organising your finances before you were an actual couple?'

'How do you mean?'

'There is a maximum amount of money anyone can put in an ISA in one tax year.'

'I know all this. I told you about it, remember?'

'You said you were onto your second ISA – which I took to mean you had one last financial year and have added to it in this new one. That would mean the first ISA started before the 6th of April.'

'Get to the point, Jinky.'

'And all this was arranged by Lucy?'

He gave a supreme sigh.

'Count back a hundred days from Tuesday, Hoogah, and see where it takes you.'

'Don't be daft, I could barely do that with a piece of paper and a pen. What are you like?'

'Okay, here's a clue: it doesn't take you into the last tax year. You have been a couple in *this* tax year only. That means your first ISA was taken out *before* the two of you were together. She was putting money into it *before* you were a couple.'

'Oh, I see.' He said the words slowly, individually.

I nodded. 'She must have been planning this, pretending to be you, for some time. That means she had information on you
215

– date of birth, employment, that kind of thing – *and* forging your signature, before she was a twinkle in your eye. Not only is that illegal, it's just a wee bit spooky as well, don't you think? What else has she been doing in your name? What else has been going on behind your back? And, just as importantly, how did she manage to get all this information?'

Hoogah gave a weary shake of the head. 'It's not right, is it? I can't let her get away with it.'

'You *could* go to the police.'

'No, no, I wouldn't do that. But what I *will* do is finish this now – finish with her.' He added, awkwardly, 'Will you come round with me to see her?'

'Not likely. This's purely a private concern.'

Five minutes later, I was driving Hoogah over to Lucy's. I let him knock on her door. He can be a very persuasive talker – and not just to get out of paying for broken windows in a manse.

By the time I arrived at The Bruce later that night all the boys were there, sitting round a table, and they were keen to congratulate me on my efforts at the hospital. I offered to buy them a round straight off, even though they didn't need one. It always helps to keep folk wrong-footed when after a favour – and a dangerous one at that.

Tread was in first. 'All this hero lark has gone to your head, man.'

'How do you mean?'

'The drinks. You know they take decimal coins in here now?'

'What will you do with that ten bob note you've been saving?' added a surprisingly cheery Asa.

I let the comment go. 'Any further word on anything?' I asked him.

Tread got there before he could reply, 'I like it, Jinky.
216

Moving on, nonchalantly. Just another run-of-the-mill day in the life of Mr. Johnstone. Merely another life saved. And not just any old person either: a millionaire at that. I wonder how much of a reward you'll get?'

'Somehow I don't think that's going to happen,' I replied, still able to hear the energy-sapping spite in Charlie's voice.

Asa shook his head, before answering my question, 'Nothing really. The poison's been sent away for analysis. Could be something like a Potassium Chloride designer derivative. That would be my guess. It does mean, however, that Manfred's body will have to be dug up and re-examined.'

Everyone, other than Asa, shivered. I got in the drinks.

When I returned I thought about telling them of Charlie's reaction – but decided against it. It was better to let the matter rest. It was over now. I chose another concern first, one that I'd been putting off, or standing firm on, for too long. I told them about Chiara, describing the way she had fled my home last Sunday. She had said she needed space but it couldn't be the whole reason: and Dorset is an awfully long way to go to get some. One of them might come up with an idea and then, maybe, I could put everything right. They obviously thought this was the subject of our meeting and launched into the problem with gusto.

Tread began, 'You said she phoned you the other day?'
I nodded.

'Why didn't you just ask her then why she ran away?'

'I don't know – never got round to it.' I wasn't going to say it was because I was crying too much.

He went on, 'What was she phoning about anyway?'
I shrugged.

Quickly, Chisel stated, 'Women don't need a reason to phone.' Everyone nodded gravely at that – it was as though Confucius had spoken.

'Was it something you said?' Asa proposed.

I shook my head. 'I'm sure I didn't say anything out of the ordinary, or different. Nothing that she could take offence at.'

'What if she's a Gretna supporter,' Tread offered. 'Strangely, there are a lot of them about nowadays. They seem to be popping up like mushrooms. And you do put them down quite a lot, Jinky.'

'*And* she would have seen your ten foot Queens flag hanging from the banister,' Hoogah put in.

'Funny. Can we get serious here? This is important to me.'

'I've got it.' It was Tread again, and he'd snapped his fingers to give his answer extra importance. I had a sinking feeling. He said, 'Who was she seeing before you – when she was staying here, in the town?'

I shrugged again.

'You never asked?' he returned, amazed. When I didn't reply, he added, 'Could it have been Rodger the lodger?' He leaned back, raising both eyebrows, pausing for emphasis. 'She goes into your house only to realise she's been there before – making hot, passionate love up on the top floor.'

'I think you'll find that's a Rolling Stones song, Tread.' Hoogah put in.

'Right, that's enough.' I said, a hint of annoyance creeping in. 'It's very unlikely, Tread. If you're not going to take this seriously…'

Asa was straight in with, 'Are you saying you're so much better looking than Rodger, that he wouldn't stand a chance? Is that why it's unlikely?'

'*Asa*,' Tread called out: a warning behind the word. He went on quickly, 'Jinky's absolutely right there. We should dismiss that idea, straight off. The odds are too much against her ever having met Rodger. Come on everyone, brains to the fore.' He lifted his glass high to show we should do the same.

I gave a sigh. It was going nowhere – and deep down Asa was still mad about last night. It was time to tell them about my

218

scheme.

A voice of sense spoke: it was Chisel, 'Did she receive a text as you were showing her round?'

'Not as far as I know. Why?'

He continued, 'You told us, a while back, that her dad hadn't been well: that's why she's never been back up. Maybe she had to rush off to see to him?'

'Surely she would have said. And, anyway, why say she was going to Dorset, then? It doesn't fit: he's in Birmingham.'

It was Hoogah: this time it was close to what I'd been thinking. 'When she saw you in your home, saw how much it meant to you, she knew you would never leave there. She's hundreds of miles away, so what chance is there of a proper relationship? She's upset – and she runs away.'

'For that to be the case she would need to have strong feelings towards Jinky,' Asa said.

'What's your point, Asa?' I demanded, staring him down. He was taking every opportunity to put me in my place.

Chisel came in hurriedly, glowering at Asa as he spoke, 'You're right, Hoogah, that's a distinct possibility.'

We finished up with this as the likeliest reason – dismissing Tread's next one of the house being haunted, never for one moment realising he was the closest to the truth.

'How come we've still never met her?' Tread asked.

'You've asked me that before.'

'And?'

I shrugged. 'I told you – she ran away before there was a chance.' I slipped in, 'Maybe that was the reason: scared of meeting you bunch. I did mention it to her. Now that's a distinct possibility.'

Tread crinkled his nose before saying, 'Is she as beautiful as Asa says?'

'I don't know what he says – but she is beautiful – and clever and...'

219

Tread stopped me, 'Okay, okay, no need to go on.'

Chisel brought in the next round. 'Tell us about the walking stick, Jinky,' he said, laying my gafoni in front of me like a bribe. Asa must have been talking – but that was allowed under our friend-sharing rule.

'It's something I'm working on,' I replied, evasively.

'Oh, we'll need more than that,' Hoogah said.

I deflected it by turning the tables on him, 'Did Hoogah tell you he's broken up with Lucy? Just this afternoon.'

The faces round the table shook from side to side, turning to stare at him: the walking stick forgotten as quickly as the need for everyday socks.

'I would have mentioned it.' Hoogah responded. 'In time.' He dealt me a sharp look. I took no notice and explained about Lucy's long-standing messing in his financial affairs.

'Just as well. I never liked it from the beginning.' It was Tread. 'I'm not saying anything against her – she might be nice enough. *But,* taking your best friend's husband, like she did – it's just not the done thing.'

Hoogah opened his mouth to say something, but Tread was in before him, 'How did she take it – the breaking up?'

'Oh, she was quiet,' he replied. 'Didn't say a word, in fact.'

I asked, 'Was that why you wanted me there? Did you think she might have reacted differently if I wasn't?'

Hoogah offered a meek nod back.

I said, standing up, 'Can I get anyone another drink – only I've a favour to ask, and it might take a wee while to explain what's needed.' I noted the order and added, 'I want us to catch Jackie's killer – together.'

Everyone jolted – even Asa. I left for the bar.

They were drumming their fingers when I returned carrying the tray. 'What is it?' Hoogah asked, in a hushed voice, as soon as I was in earshot.

'What's the plan?' said Chisel.

'I've got jobs for you – if you're interested.' I laid the tray down and a flurry of hands cleared it in seconds.

Asa spoke for the first time in a while. 'Not another of your schemes, is it?'

'*Asa.*' It was a quick and harsh word. It came from the three of them, simultaneously.

Asa said, holding his hands up, 'Okay, he did a grand job with Charlie – I'll give him that – but he doesn't always get it right, that's all I'm saying.' And then to me, 'You made a mistake with your allegations about Don Gardiner.'

'Why do you have to be so negative, Asa?' Chisel said, then leaning forward towards me, asked, 'What do you want us to do then, Jinky?'

I said, 'We're agreed we want to find this murderer, right?' I could see Asa bite his tongue, so I added, 'I know it should be a police concern, but there's nothing definite I can tell them at this moment. And, anyway, I'm not all that welcome up there. You know that, Asa.'

Chisel said, 'I like the idea of some investigative journalism, for once. Better than having to report after the event.'

'Are you in, Asa?' I asked him. 'But I don't want you getting into any bother with your superiors.'

'Count me out,' he replied, shuffling in his seat to create some distance from us.

'I'm in, Jinky,' Tread urged.

'Have you still got the keys to my house, Asa? Can you hand them back?'

I explained the plan.

'That's it, I've heard enough.' Asa stood up. 'I'll have nothing to do with this hair-brained scheme and if any of you have any sense you'll do the same as me.' He downed his drink and stormed off.

After a few moments of silence, Hoogah piped up, 'Ignore him, Jinky, we'll see to it. Right lads?'

They all nodded.

He went on, 'So what are *you* going to do while we're organising all that?'

'Me? I'm going on holiday. To France.' I swung my glass down onto the table and strolled away.

Friday 21st July

My phone buzzed. It was Hoogah. 'Jinky, where are you?'
His voice was loud, anxious.

'In Glasgow. In the passport office. What's wrong?' I stood
up from the queuing seats and walked to one side. A temporary
fan, sitting on the floor, moved its head from side to side as
though watching a very slow tennis match, as it dispensed half-
hearted air through the lukewarm office.

It had been another early start. At least the roads had been
quiet on the seventy-six mile journey up, until the edge of the
city, and then it had been horrendous. It must take a special
kind of person to face that amount of traffic every day.

I'd taken Manfred's car: it was newer than mine, probably
more reliable for the long journey to come, *and* it had air-
conditioning. It wouldn't have crossed my mind before, but I
was still a bit miffed at Charlie and this felt like getting back at
him. It was a silly, childish gesture; although after a bone-
chilling blast of cold air, I was chittering blissfully, and
annoyed with myself for not using it sooner.

'Something terrible's happened,' Hoogah was saying on the
phone. He sounded angry, tired, and close to tears.

'What is it?'

'I just woke up. And there it was – lying in my bed, beside
me. It's awful. How could anyone do that?'

'What are you talking about? Are you all right?'

There was a loud swallowing noise. 'I suppose I'll get over
it.' He was quiet for a few moments and he had calmed down a
tad when he added, 'How could anyone leave *that* on my
pillow, Jinky?'

It felt safe to lighten the tone. 'Let me guess: a horse's
head?'

'Wrong end,' he replied, wearily. There was another pause
before the rebuke came, 'This is serious, you know.'

223

'What do you mean wrong end?' Then I understood. 'Get rid of it straightaway, Hoogah. Do you hear me? Bin it. There's no point hanging onto it. Put it in the dustbin outside.'

'What about the police?'

'I doubt if they'll be all that bothered. Tell me how it happened.'

He gave a deep sigh before going on, 'As I said, when I woke up, it was there. A pony tail. *My* pony tail – lying on the pillow. Severed.'

'You didn't feel anything when it was happening: when it was cut?'

The man at the counter beckoned me forward. I had all the documents in my hand. I'd phoned yesterday for an appointment for the fast-track service, receiving this early time. It was obvious the man didn't appreciate me being on the phone, and he was right but I couldn't hang up: Hoogah was still explaining.

'I stayed in the pub after you left. Felt a touch down after dumping the girlfriend, I suppose. Had a bit of a skinful – *and* it is still the holidays.'

'You think Lucy did this to you? In the middle of the night?'

'Who else could it be? It has to be her, Jinky. Revenge.'

I handed over my forms and my photos, taken by the machine in Tesco at six this morning. The man glared again at the phone at my ear. I nodded to him in recognition of my lack of manners and gave a look which I hoped implied that the call was extremely urgent.

'You'll need to change the locks, Hoogah,' I said. 'You should have asked for your keys back yesterday.'

'Jinky, I never gave her a set of keys.'

No surprise there. I said, 'I need to go now. But try not to worry, she's probably got it out of her system – but *do* get the locks done. I know a good person. In any case, Hoogah, you said you were contemplating having your pony tail cut off for a

224

change of image.'

'I was saving it for when Queens get promotion.'

'Look on the bright side: at least your future won't be lucid from now on.'

'What are you talking about?'

'It won't be Lucy– ed anymore.'

'So now we know who's been eating all the puns.'

I was back on the M74, in the delightful cool air, with my newly printed passport in my pocket. There was another reason for keeping the air conditioning chilly – I didn't want to fall asleep at the wheel. I hadn't slept any better last night and the early return from the pub had only resulted in hours of lying and sweating, feeling the mattress burn beneath my skin. It had forced me to rise much earlier than required and, inside my oppressive bedroom, faintly light outside, I'd filled the time by packing and repacking my suitcase before soaking in another cool bath.

The long drive south finally came to an end when I reached the Warwick service station on the M40. I stopped the car and gave out a long, weary sigh. From Glasgow, the outside temperature had climbed steadily – at a rate of almost one degree per hour – and as the frigid air blew, the gauge pushed towards thirty-four degrees outside. France, according to the latest weather report, was to hit a roaring forty today. I wasn't sure I could survive in that.

It was a half hour wait before the taxi pulled up. Tiredness had closed in on me: it was an effort to stay awake. Fortunately, I spotted Chiara skipping from the vehicle in a white, sleeveless summer dress, a suitcase in her hand. I squeezed out and shouted across. She gave a wave, rushed over, and threw her case into the open boot. We kissed. There was a thrill but exhaustion managed to wipe away some of the joy at seeing her again. I moved into the passenger seat; my eyes closing again

225

as she familiarised herself with the controls of the car. And we were off, with the hint of a wheel spin.

I didn't really think she would take me up on a trip abroad: we were staying in a tent after all, not the luxury she was used to. But there had been no harm in asking – and she *had* made the comment about taking a holiday some time when I was free.

She was still in Dorset when I'd called yesterday. She'd had her meeting with the developer and needed little persuading in taking this trip; despite the fact that I asked her to book it for me, using her name, along with my address. I would be paying for everything, of course, but she would do the driving in France. By the time I phoned again this morning, to check the details, she had returned to Birmingham to drop off her car.

'New model?' she asked. 'Really splashing out on the money these days, eh?'

I gave a very brief explanation without opening my eyes.

'I want to explain why I hurried away last time,' she said, quickly. It sounded as though she had been practising the words.

I raised my eye-lids to half-mast. 'Could you tell me another time, please, Chiara? All I want to do is sleep right now. I'm really tired. It's been a long drive down.'

I saw her bite her lip and give a slight nod. I wound my seat back to the horizontal and was asleep in seconds.

We arrived at Dover with very little time to spare for the 9.25pm ferry to Calais. Fortunately, the campsite wasn't far on the other side – probably the reason why it is so popular.

'You've remembered your passport?' she asked, as we waited to board. 'It's a long way to come without it.' She gave a laugh.

'Yup, got it this morning.' Bouts of cat-naps had helped considerably. 'The last time I had one was on a cruise to Norway with the school. It's been a rush.'

226

'And you think it will be worth the effort?'

'I hope so. I've never been to France. Norway, England and Wales – that's my lot.'

'Do you ever drink red wine?'

'Not very often.'

Chiara drove on the other side of the road without any problem: I would have found it extremely difficult, especially in the dark. The gate was shut when we arrived at the campsite but the young man at the reception opened up for us. His name was Ben, he was English, and very helpful. When his phone rang, he was able to check our booking, direct us to our tent, whilst speaking on the phone in French. It made me feel rather inadequate.

I've camped with the lads once before but that was many years ago and up the Scaur valley, miles from anywhere, so I was completely unprepared for the amount of noise on the site: even at this late hour, laughter and conversations filled the warm night air. Packed together tightly, with flimsy strips of canvas for separation, privacy was a difficult beast to find.

No need for covers, we lay, cuddled, uncaring of the sticky contact of our skin. Our bed croaked like a frog. We slowed to barely moving. A man coughed behind us, a few feet away, so clear he could have been standing in our tent, watching. A Scottish voice asked Peggy for more beer. We started to chuckle. She clasped a hand over my mouth. I did the same to her. We shuddered as we held back the giggles. I rolled her off the bed: she landed on top. No springs. No noise; locked and hot together, on the earth, in a mouth-clamped, chuckling, jigglingly glorious frenzy.

Saturday 22nd July

I had my best sleep in days – the temperature fell through the night – but the awakening was harsh: the piercing whistle of a nearby boiling kettle. No-one sleeps after the early riser. Apparently, it is a motto Chiara is keen to keep with me now.

By ten o'clock, the beating sun, hovering in a deep-blue sky, shimmered impressively over the ground. I'd never felt anything like it before: my skin basted in my sweat. We sought out the large communal pool.

It was busy with thousands of bairns with their parents, mostly British, as well as lines of lithe young men of various nationalities, stacked round the edge, dangling their feet in the water, watching on.

Chiara dropped her robe to reveal a new, red bikini. All male eyes were on her as she plunged in. Swimming was difficult: an obstacle course of ball-throwing kids and somersaulting, show-off dads. Every now and then she would approach to plant a full-blown kiss on my mouth. I could feel the wall of envy in the onlookers. I was public enemy number one.

In the evening we drove to a small village and had dinner in a quiet restaurant, on their patio, under grape vines. She persuaded me to have a glass of red wine. It was good; but we limited ourselves to one. When she replaced her glass on the table and looked away, I watched her. I studied the poise of her movements, her little mannerisms, and the dignity of her beauty: still unable to believe my luck. Then she explained why she had ran from my home and we talked for hours on end until it was settled.

We stopped off at the reception on the way back to ask Ben the procedure for leaving early: our ferry sailed at five.

'Don't worry, it happens all the time,' he said. 'There'll be someone to see you out. Where are you going?'

'Dumfries, Scotland.'

'A long way.'

'I know but we're going to stop off on the way up for a rest – Chiara's originally from Birmingham. But I have to be up there by Sunday night – work the next morning. Reckon we should be back no later than nine at night.' I sensed Chiara's strange look.

Sunday 23rd July

We arrived in Dumfries at ten past four in the afternoon, taking turns to drive, stopping only for petrol and sandwiches. On the way up, I'd called every bed shop in Dumfries, asking how quickly they could deliver a new divan. They thought it was odd to be buying over the phone but I managed to find one who could deliver the next day.

I dropped Chiara off at The Cairndale, and drove onto my house. The boys had been busy and the sitting room at the front was ready. It looked fine. My bike sat in the hallway by the front door. It had been dragged up from the basement, dusted down, and given new tyres: they were still hard. And there was an envelope for me, on the floor, pushed through the letterbox.

I didn't stay, driving over to see Charlie, calling in at Tread's work on the way for the car's evaluation. I wanted this particular job finished, over and done with.

It was a woman in a uniform who opened his front door. She showed me into his sitting room. Charlie sat in an armchair, wearing a yellow and blue striped dressing gown – no sign of anything underneath. He flicked off the TV. Some of the smells of the hospital had come with him. A fan in the corner buzzed air around the room.

'Thanks, Ellie,' he said to her. She left.

We stared at each other for a while. He looked fragile: his face held the same blotchiness I'd seen on his visit to my home more than a week ago.

'She's a nurse – helping to look after me,' he explained. 'Had a bad reaction to the anaesthetic. It's held me back.'

'The hospital told me you got out yesterday.' I reached into my pocket and handed him the cheque. 'Half the money for the car, as arranged,' I stated.

He didn't look at it but laid it on the table by his side. I remained standing, adding, 'I'm about to drop it off at Tread's salesroom. Where will I put the things in the boot?'

'What sort of things?'

I shrugged. 'There's a couple of photos, jewellery, and some other items I thought you might want to keep. You can bin them for all I care.'

'You're mad at me, I know. Have a seat.'

'I'm not staying. I'll get those things and I'll be off.'

'Please.'

I hesitated, then sat down opposite him. He sipped from his glass. It took him an age to replace it on the table. 'Why do you think I asked you to go along with me to see Mrs Mann?' he said, his fluid eyes failing to lock onto me fully.

I sighed but played along. 'You wanted company?'

He shook his head slowly. 'I'd been putting it off, hour by hour. I should have gone immediately. I waited *two* days to tell her. I left it to the staff at the home to do the job. That wasn't right. I didn't want to go. I am a coward. There I've said it.'

He raised his glass once more before continuing, 'I thought if I asked you to come along with me, I couldn't back out. It was the right thing to do – to try and explain to her.'

'That's fine, Charlie, but I need to be going.' I stood up and made for the door, Manfred's car key in my hand.

'Wait,' he shouted. It took an effort. 'I need to say I'm sorry for what I said the other day. That's another thing I got wrong. Take a seat again. Please. I won't keep you long. Please.'

A little slowly, I sat back down in the armchair. For the first time I saw the suitcase I'd found in Manfred's attic, sitting in the corner of the room.

Charlie gave a cough. 'I've learnt a lot about myself, Jin. And none of it is good. I wasn't away on business when you were seeing to the house. I said I was, but I stayed here all the time.'

'I don't follow.'

'I made up that story of needing to go away on business
231

matters. It wasn't true. I just didn't want to set foot in his house. I didn't want to go in, break its threshold. It sounds terrible. It's not right – but, at the time, that was the way I felt. It would have been too painful to go in there, too awful to touch his things, his property – and disturb his memories.

He was my best friend, Jin. I can't ever remember him not being around. We never had an angry word – *never*. He was someone I could talk to, ask his opinion, and I thought I was the same for him.' He hung his head. 'Perhaps, when he needed me the most, I wasn't there. It's almost unbearable.'

He sucked in a breath: it made him cough. He swallowed heavily before going on, 'I've loved a few times in my life, Jin…' He paused, noting my increasing discomfort. 'Just let me say this... I want to explain.' He waited until I nodded, before continuing, studying his podgy hands as he spoke, 'I've loved, but it has never lasted. I never married. There wasn't the basis, the footing. I've learned that friendship is *the* necessary foundation. Everything solid is based on it. It's the most important thing in the world. Not only is it the foundation, it is the pinnacle as well. It is the pinnacle of life. A keystone holds the arch together, provides the strength – and it fits in at the *top* – like friendship. It is the base and the peak at the same time. Do you see what I mean? If you walk in that room you have the solid floor beneath you and the ceiling overhead as protection. That's what I've always thought. That was my conclusion for life. I had that room. Do you understand?' He glanced up, and went on, 'I'm trying to say that Manfred and I were friends, real, proper friends. We had that bond… There was nothing more…'

A burst of coughing stopped him in his tracks. The nurse appeared quickly and coaxed some liquid down his throat. He relaxed and went on, when she left, 'When you gave me that case,' he made a gesture to the corner, 'something happened. I realised I hadn't quite reached the pinnacle after all: there was
232

another one waiting for me, the ceiling was higher then I imagined. Manfred was my brother as well. *You* found that out. But it was too late. He had gone. It made it worse, much, much worse. I blamed you for the pain I felt. I wished I hadn't woken up after the operation. I wished that Lionel had succeeded with his plan. I wanted to die. It felt as if *you* had taken everything away from me: my nephew and my death.

I don't hate Lionel. I even wish he was still around – but I won't be visiting him in prison. I won't go that far. They say he was after my money?'

I gave a nod – there was no point raking up Lionel's hatred.

Charlie went on, 'Why do you think Manfred never told me about the note?'

'I'm not sure. Perhaps he didn't want things to change between the two of you. He was happy the way things were: he didn't want to risk things turning for the worse. Maybe he was worried that the dynamic might alter: you might feel obliged to give him money, or amend your will, and that could lead to resentment elsewhere.'

'You're wrong, Jin. There are three reasons.'

He didn't go on. I wanted desperately to leave but my curiosity took over. 'What are they, then?'

'I'll tell you. The first thing is that it would have taken him a while to come round from the shock of it. Don't forget it would have meant that he never knew his real, biological father. Believe me that would have been a big thing for him. He might even have started a search for him. He would have wanted to know – of that I've no doubt.

Then there would have been anger: anger that he'd never been told before. And that anger would have bothered him: he would have been furious with himself for feeling that way towards his adopted parents. It would take time for him to get over it as well.

But the biggest reason, the one that stopped him short, was to
233

stop the news hurting *me*.'

'How do you mean?'

'He knew I worshipped my mother, put her on a pedestal. I freely admit that. Manfred wouldn't have wanted to change that in any way. He wouldn't have wanted to tell me she'd been unfaithful to my father – a floozy. There was no excuse for it: not even in wartime. Manfred would know how badly I'd take it. He kept quiet to protect *me*. I see that now.'

I remained in my seat: unwilling to speak.

'And that was another reason to hate you, Jin: you who brought me this news, this revelation about my mother. I didn't want to hear it or believe it. I still don't; but, at least now, I realise it's not your fault. Can you accept my apology, Jin?'

I walked over to Jill's flat. It was half past five. The town was quiet. The temperature might be retreating, or else I was adjusting to it. Either way, it felt more comfortable. Jill smiled when she saw me. She ushered out her daughter – I'd asked if we could talk alone – and offered me some tea. I declined.

The morning after Sanny's flit, there had been four bottles of his wonderful liqueur at my back door, along with an envelope containing fifty crisp £1 notes for the van hire: although I would need to check to see if they are still legal tender. I had one of those bottles with me now and suggested to Jill that we have a drink.

She found a pair of crystal glasses in a box in a kitchen cupboard and I poured a large whisky measure into each one.

'What brings you here, Jinky? And the drink? It's still early.'

'Thought you might like to try it. And it's an hour later in France – so it's fine.' She eyed me warily. 'It's very good,' I coaxed. 'Try it. Onion Sanny makes it from local produce. You can have two glasses of it – no more, no less, that's what he says.'

234

'I didn't think anyone spoke to Onion Sanny, far less got presents.'

'It's a story for another time.' I downed half of my measure, adding, 'I'd like to invite you round to my house tonight for half past eight.'

'A party, is it?'

'There'll be a few folk there, right enough. But really it's to catch Jackie's killer. I thought you might be interested.' I finished off the rest of the liquid and slowly placed the tumbler onto the coffee table between our seats.

She stared at my glass, her eyes wide, her drink untouched, motionless, in her hand. I indicated to try some. She did. Her quickly raised eyebrows registered the afterburn and the smooth fire down through the centre of the body. It was a moment before she spoke. There was a growl of disgust in her lowered voice, 'Who is it? Who did it? Tell me who did it.'

I backed up a little. 'I reckon there's a good chance of getting him – but I can't be totally certain he will come. If not tonight, we'll get him soon after, don't worry.'

'Tell me who it is,' she demanded, becoming increasingly animated.

'I can't, Jill.'

'Why not – I have a right to know!'

I raised my hands, offering a calming gesture. 'Why are you so bothered about this anyway, Jill? You had gone your separate ways. You were no longer together.'

'Doesn't stop you caring, does it?'

I nodded. 'That's what I thought. But at this moment it is better if I don't say. You'll need to be patient.'

She bit her lip and this time her tone was a touch lighter, '*You* are going to catch him? What about the police?'

I motioned to her glass again and said, 'This is what I know...'

It made her sit forward. She swigged back the remains.
235

'There's a group smuggling items into Britain. I'm not sure where the line starts but it passes through a man called Ben, who works in France. He's the important part in the chain. It's his job to attach packages to the underside of cars travelling back home. The unsuspecting motorist then drives into the country, bringing in the parcel. All the smuggler has to do is sit back and wait for the goods to come to him. There's very little risk: if the vehicle's caught, the car owner will be the first one suspected.

From their bookings, Ben has the names and addresses of everyone staying in his campsite, and he knows when they will be returning home – even the ferry they're taking. Once the package is on its way, he phones his contact in this country, ready for the pick-up. That's what Bones forced me do in Gretna.'

I refilled our glasses with the pale, reddish liquid. The glug of the bottle was loud in the stillness of the room. 'I've been there, Jill – to where Ben works – his campsite. I'm just back and still on continental time. We said we'd be home by nine tonight: I expect someone will be round a little later. The package is there – underneath – at the back of the car. I've checked. And, I bet it's not just the one campsite doing this either. It's bigger than that.'

Jill waited, her eyes flickering. Then she said. 'And you think the person picking up this package is the same person who killed Jackie?'

'At this moment, I can't be completely sure. But there are a few pointers making it seem likely.'

She stood up and, head bowed, paced the length of the room.

'Do you want to come along tonight to help?' I asked.

She stopped. As she opened her mouth to speak, I cut her off, 'But of course you know all this, don't you, Jill? You're not the slightest bit surprised by any of it. You didn't even ask what this had to do with Jackie. You *knew* he was involved.' I picked

236

up her glass and handed it to her. She sat down heavily.

'You seem to know a lot, Jinky.'

'I've put a few things together. Anything more might help us tonight or later.'

There was a long pause. 'I should be grateful to you, Jinky, for helping.' She sipped the liquid and emitted a sigh, her shoulders lowering a couple of inches. 'There's not much else to tell.' She pulled her lips together as though about to deliver a kiss before adding, 'Jackie and William Bones worked together picking up the parcels as you said. They were covering a good stretch of the country and making good money. They took in the south side of Glasgow, Ayr, Carlisle, Newcastle and, of course, Dumfries. That's a large area.'

'Who gave the commands? Who told them where to go, Jill?' I knew the answer.

She didn't reply. Her mouth had tightened again, her lips whitening, in an attempt to stop any words spilling out.

'It's over, Jill. After tonight the smuggling ring will be finished.'

A sudden burst of anger detonated in her eyes. She jumped to her feet and shouted at me, 'What *right* d'you have to go messing into this, eh? It's none of your business.' She leant forward, towering over me, her free hand raised as if to deliver a clout. I shirked, involuntary. Not again. Why is everyone against me when I'm trying to help?

A voice sounded from the other side of the door and the door started to open. 'Are you all right, mum?'

Jill sat down quickly, bringing her arm to her side, smoothing her skirt. She forced a smile onto her face. Her daughter, key in hand, entered the room. I don't think she had moved far from the other side of the door.

'I'm fine. Off you go now,' Jill said. 'I'll catch up with you later. Don't worry – Jinky's an old friend. I just had some bad news, that's all. Off you go – and properly this time.'

The daughter glanced at me, noted my reassuring nod, before, reluctantly, closing the door gently behind.

'Take a drink, Jill,' I said softly – and waited until she had. I continued, 'It's Wallace Lemon who gives the commands. He's the one receiving the calls from France. He passes the information onto Jackie and this Bones fellow. I heard one of the messages on his phone. I pressed 1571 and there it was – exactly the way you showed me in Jackie's flat, remember?' I swallowed another half of the liqueur. 'It gave the address, car reg, and probable arrival time.'

Jill sipped. 'How could you hear his messages?'

'I was in Lemon's house on Wednesday night. And do you know what that message was?' I didn't wait for her to answer. 'It was the same address you and Bones sent me to the next morning, the one in Gretna. Lemon was in the pub getting drunk that night – as he does every Wednesday. Probably doesn't expect many calls then. I imagine the weekends are the busy times. He doesn't go to the pub on a Friday or Saturday. I thought that was very odd at the time. I should have twigged something wasn't right straight off.

And he's not the smartest one either: when you hang up after listening to a message, it's automatically saved. He was either too drunk or too stupid to delete it.'

'Or he wasn't expecting someone to break into his house,' she retorted.

I didn't respond but stalled for a moment. We drank until our glasses were empty. Jill's eyes stared at the floor and she nodded slowly – perhaps sifting and ordering her thoughts. It was a full minute, feeling like five, before I said, 'There's something I'm not sure about, Jill. Why did you stab William Bones in that toilet?'

I knew it was a risk: she was as strong as me, but, as far as I could see, she didn't have a weapon close to hand. I had checked the distance to the kitchen area and how I could stop

238

her. There were no knives visible on the work surfaces.

She peered up at me. She was calm, perhaps forming for a plan. She showed no emotion, her words were flat. 'Why would you think that?'

There was no harm in going on, 'The knife used against Bones was short-bladed and paint-speckled. I saw that knife in Jackie's flat – the one his brother uses for decorating.'

'That proves nothing. There must be thousands of knives like it.'

I shook my head. 'You were quick enough to give your boyfriend an alibi for that night: you told me he didn't go out. But it was *you* who went out. You left his house in Georgetown to attack William Bones. Gardiner told me.'

She waved it away. 'I went to the supermarket, that's all.' Then she eyed me suspiciously. 'When were you talking to him?'

I pulled a piece of paper out and unfolded it. 'This is a receipt for a brown tracksuit, bought on Monday afternoon at the Gretna outlet place – that's your day off – and only hours before you came into the pub, looking for me. You picked up the knife in Jackie's flat when we were there – probably hidden in a bundle of clothes – or else you went back for it later.'

'Where did you get that?' She tried to snatch the receipt away. I was too quick. She slumped back down, her hands returning to her knees.

'It was found here, in your home. You were so keen to search Don Gardiner's home; he thought he would return the favour. He was disappointed by your lack of trust in him, he said.'

She was still composed.

'Why did you call the police on me, Jill, when I was sitting outside his house? It *was* you, wasn't it?'

She shrugged. 'I was trying to do you a favour, Jinky. If I found out *he* was the murderer, I didn't want you involved. It was to keep you out of it – for you're own good.' She crossed her legs. 'Are you going to the police with this?'

'No.'

She expected me to go on. I didn't. It sparked something inside her. Her words poured out in a tumble of anger and revulsion, her face twisted. 'I'll tell you, Jinky. I'll tell you all about it. D'you want to hear? I'll tell you. It's true, I wanted you to find his killer. I wanted him found more than anything else in the world. I needed to settle the score for what he did to my dear Jackie.' Tears rolled down her cheeks. She didn't wipe them away.

'I've been looking as well, Jinky. I've been trying to find out who did it. I want this…this evil…' She struggled for a suitable word, in the end giving up; picking up and holding out her empty tumbler instead.

I shook my head: she'd had her two glasses.

She rose to her feet and began pacing the room, slowly, methodically: my eyes never leaving her. She said, quietly, 'Some of the smuggling was for kilts, vacuum-packed. As you know every man in Scotland has at least one nowadays and every boy coming of age has one bought for him – and they're not cheap, not by any means. These ones were brought in from Eastern Europe – for a fraction of the price but with fake Scottish labels, which makes them worth a lot more, of course. But that wasn't the real earner. The big business was in sporrans – the fancy ones, the exotic types.'

'Illegal skins?' I gave a nod.

She returned it. 'Right. They make the most money. Hundreds of pounds each – and there'd be seven or eight in each parcel. Jackie and Bones were paid £100 per package, plus travelling expenses. It doesn't sound like a lot but they could collect ten in a week, minimum. And a lot more at peak season.

Jackie didn't want to tell me about it: he wanted to shield me from it. I had to keep on at him just to find this out. But

240

then he changed: something happened and he became very nervous. He wouldn't say anything about it, mind, but he was worried about his safety – and *mine*.

I didn't think William Bones had murdered him. I couldn't see the reason: they were a team. But I wanted to scare him into talking. I needed to find out what Bones knew and why Jackie was so scared. That's why I went to that hotel, but it didn't go well. I thought the tracksuit would give me an edge: he'd have heard about the sighting of the jogger and would have feared for his life. That's how I wanted him to feel. But he was too quick. He turned. I wasn't expecting it. The knife caught him and it shot from my grip. I ran. I had the hood up the whole time. He wouldn't have known it was me.'

She sat back down, tapping absently at the glass in her hand. A weak smile emerged. She reached for the bottle – I drew it away.

'You were always going to leave the knife, Jill. You wanted Jackie's brother blamed: you never liked him. You must have been disappointed when there were no fingerprints on it?'

'I forgot he always wore gloves when he decorated. Always liked to keep his skin nice,' she said in a mocking voice, caressing the back of her hand.

'But I don't understand why you've done all this. Why this desperate need for revenge? You were separated from Jackie.'

'We filed for divorce.'

'Even more so, then, Jill. You had moved on. It was all behind you. You had a new man and a business to run, why take the risk?'

'It was never like that, Jinky. It was a ploy – that's all it was. It would have been a paper divorce. It didn't mean anything. Jackie wanted to make sure nothing came back on me. He was *that* worried, d'you see? No-one would think I was involved. He even moved out from here well beforehand to make it look right. He needed me to be safe but we were still a team – as always.'

She added, determinedly, 'We were together, don't you worry about that. We were always together. Jackie was taking risks for me.'

'But your business, Jill?'

'That's just it – I needed the money. I still need the money. I must have this income, Jinky. That's why I went to Lemon: to ask him if I could replace Jackie, to do his work, share with Bones. I pleaded with him. He agreed: he probably had no choice after Bones' injury. That was one good thing to come out of my fight with him – Bones couldn't drive. So I was probably the only one Lemon had.'

'What about the dangers though?'

Her shoulders slumped. 'My business isn't doing well. I overpaid for it – I'm not getting enough customers in to break even. I need the extra money or I lose the salon. I employ two people, Jinky.'

'Then get rid of one of them.'

She shook her head. 'It doesn't work that way – not in hairdressing. If I get rid of Nancy, she'll take half the clientele with her. And I'm not going to sack my daughter.'

'What happens to your daughter if you're caught and locked away?'

She gave a vague shake of the head, before catching me with imploring eyes. 'Jinky, we can still catch this killer and the smuggling can continue. Why not? You don't need to tell anyone about it. I can still take over from Jackie. Where's the harm anyway in a few sporrans coming in?'

'That's not going to happen, Jill. It's over.'

She didn't like the answer: her face hardened. I moved on, 'What made Jackie so frightened?'

'I don't know – really I don't.'

I didn't take my eyes from her.

She hesitated. 'At a guess, I would say he thought someone
242

was trying to take over the scam and they were vulnerable. Someone wanted them out of the way. Jackie was the first.' She stared into the distance.

'Look, Jill, you can be there to catch his killer – isn't that the most important thing?'

She leaned forward, laid the glass down, and placed a hand on my knee. She had brightened up all of a sudden. I shuffled in my seat and distracted her with a question. 'And that business with Bones and the package – why did you rope me into going to Gretna to fetch it?'

Her grin didn't change. 'He came looking for me. Bones. He heard I was taking Jackie's place, but he didn't want to split fifty-fifty. He wanted the bigger share – probably because I'm a woman. But, of course, he couldn't drive with his wound. The man's an idiot – he doesn't even have his own car, he travelled in Jackie's. He threatened me. I had to pass all the parcels onto him or he would see to it that my shop burned.

I told him I didn't have a car either and that the police hadn't released Jackie's one yet. I thought that would buy me some time – until I could go back and talk to Lemon. But it didn't work: he wanted me to call someone right away to make the pick-up, someone I trusted, someone who would keep quiet. I thought of you. I knew you wouldn't tell anyone. Jackie was smarter than the lot of them: I don't know how he put up with them.' She sat back, her hand leaving my knee, the smile undiminished. 'I lied to you, Jinky, about it. I'm sorry. I had to.'

'I have to get going, Jill.' I rose and stopped at the door, bottle in hand. 'One thing I'm not sure about – where does Don Gardiner fit into this? Why did Jackie give me that job to investigate him?'

She gave a shrug. 'I imagine he wanted to make sure Don was all right for me.'

'But you were still with Jackie – unofficially – or did I get that wrong?'

'Jackie was playing it safe. He liked the idea of someone around, protecting me – as long as it was the right kind of person. He didn't want me to be alone after he moved out. We only ever did what was best for each other. Right from the start, we devoted ourselves to that. Then nothing else mattered.'

I understood. I'd heard it before. I'd felt it before. I turned the handle to leave.

'If it wasn't for these happy pills, I wouldn't have coped. I'd be in pieces right now.' She hesitated, biting her lip. 'Jinky, if Bones ever found out it was me who stabbed him…'

'Don't worry, I won't say anything.' I paused. 'Wait a minute, Jill. You weren't so worried about him before – you attacked *him*. How come you're so scared now?'

'He's stupid but he's also dangerous – I didn't know that then. Jackie sheltered me. He told me Bones was a big softie: wouldn't harm anyone. He only said it so I wouldn't worry. You saw what Bones' like: you need to be careful, Jinky.'

I nodded. 'I will. See you later. Half eight?'

As the door closed, I heard the clink of glasses as she tidied away and I heard her start to sing to herself. I clipped down the stairs, whistling tunelessly.

As arranged, both women arrived at half past eight at the back door. I led them through the open connecting door, into the never-used sitting room at the front of the house. I introduced Chiara to Tread, Chisel and Hoogah. Flamboyantly, Tread kissed the back of her hand, then seeing Jill, felt obliged to repeat the gesture. Jill gave him an incredulous glare, wiping the back of her hand on her denim skirt the moment he turned away. It took a while for the enhanced redness to disappear from Tread's already sun-pinked face.

Hoogah was sporting a new haircut; the ponytail just a memory, lying in a bin somewhere. Or, more than likely, in a display case on his wall. His new style was similar to the one he had as a wee boy but without his hair tugged back and clasped, his skin appeared looser and his face held considerably more wrinkles.

I brought through six mugs of tea and laid them on the sideboard. No-one touched them. A net curtain had been fitted to the bay window. I eased it back a fraction and peered out. It was light outside. Manfred's car had been reversed into the front garden, giving a clear view of its rear. The holiday had been booked in Chiara's name: as long as my address wasn't known, everything should go to plan.

In the room, no-one talked, everyone stood.

'You've done a good job,' I whispered to the boys.

They returned crisp nods.

The car's image on the computer screen was addictive. We watched the stationary vehicle for minutes on end, in silence. Chiara didn't seem any more relaxed this time: she was fidgety. But she had a job to do: it might take her mind off things.

I left and returned a minute later with two boxes, handing each person a long, heavy, rubber-cased torch – robust enough to be used as a cudgel, if necessary. They seemed to understand the dual purpose: Chisel trying it out, smacking it into the palm of his left hand. It brought a moment of doubt to him. 'Why don't we call the police now, Jinky? We know the package is there. Let them take it on from here. This could get dangerous.'

'If you want to back out right now that's fine. I mean it. It won't be a problem. It was difficult for Asa and it could be the same for you, with your work, but I'm going ahead with it, no matter what.' I paused. 'Look at it this way: we're just being responsible citizens. I'm simply doing some flushing out. They were happy enough using me before, so they can't object this time round. And, besides, this is for Jill.'

She looked up and nodded, her voice was hard, 'I want him caught more than anything, Chisel.'
245

I added, 'There should be no danger: not if we do it right. And don't forget, it might not happen: maybe no-one will show for the package. Then what would the police say? I'd be wasting their time again and they don't like that. And...'

Chisel cut me off, 'Okay, okay, you've made your point. I was just saying, that's all. I'm still in.'

For one awkward moment I thought Tread was going to administer a consoling pat to his back so I opened up the other box quickly. It was a quad-set of walkie-talkies. I handed one to Chisel, one to Hoogah and kept the other for myself. We practised for a minute, ensuring we could work them. To avoid any misunderstandings, all messages would start with the name of the person speaking. Tread's suggestion of having codenames was duly turned down.

Chisel noted the empty box. 'Who's got the fourth?'

'Is Asa here? Is he coming?' Tread butted in, excitedly.

I shook my head. 'Unfortunately not: no change on that front. We could have done with him, right enough. I've enlisted someone else. No-one you know, Tread.'

The clock on the wall said twenty to nine. I left to check the tyres on my bicycle again. Hoogah came with me. 'Another good job,' I said to him. It had been his task to make the bike roadworthy and there wasn't a cobweb to be seen. 'What about Rodger the lodger?' I asked.

'He's been told to keep out of the way, and definitely not to use the front door. I told him he could use the back one and then out over the garden wall into the lane if an emergency arose. I don't think it's likely though.'

We returned to the front room. 'It's time,' I said. Everyone nodded – they hadn't moved. 'A quick run-through before we take up our stations. Torches?'

They replied in unison, 'Check.'

'Walkie-talkies?'

'Check.' Male voices only this time.

246

'Web-cam on and computer recording?'

'Check,' answered Chisel.

'Car keys?'

'Check.' Tread replied.

'Mobile phones switched on?'

A delayed 'check' was called, one at a time, from each person in the room.

'Then it's time to take up positions.'

Tread and Hoogah left by the back door – Tread giving a quick salute on exit. Chisel sat down on the stool in front of the computer, while I took my place at the door-jam, able to see my bike by the front door as well as the computer screen. Jill knelt by the window, peering out through a tiny gap at the bottom of the curtain, while Chiara stood by the new outdoor light switch, away to one side.

I heard a noise from upstairs and saw Rodger wishing me good luck in the form of a thumbs-up signal. Then he disappeared back up to his flat.

The web-cam and light had been installed by the boys in my absence. Both stared directly at the back of the car. The plan was simple: someone was coming for the parcel and we would make sure he was caught. Tread and Hoogah were now along the street, in a car, and I had my bike for added support. The moment we spotted out target taking the parcel, Chisel would phone through to the authorities and we would follow the thief at a discreet distance, relaying our positions, via Chisel, until the police intercepted. It should be simple enough.

The minutes ticked slowly past. Nine o'clock – the time we told Ben – clicked away. The clock was noisy. The streetlights came on but their low, yellow light failed to penetrate. The image on the computer was becoming increasingly grainy; the new wall light would be needed to capture a good image. It would spook the smuggler but it would be worth it. If he managed to discard the package at some point, we would still have evidence: we had our own CCTV.

Our room became gloomy too. It exaggerated the glow of the laptop. Chisel adjusted down the screen's brightness from time to time. Chiara rocked from one foot to the other. Jill shuffled into a more comfortable position.

At twenty past nine Chisel's phone gave a harsh buzz. He pulled an apologetic face, illuminated in the screen, before taking the call. He didn't say anything other than the occasional 'right', accompanied by the occasional nod: his eyes never leaving the computer. He clicked his phone shut, and backed over to me, eyes still on the laptop.

'Bit of news,' he whispered, but it was loud enough for everyone in the room to hear. 'William Bones has been found – stabbed. It happened about half an hour ago. He's dead.'

Immediately Jill turned from the window to stare at me. I couldn't see her face in the shadow but I returned her gaze, saying nothing. She turned back to her vigil.

Chisel went on, 'He was hanging out his kilt on the washing line when he was attacked by a man in a tracksuit. His wife witnessed it. No knife found. Does that change anything, Jinky?'

'I don't think so. In fact, it makes it clearer.'

Perhaps, I should have felt sad for Bones but I could only think of the difficulty of hanging a freshly washed, heavy kilt onto a line, with only one good arm.

Ten o'clock passed.

Chisel jerked. He motioned to us to be quiet: no-one had been talking. He pulled out his phone. Jill shrunk back and raised her hand, ready to signal to Chiara. From where I stood, the image on the screen wasn't obvious. I could make out a shape moving to the back of the car but little else. Jill's view, peeking out of the corner of the window, would be better. I held my breath. She knew she had to wait until he had the package in his hand before making the signal.

Right at that moment I saw my mistake. Jill shouldn't be on look-out. I should have swapped her with Chiara. What was I thinking? She wants the smuggler to escape. She wants the operation to continue. She needs to be in on it for the money. She won't let him get caught. She'll wait too long: give him time to escape. Chisel isn't getting a good enough picture on the computer. He can't see what's happening: the image isn't clear enough. The recording will be useless. I told Jill it was *probably* the murderer – that's all. It won't be enough for her. I shouldn't have trusted her.

I ran forward. At that instant, Jill's arm plunged. Chiara flicked the switch and the outside light blazed. I stopped. On the screen I saw a hooded man in a tracksuit bolt round. His face was shaded, hidden: the rucksack on his back was big. The package would fit easily inside.

In a second he was gone.

We were off!

'Which way?' I shouted, running to the hallway.

'Can't see him,' Jill called, breathlessly.

She's letting him go.

A second later, Chisel yelled, 'He's gone round the back. *Listen.*'

We froze.

A thump of footsteps round the side of the house.

'He's going over the back wall. Into the lane,' I hollered.

I grabbed the walkie-talkie and shouted into it, *'Jinky here: Hoogah you need to go to the north end of my back lane. It comes out in Rae Street.'*

'Hoogah: proceeding there. Check.'

I flung open the front door, and pushed my bike out.

'Jin here: Poseidon, you need to go to the south exit of the lane. It comes out in Newell Terrace. Don't get close, remember. Only follow. I'll be there in a moment to help.'
249

Chisel should be onto the police by now. I jumped onto my bike and headed for the south exit: making it two at each end.

'Hoogah: no sign here. Anyone spotted him? Tread is asking why you didn't allow us codenames. He wants to be called Zeus from now on.'

I charged on and into Newell Terrace. It was the long way round. The jogger only had ten, twenty yards, at most, to run from my back wall. The street was deserted: no-one to be seen. I jammed on the brakes. They squealed. I came to a halt. It was quiet. A solid hush. Nothing at this end. I waited to hear from Hoogah. There was another squeal – like a cat. Ahead of me. I peddled on. There was another noise to the side. Maybe from the council car park?

I rushed in and saw a shape lying in the dim, empty tarmac, lying across a parking space like the middle bar of an H. I jumped from my bike before it had stopped. A peddle scraped and the machine clattered to the ground. I clicked on my torch and edged forward, holding it firmly at its end, ready to use as a weapon.

The shape gave a groan. The beam picked out a man in a tracksuit. I couldn't see his face but I saw blood running down his shaking hand at he pointed.

'Jinky: accident here, Chisel. We need an ambulance right away to the council building car park, off Newell Terrace.'

'Chisel: check.'

I rushed to the man and knelt by his side. 'There's help on the way.'

Don Gardiner's head turned. He looked up. There was blood on the side of his face as well. He gasped, 'It happened. So fast. Before I knew. That way.'

He pointed to the path leading from the back of the car park into the cemetery and I started to run.

'Jinky: he's gone into St Mary's graveyard. There's only two ways out. I'm blocking off the back exit. Hoogah, can you get
250

round to the front, on English Street, and see where he goes from there? Don't try to stop him – he's dangerous. One man down.'

'Hoogah: copy that.'

I heard a siren. I didn't know if it was police or ambulance. I ran on.

The path from the car park runs between a high wall and a large hedge. It was like a black tube. I stopped at it entrance, shining a beam along. It was empty. I could see the old wooden door at the far end, slightly open, and through the gap loomed the headstones in the cemetery beyond. I dashed along, the light flashing wildly, my legs aching now. I wasn't used to this. The door squeaked as I closed it behind. It was rotten, fragile. There was a small bolt. I threw it across: better than nothing. I bent double to heave in some air.

The night was still. My breathing eased a touch and I took a step forward, casting the beam one way then the next, and back. The siren was approaching. I couldn't hear anything else. He might be out the front gates by now, setting off along the street – but which way? We may have lost him.

I clicked away the beam and crouched into the shadow, still panting. There was some light left in the sky: the headstones were black against it. But the light wasn't enough to break through all the murk. I inched forward, cowering behind a slab of stone, waiting, listening.

It would be foolish for him to turn back but he might panic in the face of the siren. I had to secure this exit. Stop him at all costs – if he came this way. A surprise attack.

I heard a noise – a scrape. To my left. I couldn't bear the darkness. It threatened me. It was suffocating. I clicked the torch back on and stood up. A noise at my side. I twisted round, the beam shining. A blast of light hit my face. I shrunk back.

'Johnstone, what the hell are you doing here? Get out of my way.' The light dipped.

251

I saw a hobbling figure coming towards me. 'Mr Lemon. What are *you* doing?'

'Heading for home, of course. Short cut. Let me through.' He was wearing black trousers and a t-shirt. The straps of his backpack dug into his shoulders. He waggled his walking stick in the direction of the gate.

I didn't budge. 'I can't do that. No-one's to leave. I thought this was your pub night.'

He reached me, faced me, and pushed. 'Out of my way, man.'

It happened before I could move. The handle of his stick hooked round my neck and yanked me forward. I lost balance. His fist smashed into the side of my head. I staggered and fell. He was on top of me, twisting me onto my back, his stick, held in two hands, under my chin, across my throat, throttling. I struggled for breath, trying to call out. My mouth was open. His weight was on my chest, his arms straight, all his might choking away my life.

I couldn't breathe. I flailed at his hands, dug my nails into his skin, trying to prise them off. I reached for his face, to gouge an eye: he was too far away. His grip on the stick was too strong. I was becoming light-headed.

The torch. Where was my torch? It was solid. It was a weapon. I was weakening. I ran my hand over the ground, the earth of the dead. My fingertips touched something. I sensed I was floating, soaring. And there was pleasure.

He released the pressure, air gushed in through my open mouth and into my lungs. My body wracked and I gave a long, wheezing gasp. He shuffled quickly, pinning my arms under his knees as I clutched at my torch. I couldn't lift it from the ground: his weight on my elbows. I fought to raise my hand. The angled beam lit up his head. His eyes were cold. They were black. He raised his right hand. It held a knife. The torchlight flashed off its long blade.

He muttered, his voice harsh, 'You get what you deserve, Johnstone.' He was smiling.

Over his shoulder, caught in the torch beam, I saw an angel – glowing milky-white. I stopped squirming.

He laid *his* torch on my chest, pointing at my face. 'I want to see this. I want to see the look you give. With Gittes, it was a surprise. I've seen the look of shock: I want to see *this* one – when you *know* what's coming.' He held the knife in both hands above his head.

The angel was a statue, perched on top of a headstone.

A roar sounded, like a volcano exploding. Something splattered. In a fraction of a second, my attacker had gone, his bulk lifted cleanly from my chest – as though he'd pressed the button of an ejector seat.

I turned onto my side, coughing. In the torchlight I saw Lemon, flat on his back, unmoving, a heavy shape leaning over him.

There was noise behind me, from the path.

'You okay, Jinky?' Asa said, still bearing down over the listless shape on the ground. 'He's out cold. Why was he trying to kill you? Where's the guy in the tracksuit?'

A woman's voice shrieked. I saw Jill, Chiara, Chisel. Jill ran past. Chiara knelt at my side and put a hand to my head.

'He's the killer, he's the jogger,' I rasped, clutching my throat.

There was a scream and a thump: Jill had kicked the prone figure with the toe of her flip-flop. The body didn't stir.

'How can it be him?' she screamed, and lashed out again: not waiting for an answer. She tried another blow, this time from her torch, but Asa grabbed her middle and lifted her off her feet, taking a step back, whispering in her ear. She struggled. She pleaded with him to let her go. He wouldn't.

'I didn't let on I knew,' I mumbled. 'I tried to keep him talking until someone came. He attacked me. His tracksuit is in
253

the rucksack.'

The police came running from the front. Hoogah and Tread following. They handcuffed Lemon. He still hadn't moved.

'How can it be him? He's lame. How could he do that to my darling Jackie?' Jill shouted. Then the energy left her, she started to bawl, and sagged over Asa's big arm like a folded blanket.

It was the early hours of the morning. We'd been at the police station for a long time. I'd been examined by a doctor. There was bruising and swelling – no serious damage but it was difficult to talk. I poured Sanny's liqueur into six, crystal glasses and handed them round to the same people seated in my front sitting room – except the newly arrived Asa had replaced Chisel, who was already at his newspaper office, working away. The room was as we'd left it, except the police had my laptop now.

'Here's to us,' I croaked, lifting the glass into the air and knocking back the tipple in one go. It snarled down my gullet. Surely this could be counted as a new session: it must be safe to imbibe again.

Everyone followed.

Apart from a few short naps on the way up from France, I'd been awake for twenty-four hours, most of it living on adrenalin. Now I was dying on my feet. I filled up the glasses. 'By the way, Hoogah, there's two bottles for you as well, left by a grateful hermit.' My voice was little more than a whisper: the fire of the liqueur was harsh.

'I'll drink to that,' he replied, with a grin.

Asa's face remained as serious as when he arrived. He was quiet, unusually so.

'Did you really know it was Wallace Lemon who was…doing it, Jinky?' Tread asked, casting a glance towards Jill, trying not to be too blunt.

I nodded.

'How?' Asa asked.

I turned to him. 'Did the police ever interview Lemon in his slippers?'

'Why would the police be wearing Lemon's slippers?' Tread shot back.

I pretended not to hear him. 'Lemon's left shoe was worn down at the heel, but his right one, where the walking stick takes the strain, wasn't. Yet the worn patches on his slippers were oddly even.'

'Oh, I get it,' said Hoogah. 'When he's inside, in the privacy of his own home, he can't be using his stick to get around. So he can't be lame. It was all a show.'

Asa took over, 'The curtains in his house were always drawn in case anyone caught sight of him rushing around. The DVD watching was a cover.'

I added, 'I reckon he did a bit of training in there as well – on the stairs. They're thread-bare on every second step.'

Nobody took me up on how I knew their condition. So I went on, 'I think he *was* injured at one time, but got better. It happens. People are told they'll never walk again, and they do. Lemon must have decided it was good cover for all his activities.' My voice was improving a touch.

Asa took over, 'He probably started this smuggling business when he was driving his lorry round Europe.' He directed the next comment at me. 'Still, it's not a lot to base it all on, is it really – the worn slippers?' Then instantly he held his hands up. 'Not that I'm trying to be negative or anything – just pointing it out.'

Something was bothering him still.

'There's more than that, Asa,' I said. '*You* were with me in that pub. I had one of those small step counters hidden in the hollow tubing of my walking stick. I switched the stick with his one and counted the number of steps he took to his home.
255

When I retrieved it later, there were only a handful of unaccounted ones. It meant he never needed his stick in the house, only when he was out. It's sixteen steps up to his toilet: he was up and down that night.' I took a sip before going on, '*And* there was the timing as well. According to Miss Welch, the jogger passed by at 5.08. She was only away from the window for three minutes between 5.09 and 5.12. Lemon said he saw the jogger from the rise and stated it would have taken him as much as ten minutes to get over from there to the houses. He could only have escaped Miss Welch's view if *he* was the jogger – the only person she saw.

Lemon's everyday clothes were in the rucksack, all he had to do was nip into his garden first, change, put his stick together, and turn up at next door's gate looking distressed. That was why he used to go for walks round the field in the first place: so he could change and be away doing whatever. He did it all the time.'

'A bit like Superman,' Tread muttered.

'Aye, Superman with a collapsible walking stick,' Hoogah chuckled.

Asa cast an alert eye in my direction. I hadn't told him about Miss Welch's timetable nor did I wish to explain the method used to derive it.

Hoogah said, 'The dismantled walking stick would fit into his rucksack. But I still don't see why he changed in the graveyard and turned back. Why didn't he keep going?'

I said, 'He would have heard the siren: the police station is only a few hundred yards from the front gate of that graveyard. If the police had spotted a jogger coming out, or anyone, in fact, they would have been suspicious. This was the better way. He could nip back into the dark, quiet car park and out through its other exit, opposite The Cairndale. Don't forget, he didn't know Poseidon had followed him. And he didn't know I was on his tail either.'

'But why kill my Jackie?' Jill asked, sadly.

I shrugged. 'If I were to guess, I'd say Jackie and Bones were doing some business on their own, possibly receiving direct calls from France – straight to Jackie's flat.' I gave a slight nod in Jill's direction. She returned it.

I went on, 'I think they were trying to get one over on Lemon – cut out the middle man. But Lemon found out and wanted to show he was the boss. It would be a warning to Bones – and to anyone else thinking of moving into the business. Hence the show of the kilt over the body: it was a sign.'

'But why kill Bones then?' Hoogah asked.

I ran a hand round my neck. 'That's hard to say. Perhaps someone let on about Bones still wanting to go it alone: as a way ingratiating themselves to Lemon.' It was a pure shot in the dark. I cast another glance at Jill. She betrayed no emotion.

Asa said, solemnly, 'It's not quite as simple as that, Jinky.'

'How do you mean?'

He went on, heavily, 'We found ten, almost certainly, illegal sporrans in Lemon's rucksack and there was a brown-handled, long-bladed knife in there as well – very similar to the one used on Jackie. The one he was about to use on you was black-handled, by the way.

The sporrans will have to be taken away for examination but we'll soon find out what they're made from.'

Everyone gave a satisfactory nod.

'But that's not the end of it,' he sighed. 'In each sporran was a stash of drugs – class A.'

There was a hush.

Asa nodded. 'All Lemon is saying right now is that he was told to make the killings. He's not telling us anything more.'

'Who told him then? God?' Hoogah threw in. The joke fell flat.

Asa continued, 'We haven't heard the end of this – mark my words. Lemon's home has been searched. We found more sporrans with drugs.'

'Any idea who he was passing them onto?' I asked.

'Not at this stage.'

I took a few steps to the window, tasted my drink, and peered out. It wouldn't be long before the sun rose from its bed, lifting away the darkness. At this moment, there was no light. Did Jackie know he was dealing in drugs? Perhaps not at first: he wasn't getting paid nearly enough. He was simply passing on the packages thinking they were nothing more than sporrans and kilts. Maybe he only found out after one of the direct deals from France. Was there a stash in one of those packages? Was that the moment he became scared, suddenly immersed in very serious crime? It didn't stop him though: he continued for weeks on end, taking steps to keep the danger away from Jill by splitting from her. Doing it because she needed the money.

Asa broke through my thoughts. 'Sorry to mention this, Jill, but we also found some homo-erotic material in Lemon's bedroom. That might be why Jackie was found naked. I think Lemon stripped him – for pleasure – and the kilt was an afterthought. As Jinky said, as a warning to Bones.'

The air was tense. For once I was glad when Tread piped up: he sounded a wee bit miffed, 'Who's this Don Gardiner fellow, anyway? And how come *he* was allowed to have a codename? And who chose Poseidon anyway?'

I looked at Jill. 'Do you want to explain?'

She shook her head and pulled out a hanky to blow her nose.

'He's Jill's friend,' I said. 'Poseidon is his *actual* name – he shortens it to Don – but that's what his parents gave him. To my mind it sounds grand. I told him he should use it more often, and not just in the phone book.'

'Do you think he'll be all right?' Jill asked, suddenly.

Asa answered, 'Last I heard, he's going to be fine but it'll take time for the wound to heal.'

I added, 'He was trying to impress you, Jill. That's why he

258

offered to come along and help. I think he wanted to show he wasn't afraid, and that you could count on him. He wanted you to be safe – that's what he said. And he wants you out of that business. You know what I mean?'

Before anyone could ask, I said, 'I should never have let him help, though. It was my fault he got injured. I thought it would be good to have someone who was fit in case I couldn't keep up or couldn't follow easily on the bike. Lemon caught him by surprise. Gardiner's new to the area: he didn't understand my instructions, didn't know the street names. But, even after the attack, he tried to follow Lemon, until he collapsed. We have a lot to thank him for: I doubt if we would have looked in the car park. You should go and visit him in hospital, Jill.'

She nodded.

Tread said, 'That was some tackle, Asa: the way you took out that Lemon guy. Where did you learn that?'

Asa tilted his head. 'I had the misfortune of watching Gretna last season. Never thought it would come in handy.' He shot a look in my direction and gave a wink. Then added, 'It helped when my weight landed on him, not to mention him banging his head on the side of a headstone on the way down.' He asked me, 'Why didn't you shout out, Jinky? Call for help?'

I rubbed my neck again. 'Not easy when you're being throttled.' I wasn't going to say any more. I certainly wasn't going to tell them that I thought I'd caught sight of my guardian angel and felt safe. So I asked Asa, 'And what about you? You said you didn't want to be involved. That's what you told us. What happened there?'

He shrugged. 'I had second thoughts. Chisel phoned me after he called the police and told me what was happening. Things weren't looking too good. He told me where to go. I was never all that far away. I was on lookout the whole time – and this time I didn't run away.

Monday 24th July

My last sleep in my old bed was not as good as I would have liked. Unlike France, the warmth of the day didn't subside. It meant I was up early, which was just as well as it was going to be a busy day: and, sadly, no time for golf again. Unbelievably, I had more important issues to attend to.

I started by clearing out my apartment. The men who'd emptied Manfred's house so efficiently weren't available until later on in the week, so, in the meantime, it was down to me to do as much as I could.

I stashed anything 'loose' into boxes: vases, books, cutlery, etc. – piling them up in the garden shed. Then I took out all the easy-to-carry items: small tables, bathroom cabinet and so on, and laid them outside. The idea was to leave my flat as empty as possible. I had to hope this initial assault would be enough for Chiara.

The newly purchased bed arrived at eleven and by one in the afternoon I'd stacked away my last item. I made a list of necessary things for the short term: linen, towels, kitchenware, and so on, and headed out for the normal Monday shopping.

It was four o'clock when I knocked on Miss Welch's door. She answered quickly, already dressed for going out: a crocheted green cardigan over a white blouse and green tweed skirt. I'd parked carefully at her front gate so she could see my aunt in the front seat. My aunt gave her a wave.

Miss Welch locked her front door, pulled at it, testing it was secure, and pulled at it again. Then she patted round her hair to make sure it was lying flat to her scalp, before trailing me to the car. She may not get along with my aunt, she may not enjoy the experience of a Tesco supermarket, but, as I'd said to her earlier in the day, over a cup of tea, "why not try it this once and see what happens." I added that it was a thank-you for her help with the list. She gave me her first smile.

I collected Chiara from The Cairndale – where she had stayed the night – and led her into my kitchen. I hadn't unpacked any of the newly bought bits and pieces: we would do that together. I explained that all the old furniture, carpets and cupboards were going later in the week. We made a date to shop for replacements, once the entire apartment had been painted.

She looked a touch more comfortable.

The money from my share of Manfred's car had vanished, spent on the trip to France, and these recent purchases. Fully kitting out my place would be expensive too – but it would be well worth it. I should have done it years ago. I could see now what had troubled her, it had been creeping up on me too.

For almost twenty years, Chiara has lived in fresh houses, done up like show homes: everything new. She has no feelings about anything she's bought: it's done on a purely practical level, whatever creates the best impression. When she steps into other people's homes, she feels overwhelmed. Every object in every room cries out to her, points at her, tells her she doesn't belong. Each possession holds a trace, a memory, a ghost of someone. And photographs of unfamiliar faces stare back at her, making her ill at ease, isolated. They choke: they suffocate. She is distant, an out of place stranger. And I'd felt that too, though not nearly as strongly, in Manfred's house, in the houses of my uncles: every single time I've had to sort through other people's belongings, encroaching on their history.

We stood. I studied the kitchen table in the middle of the floor. This is where I found my father ten years ago, slumped, his head resting, dead. If he'd blown his brains out, I wouldn't have kept the table. It would have been discarded, broken up, shoved in a skip: for it would never have been clean.

But I did keep it, and, as the years have passed, that dreadful moment of discovery replays in my head with increasing frequency. It is not right: it is time to move on and discard the past in favour of the future. My future is with Chiara. I want everything in the house to be a shared memory of *us*, nothing else. We will be starting afresh from this moment.

We sat in my own, bare sitting room at the back of the house, drinking French wine from paper cups. She was happy. I picked her up, my left arm under the backs of her knees, her left arm dangling over my shoulders, and carried her along the corridor to my new bed, and the bowl of fruit beside it.

She asked me if I believed in love at first sight. I said I didn't. She asked if I believed in friendship at first sight. I said I hadn't thought about it. She said the moment she first saw me she knew we would be friends. A week ago, a month ago, it would have been a nice thing to say, but it wouldn't have meant all that much. Now, it meant everything.

THE END

The trilogy concludes with: The Case of the Hermit's Guest Bedroom.

6671715R00146

Printed in Great Britain
by Amazon.co.uk, Ltd.,
Marston Gate.